by what we Love

ALSO BY CHARLENE CARR

A New Start Series
When Comes The Joy
Where There Is Life
Forever In My Heart
Whispers of Hope

Behind Our Lives Trilogy
Behind Our Lives
What We See
The Stories We Tell

Standalone
Beneath the Silence
Before I Knew You

By What We Love

A New Start, Book 3

Charlene Carr

Published by Coastal Lines, 2019.

Published in Canada by Coastal Lines
www.coastallines.ca

Library and Archives Canada

By What We Love
Book Two of the A New Start Series
ISBN: 978-1-988232-17-1

Typography by Coastal Lines
Cover Design by Coastal Lines

Second Edition, September 2019

This work is also available in electronic format:
By What We Love
ISBN: 978-0-9939238-4-5

*For my niece, Alysis, who taught me what it is
to fall instantaneously in love.*

CHAPTER ONE

My breath catches as I step out of the elevator. I can't get air. All I see is the image before me: red, angry blotches against a white backdrop. My sight blurs, melding this nouveau art into something more incomprehensible than it already is, something I've seen before. My limbs stiffen, as they did back then…the blood on the white tile, the brightness of it, the fear and knowing seeping through my veins as I stood outside the bathroom, unsure whether to step past the partially open door or run away.

I blink, and that action frees me to see what's actually before me—the office doors, the starkly decorated hall, and the painting. It is just a painting—some new, most likely coveted acquisition of Mr. Everdeen's.

My breath comes easily now that I see the canvas for what it is, though it baffles me that anyone could label this abstract mess art. I could create this. A woman dying could create this.

Turning my gaze from the painting, I draw my focus to the large double doors. Julie, the receptionist, can't see me yet. Breathing deeply once more, I erase all thoughts that led to my stilted breath. I tuck the memory away—I'm good at this. I adjust my pencil skirt, making sure the belt lines up with the slimmest point of my waist, then tuck in my blouse. Perfection. I scrunch my curls, glad it's not a humid day. No need to worry about flyaway frizz. I am stunning. Stunning and confident and professional…whatever Everdeen throws at me, I can handle. Closing my eyes, I inhale confidence and exhale any fear that threatens. So what if Carl implied bad news may be coming my way? Bad news is what you make it.

I will not fear this meeting. With a smile on my face, I push open the doors and stride towards Julie.

"Eloise, hello." The receptionist smiles with her perfectly white teeth and glossy red hair, a shade not found in nature. "Mr. Everdeen will be a few more minutes. May I get you tea or coffee?"

"No. That's fine. Thank you, Julie." The plush leather armchair is harder than it looks, but I don't let this phase me. I cross my legs and lean against the chair-back. My body presents the perfect mix of poise and ease. My heart pounds.

Mr. Everdeen never calls people to his office for private meetings. Meetings are held in the boardroom. This invite is unheard of for someone as far down the chain of command as me. What lies behind those doors is a mystery. My colleagues joke about it, coming up with scenarios more and more absurd—He's hiding a buffalo head, a tight-rope walking midget, a portal to another world.

One part of my mind concentrates on maintaining a serene smile, the rest is on overdrive, trying to determine what I could have done wrong. But I've done nothing wrong. I work my ass off, doing everything I'm supposed to do and more. I've secured more clients, big clients, than anyone else in my division. I've opened new doors. I've excelled. Perhaps I let my attitude take over once or twice, mildly, but that's nothing compared to all I've done right. I bite my lip, shift in my seat. Flippant would be a good term for my behaviour…and those men who think the corporate world is an old boys' club, who think they can say whatever they want whenever they want, and no one will mind. They call me endearing, precocious, fiery.

Julie's voice draws my attention. "Mr. Everdeen will see you now." I nod and make a straight line for the office door. It opens before I have a chance to grasp the handle.

Lancelot Everdeen isn't known for his smiles and he's not smiling now. He could have been a linebacker in another life. "Please, have a seat." He points to a chair in the middle of the office, with another chair right across from it. Surprising. I expected him to address me from behind a large desk. Following his direction, I sit, the ever-present smile on my face. He makes his way to the office's floor to ceiling window as if I'm not here.

Everdeen is a taskmaster. He built his empire from the ground up. A modest empire, but impressive nonetheless. Everdeen Enterprises is growing. It has satellite and partner offices in five countries. It has the potential to be one of the country's top Public Relations firms. It's already the best in our city, and whether Everdeen recognizes it or not, that's partly thanks to me.

But Carl's words plague me, have me stealthily wiping the sweat from my palms. Tipsy from too much complimentary bubbly at a big PR event the other day, Carl slapped his hand on my shoulder. 'We'll be sad to see you go.'

'What?' I hissed between smiling teeth.

'Oh.' His eyes widened. His words caught in his throat. He coughed. 'You're going to the UK again next month? Right? The office is never the same without you.'

I have no trips planned, and Carl, who approves all travel, knows this.

Everdeen turns from the window. "You're probably wondering why I've called you here."

"Yes, sir."

In five brisk steps he's towering above me, then sits as if he's never rushed in his life, crossing one ankle over his knee, folding his hands in a controlled manner. "I've been following your career, Ms. Grant. Your methods are unconventional." He's silent while I wrestle between wanting to defend myself and waiting for permission to speak. At last he continues. "An old friend of mine, Thomas Richardson from the London branch, called you 'a little spitfire.' Now that's a direct quote."

"Is that so, Sir." My voice holds no question. I know exactly the situation that prompted those words, but I don't let my confident smile waver. Richardson, one of the 'old boys' who thinks it's appropriate to comment on a woman's exoticness and fresh face, got far less 'spitfire' than he deserved.

Everdeen leans back in his chair, eyeing me. "He also said you were one of the most engaging reps he's ever had the pleasure of spending an evening with."

I nod, confused.

"A respected client of the Tokyo branch said you make the men feel as if you're one of them, joining in, not judging their thirsty tendencies as so many Western reps do, not seeming bewildered by the many cultural differences, and you always manage to keep your wits about you."

I stare at him, silent. When he wants me to talk, he'll tell me.

"You've climbed faster than all the colleagues you started with. You've signed more clients, created more relationships, garnered more campaigns, and convinced James to rework the whole way your team operates, improving everyone's numbers."

I nod again.

"Tell me," says Everdeen, "what are your connections?"

"My connections?"

"Yes. Do you have children? A husband?"

"No, neither."

"And do you want these things?"

I think of Moses. "One day. A husband, at least."

"I see." He leans forward. "And what are your goals? Do you want to take my role one day?"

"Pardon me?"

"If you could, would you weasel your way in deep enough that when I kick the bucket or simply get too old and senile to think straight, you'd be ready to step in?"

"Yes, Sir."

Everdeen's brows raise before he laughs—a deep belly laugh. "Oh, really?"

"Well," I swallow. My confident facade wavers for a moment, but I call it back. "I love my job. I love scripting. I love securing clients and creating visions they never even knew they had. I love helping companies and clients flourish and flourishing myself in the process. At the same time, I imagine a day will come when I'll want more than this. And," my face is all business, "with all due respect, Sir, no one lives forever."

"No, my dear." A grin replaces the gruff expression Everdeen's known for. "No. They don't." He rests his head in his hand and rubs his chin. "I don't know if I want someone like you in my office eagerly waiting for me to take my last garbled breath."

I suck in, as if I've received a punch to the gut, then spew the words out. "Oh, but I didn't—"

He raises his hand. "I think it would be better to put you in the position to run your own little empire. You would thrive under a bigger challenge. It's time for your days here to come to an end."

I stare at him, my lips parted. This can not be happening. Failure is not in my vocabulary. I've done everything I'm supposed to do. More. I've worked like a madwoman, never complaining once. This is my life. "Mr. Everdeen—"

He cuts me off again and as he speaks his other words register in my mind—a bigger challenge. My own empire.

"I've been looking for someone to turn things around at the Tokyo branch. It's a mess there. A real mess. I'm sure you've seen that." He shakes his head. "We could be doing so much better—expanding. The market is huge and we're barely skimming the surface." He stands, paces, swings his arms as if he's conducting an orchestra. "I need someone with drive. I need someone who's not afraid to push past cultural barriers while remaining charming and savvy." He turns back to me. "I've considered some of my senior people, but they all have ties here—children, spouses, grandchildren." He drops these words, as if they're needless trinkets. "I know some of them would leave but they wouldn't be happy. I need someone who is young, energetic, smart and, most important, open enough to have me groom them, while pigheaded enough to disregard my advice when they know I'm wrong."

I stand, surprising myself. He brings his face close to mine. "Can you be that person for me, Ms. Grant?"

"Yes." I squeak, trying to believe this is real. I smile broadly, bringing an even tone back to my voice. "Yes. Absolutely. Yes."

"Well," he steps back, "don't answer so quickly. Take some time to think on it. This is a big commitment, Ms. Grant. You would relocate to Tokyo. Not immediately, of course. You'd have a good six months before you took on the role full time, maybe longer, but during those months you'd travel more than usual, to Tokyo as well as some of our other sites. See what works, what doesn't." His smile is large, his shoulders back, his chest thrust out. "You'd be made privy to the inner workings of this branch." He spreads his arms. "You'd be my protégé."

I nod, unsure whether to smile, to shake his hand, to speak.

"The job includes a substantial pay raise, so it wouldn't be too difficult for you to come visit on your vacations. And, of course, we would fly you in for all necessary company-wide events."

"That sounds wonderful."

He waves his arm, conducting again. "Take the rest of today off, but I won't take your answer until this time next week."

"Yes, Sir." Tokyo. Head of the branch. Me.

Everdeen walks to the door. "Ms. Grant, do think long and hard. This is no small thing I'm asking. This is the type of job that becomes a life."

"I understand."

He shakes my hand. "I'll be disappointed if you turn it down. It won't destroy your position in the company, you'll just have to work your way up like everyone else, knowing you may hit a ceiling. This offer is the equivalent of a rocket, shooting you to the top. Well," he laughs his gruff laugh, which seems friendly now, "almost."

BACK IN THE RECEPTION area I smile the same confident smile at Julie as I wore a short time ago, not letting my excitement show. Once I've stepped through those big glass doors, however, the strength of my smile stretches my face. I run down the hallway, open the door to the roof, and take the steps two at a time. The sun lights the glass buildings around me, making my whole world sparkle. I grab my phone and dial Moses, who answers on the third ring. "Hey, dar—"

"I just had the best news of my life! You won't believe it."

He laughs. "Won't believe what?"

"Well, what am I saying? Of course you'll believe it. You know more than anyone how hard I've worked."

"Let me guess. You finally convinced that client to sign on—what was it, the speed reader?"

"Better than that."

"Better than—"

"I got a promotion. More than a promotion! Mr. Everdeen, the Lancelot Everdeen, invited me into his office to offer the Tokyo division to me. He's going to groom me and—"

"What? What does that mean?"

"It means I'm going to be the top. I'm going to—"

"Tokyo?"

"Yes, I—"

"You didn't take it, did you?"

I pause. "What do you mean?"

"I mean, Tokyo. You'd be working in Tokyo? Full time?"

"Eventually, yes." The wind whips around the building, a horn sounds in the distant street below, but I hear no response. "Moses?"

"That's really amazing, El, that he thinks so highly of you, that he recognizes your talent and how hard you've worked. I'm proud of you."

"Well, I should hope so." I brush my curls out of my face, trying not to read anything into his tone.

"It's an honour."

"Yes, it is."

"But," his pause is long, "you haven't taken it, have you?"

"Well, no. Not yet." I tell him Everdeen's stipulations. "But I can't turn something like that down." He's silent again. "Mo—"

"We'll talk about it tonight, okay? da Maurizio, seven o'clock."

"I don't see what—"

"Tonight."

CHAPTER TWO

Moses and I say our goodbyes and I hold the phone in my hand, staring at the screen. What must Moses be thinking? Tokyo's far and my travelling has already taken a toll on our relationship, but he doesn't know all this job can do for us. Right now, all he knows is his girlfriend is thinking of moving to the other side of the world.

I shake these thoughts away. I can't let this moment be ruined. I won't let it be ruined. It's nothing short of amazing that the scrawny, scared, destitute little girl I once was has made it here. All of the long nights. All of the jet lag. All of the studying and prepping and sacrificing were for this moment. I pull my hair back so it doesn't blind me, breathe deep, and let the wind wrap its arms around me. I've made it.

I don't even bother returning to my office. My news is too good for small-talk or nosy questions. On the drive home a text from Lori interrupts my Sirius radio. 'Pop wants to know if we're coming for dinner this weekend. What should I tell him?' I ignore the text and turn up the music. It would be nice to tell the whole family about my news, but I'd much rather take everyone out to dinner to do it. Nine years have passed since I've called that house my home but being there still makes me feel young and weak and defeated.

Looking at the time, I realize I have two hours to kill before my guest talk with the Aspire to Success young women's group. The perfect amount of time to indulge myself. "Siri, call Suzy's Salon," I say. Two minutes later I'm on my way to a mani/pedi.

RELAXED AFTER MY SALON visit, I pull up in front of my old high school, where Moses and my friend Tracey both work, and gather my materials. Before I have the door closed, a group of girls rush my car.

"Eloise! Hi!" They laugh for no apparent reason and each take an item or two out of my arms as we walk toward the large stone steps. It's only my second Aspire meeting, and the first was three weeks ago. Seeing as I'll just be volunteering my time every few weeks to talk to them about aspects of business, I'm touched they remember my name and are so excited to see me.

"Sherry, Jolie, and Jayden?" Their faces light up.

"You're good," says Sherry. "Super good!"

"Well, you all remembered me, didn't you?"

"That's different." Jayden twirls a long dark spiral of hair around a finger. "You were like standing in front of us for an hour! And you had all these cool travel stories. Plus," she flips her hair back, "there's one of you and eleven of us."

"Well, here's a mini-lesson. Remembering names is one of the first tips to success in business."

"We didn't even have name tags though." Sherry pushes open one of the school doors. "How'd you do it? Do you have a wicked memory or something?"

Laughter echoes through the halls. Being back here is the one thing I don't like about these sessions. I wanted nothing more than to get out of high school, start my real life, and here I am, over a decade later, walking these corridors again.

"I do have a pretty wicked memory. But it's more than that. You can find something about each person that will help you remember their names. So," I gesture to each of the girls, "Sunny Sherry, because you smiled through the whole first session. Jokey Jayden, because you kept cracking jokes, and Generous Jolie, because I saw the way you were eager to help out your classmates."

"Yeah, but generous starts with a G, not a J," says Jayden.

"I still remembered it, didn't I?" I wink.

"But you have to remember our names long enough to learn something about us, right?" Jolie's cheeks redden. "Names usually fly out of my head the second I learn them."

"Repeat the name as soon as you hear it," I say. "In your head, if necessary. Even better, repeat it out loud. Let's give it a try. Jolie, can you introduce yourself to me?"

"Uh, sure," The petite girl steps toward me. "Hi, I'm Jolie, and you are?"

"Hi, nice to meet you. I'm Eloise."

"Hi." Jolie giggles. "Nice to meet you too."

"All right, criticisms?"

"Criticisms?" says Sherry. "You introduced yourselves. What's to criticize?"

"Neither one of you used the other's name." Jayden bounces in place. "It should have been," she pops over beside Jolie and mimics her, "Hi, I'm Jolie, and you are?" then pops back over to mimic me, "Hi, Jolie, nice to meet you. I'm Eloise. Hi Eloise."

"Exactly." I laugh. We continue our walk to Tracey's classroom. "This way each person has already said the other's name, cementing it in their brains a little bit more."

"Could work." Jayden twirls her hair again. "Worth a try I guess."

"Definitely." Sherry smiles. "That's so smart."

"Well, I didn't come up with it," I say as we approach

the classroom. "But I like it."

"Eloise, hi!" Tracey waves me over to the front of the room and wraps her arms around me. Her hazel eyes sparkle and her hair falls in luscious waves around her face. She practically glows. "You should have heard the girls talking about today. They were so excited for you to come in again." Sherry, Jayden, and Jolie join some other students at the back of the room. Tracey glances toward them. "They're so excited about this project. They've already got orders and everything. Today you're talking about writing compelling copy, right?"

"Not just talking." I can't help but smile at the sound of the girls chatting. "We'll write and polish some copy, break into groups, and brainstorm for our specific target audiences."

⤬

AFTER THE SESSION, I'm grinning so much from the girls' enthusiasm it almost dims my excitement about the promotion, and the excitement about seeing Moses for our anniversary dinner. I consider checking his classroom and saying a quick hello—I almost never visit him at work—but decide it will be better to see him when there's no chance of his students interrupting our conversation. As soon as he hears everything explained, I know he'll be on board.

Once home, I pick out one of my favourite dresses and open-toed heels to go with it, happy my nails are now flawless. Next, I take extra care with my hair and makeup. This anniversary dinner has been planned for over a month but with this new reason to celebrate, I'm practically tingling. I take a taxi to the restaurant so we can drive back to his place together.

da Maurizio is one of my favourite places. An Italian restaurant with amazing attention to detail, it rarely disappoints. The Maitre'D shows me to our table, where Moses stands. His beauty strikes me as if I'm seeing him for the first time. He's six foot three with naturally sculpted muscles, dark smooth skin, eyes that look deep into mine, and a smile that could make a woman swoon from ten feet away. More than that, he's smart, kind, sensitive, the only man to make me dream of a future. I step toward him and rise on my tiptoes to let our lips meet. He is everything I never knew I always wanted. I glance at our reflection in the mirror that runs across the width of the restaurant. It doesn't hurt that we look like the perfect power couple.

"You're breathtaking," he says.

I do a little turn so he can see the full effect, then grin. "You don't look too bad yourself."

"My lady." He pulls out my chair, grinning back. We take our seats and order our wine. He reaches for my hand across the table and caresses my fingers. "It's been a good three years."

"Wonderful." I squeeze his hand in response. "And it's about to get better."

He takes a deep breath, staring at our hands, then looks at me. "I hope so."

"How could it not? You'll be finished your doctorate soon. I've gotten this amazing promotion. Our lives are set."

There's something in his eyes I can't read; whatever the emotion is, it doesn't mirror mine. "You haven't decided on the position yet, though? You have a week to decide?"

"Well, yes, but—"

"I had my own question to propose to you tonight," he clasps his other hand around mine, so he's cradling it. "I wondered if I shouldn't, with your news, but I planned to, after dinner, on a walk by the water." His words are shaky, stilted, not smooth and assured like normal. "But I don't know how I can go through a dinner with you, talking about this promotion, without my prospect on the table…"

"Your prospect?" I lean forward. "You've been offered a university position?" I sit back, shaking my head in wonder. "That's what it is, isn't it? That's why you were so hesitant about Tokyo. Someone you met at the conference last month? I just knew—"

"No. No." He shakes his head and breathes deep. "It's nothing like that. I don't even know if I want to switch to university. I love my students and—"

"Moses. Not be a professor? Not pursue research?" I offer a hesitant smile. "Don't be silly. That's what you've been working so hard for—studying on all the nights and weekends and—"

"It's not silly, and I know that's what I've been working toward. I know. But that's not what I was going to say."

I pull my hand away. "Then what?"

A young man with slick blond hair and a wide-mouthed smile stands before our table. "I'd like to tell you about this evening's specials."

I listen with partial interest as the server lists the night's delicacies, then order one without bothering to look at my menu. Moses does the same. As soon as the man walks away, I ask, "Then what would you do?"

"Well, stay teaching high school. But Eloise, that's not what I want to talk about."

"Well, it might be what I want to talk about." I try to keep my voice even. "I thought this was your dream."

"My dream was to study…and I've always dreamed of teaching, but I'm doing that now. These kids are smart. They can take a real challenge. My degree will only help me prep them better. I'll have an extra level of calibre to bring to my students, to help guide them to succeed when—"

"You're not wasting a doctorate on high school students!"

"It's not a waste."

"And the pay? It's not even comparable—"

He laughs—the sweet, loving laugh I'm more used to

hearing when he's talking to my younger sister. "It's not about pay."

"I know, but that is—"

"Eloise." He reaches for my hand again. "There's something else I wanted to talk about, okay? Get out of control-the-world mode."

"Okay." I nod and push down the questions and concerns threatening to burst from my throat.

I shift and a slight chill makes its way through me. He squeezes my hand. "From the first moment I saw you I knew I wanted you in my life. We've had our ups and downs, but through it all my love for you has grown. You're not like any woman I've ever met. You're determined and tough and voraciously ambitious." He smiles, and I cup my hand across my cheek. "But you're also sweet and kind and you love the people around you with a fierce tenderness unlike anything I've ever witnessed."

My mouth goes dry. I take a sip of wine. I should have expected this, months ago I had expected this, but today it was the last thing on my mind.

"We've been building a life together and I want to continue building that life for many years to come. I love your family like they are my own. I want them to be my own, as I want to know you will be my own, forever." He slips out of his chair and down on one knee, grinning like a little boy. "What I wanted to ask is, will you be my wife?"

CHAPTER THREE

"I..." My face feels numb. It seems like the room's about to spin. "I mean, I...Of course, I...you don't have a ring?"

"Oh!" He laughs and reaches into his coat pocket. "I guess I was a little nervous." He flips open a black velvet box and my breath catches. It's beautiful. It's perfect. Well, I wouldn't have gone for princess cut myself, but beyond that, it's perfect.

"Wow. I—" I stare at the ring. As his hand shakes, the diamonds shimmer. "We hadn't really been talking about this. Lately, I mean."

"Yeah," he says. "You're right. I—"

"Hypothetically, I know. We've. And I've...I'm just surprised. I didn't—" His face falls. He pulls back the ring. "Yes!" I squeak. "Yes. Yes. Yes."

"Really?" Relief washes over his face like a wave, the smile back.

"Really." I hold out my hand as the cool metal slides onto my finger. Moses jumps from his knee and pulls me up into an embrace, cupping my face and drawing my lips to his.

"She said yes!" He holds up my hand to the room. "She said yes." He's positively giddy, and I smile along beside him as the other diners clap and cheer. Behind the smile, my mind races...what did he mean he might not seek a university job? How am I supposed to plan a wedding while

I'm training to take on a division?

Once the cheering settles we return to our seats. The server places our meals before us. We smile almost awkwardly, at least mine feels awkward, as we take our first bites. "So," I say. "What are your thoughts on how this will work, the time-line and everything?"

"You don't want to enjoy the moment?" His smile seems deeper than I've ever seen it. "Figure things out a little later?"

"Well." I set my fork down, striving to keep all emotion out of my voice. "Isn't that why you asked me now, before dinner, instead of waiting until afterwards? Didn't you want this 'on the table' so we wouldn't talk about my promotion without putting wedding planning into the equation?"

"Sort of." Moses sets his fork down as well. "I didn't want to get into some big fight about it when I imagined the proposal may sort of make it a moot point."

My chest tightens. "A moot point?"

"Yeah, it's when—"

"I know what a moot point is." My voice comes out as more of a snap than I want it to. Putting on my client face, I return to an easy, conversational tone. "I mean why would the proposal make it a moot point? It would be hard to plan a wedding and do the training at the same time. But maybe that means we can have a long engagement and plan the wedding after I take on the role in Tokyo."

"After you take on the role?" Moses takes a sip of water. "You're talking like you've decided—"

"I basically have."

"You've basically?" He sits back, a look of disbelief on his face. "You've dropped hints for me to propose for over a year now. You've talked about wanting to solidify our lives together. How is living on opposite sides of the world going to do that? You want to plan a wedding and start our married lives long distance? How long would you even have to be in Tokyo before you'd come back or—"

"No," I say. "No, of course not. I thought you could move to Tokyo with me and we could—"

"Me move to Tokyo?" He tents his hands in front of his chest. "Why would you think that? Have I ever showed any interest in moving to—"

"It's never been an option before."

"Eloise." He shakes his head. "I have no desire to move to Tokyo."

"But you have a desire to be with me, right?"

"Of course, but—"

"And if that's where I'm going to be, then why wouldn't you want to be there with me?"

"This was an offer, Eloise. It's not like you're fired if you don't take it, right?"

I hesitate. "Mr. Everdeen didn't say that but obviously it would hinder the trajectory…" I stop and stare at his annoyed expression. "I have every intention of taking it."

"You have every intention of taking it without us even discussing how it will affect our lives?"

"Well, you seem to have every intention of me not taking it even though we haven't had a discussion."

"Our lives are here. Our family is here. What about Lori? Would you pack her up to Tokyo too or kick her out on the street?"

"Don't be ridiculous," I say. "She could come to Tokyo if she wants. Anyway, she'll be weeks away from graduation by the time I'm there full time. And she's responsible. She could handle the apartment by herself when I'm away before then. She does already when I travel. It's fine. It's not even an issue."

"Making an impulse decision to leave your family and fiancé is not even an issue?"

"It's not an impulse decision."

"You mean you've been planning to move to Tokyo?"

"No. But I've been working to move myself up in the company. This is just the route it's taking. And you weren't my fiancé when I made this decision."

"So, you have already made the decision?"

"Well, not officially, but…" I let my voice trail off, uncertain whether he's the one being unreasonable or I am.

Moses picks up his fork. "Our food is getting cold. Let's eat, we can talk more later."

"I guess." I push the pasta around on my plate, no longer hungry. I take a bite anyway.

We pass the rest of the dinner with little conversation. When we do speak, it's about pleasant, unimportant things, like a movie we're thinking of seeing on the weekend and a new installation at the museum.

"Do you still want to go for that walk?" Moses asks when we leave the restaurant.

"We could."

"Well, do you want to?"

"I don't know, Moses," I say. "Perhaps I should think about it a bit more. I wouldn't want to make an impulse decision."

He takes a deep breath in, his nostrils flaring slightly as he does. "Please be fair."

"How am I not?"

He wraps my hand in his and leads me along the street, motioning for me to join him on a bench.

"Don't you have your car?" I ask. "This is a bus stop."

"I'm trying to talk to you for a second."

"Talk then," I say, hating the petulant tone of my voice.

"You have to realize why I'm so thrown off by this. Yes, I know your job involves travel and that's been hard, having you away for weeks at a time. But you always said it was because you were trying to work your way up in the company—that's why you worked the long hours, why you gave the job so much of yourself." He smiles. "I haven't always liked that, but I respect it. And I've accepted it because I thought you were trying to work yourself up in the company *here*, and once you did, once you were no longer in such a strong sales position, the travel would be cut back. Isn't that what you implied?"

I purse my lips. "Yes. And it will be cut back once I'm in Tokyo." I smile back. "Once I'm in management, I imagine I'll hardly travel at all."

"Okay." He caresses my hand with his thumb. I look at our entwined fingers. From our first date I've loved the way my hand fits so perfectly in his, like they were made for each other. "Why is this so important to you?" His voice is a whisper. "I want to understand. But I don't. Why can't you just stay here, work your way up in this branch? Why do you need to work your way up at all? We're doing fine."

"It's not like I planned this, Moses. It's not like I've been vying for a position across the world. It just happened."

"I know."

"And what do you mean by 'why do I have to work my way up'? We should always strive to better ourselves and—"

"Okay, I know that's important to you but—"

"I feel like you're not happy for me. Like you don't support me."

"Of course I support you. But see it from my side, here you are ready to make a huge life decision without even considering how it affects me. How it affects us."

How do I explain it to him? He's right, from his perspective, but I don't know how to make him understand mine without explaining more than I want to. Moses knows a lot about my past—in snippets—but not the deep stuff. I take a long breath. "I need to be secure. I need to know I'm successful."

"You are successful."

"I need to know they need me, that they're never going to let me go because no one else could do the job the way I can do it. This position is my chance to prove that."

"El," he lets go of my hand, and places his on my shoulder. "I don't know that there's ever any way to assure that. You're unique. You're talented. You're wonderful. But

I think in life there's always the chance of there being someone better than us, more qualified, more—"

"There doesn't have to be. If I prove I can do what no one else has, then I'll be in control."

"So what do you propose? That we live long distance indeterminately?"

"No, I said—"

"I have no desire to move to Tokyo. My life is here. Our life is here."

"We were just over this," I say, angry at how vulnerable this whole conversation makes me. "You don't want to move. I can't stay."

He leans away from me. "You can't stay?"

"Well, I…I mean…what if I take the job and we see how things go? You can come visit me a few times when I'm over there. It's a fabulous city. So full of life, energy." I grasp his hand. "And it's becoming westernized. You would get a job as a professor in no time." He looks at me with an expression I can't decipher. "Or high school. That could work too. You'd get into any international school you wanted, I'm sure." I smile, suddenly terrified. Though I don't know what terrifies me more—that he'll leave me over this, or that I'll let go of what could be the best chance of my life. "You may really like it. You'll never know unless you give it a chance."

"Can't you speak with your boss? Maybe if you say you have a family here, maybe he'll be willing to promote you in the branch here."

"He's not my boss. He's my boss' boss' boss." My throat feels tight. "And that wouldn't work. Part of the reason he sought me out is because I'm young and unattached."

"Unattached?"

"Well, it's…he knows I'm not married."

Moses laughs. "So if I'd proposed sooner we wouldn't be facing this problem?"

"It's not a problem. It's an opportunity."

"It's a problem."

"So what do you propose?" Fear and confusion bubble inside me.

He smiles. "I already proposed once tonight. You want me to again?"

"Moses."

"That you go tell your boss thank you very much for the offer, you're honoured, but your life is here, and you'll do your best work for him here."

Car after car drive past us. I glance over at Moses, then shake my head.

"He gave you a week to decide, didn't he? He knew he was asking a lot. He wanted you to be really sure this was the right thing, sure it's best for you so you wouldn't have any regrets. Can you honestly say you're sure you won't have any regrets if you make this decision?"

"Nobody can ever be sure of that."

"Yeah. But I think you would."

"And I think we could make it work."

He turns to watch the cars drive past. "I don't know that we could."

"I would have regrets if I gave this opportunity up."

He sighs, looking defeated. "Maybe you'll have to figure out what regrets would be worse."

"What are you saying?"

Moses puts his head in both of his hands, his elbows resting on his knees. "I don't know."

I look at my hand, the way the streetlight makes the diamonds glint. "Do you want this back?"

"No." He shoots up and smiles at me sadly. "No. Is that...is this promotion that important to you? You'd give up us for it?"

"No. I mean...I don't want to. It's important. It's really important. I just thought you—"

"No." He shakes his head. "No."

"So..."

"I don't know."

I take a deep breath and let it expel. Words are generally so easy for me, but I don't know what to say. I shrug. "How about we just give it some time?"

"Give us some time?"

"No. Give making any decisions some time. I have a week. I'll take that time to really think about it, like Mr. Everdeen said. And you can take some time to think about it too. Try to open your mind to Tokyo, do some research. It really is an amazing place." He wraps his arm around my shoulders and the warmth of him seems to wash over me. "But not more amazing than us."

He pulls back so our gazes meet. "This is really important to you, isn't it?"

"It is." I stare at him, as if I need to memorize the lines of his face. "Will you do that? Take some time to consider?" His eyes are so tender and deep. I don't want to think about any of this right now, I want to sit here, lost in the gaze of my fiancé.

"It seems fair," he says. "But it isn't a lot of time to make such a big decision."

"Well, I could always take the job, start the training, and you could come on a trip or two with me. See what you think." I lean into his shoulder. "It's not like taking it would lock me in for life. It would make sense for you to see the city before deciding to move there."

"And if I decided I wasn't willing? You'd give up the job? Or would you give up me?"

Hating the words, I say them anyway. "I don't know."

He looks away, and I know I've hurt him. "What if you left the job after Everdeen invested that time and money into you?"

"It wouldn't be good. But I guess we cross that road if we come to it."

"Okay." He tilts my face up and kisses me gently. "That's the plan, then? You think long and hard this week, and if you do make the decision to accept, I think long and hard afterward, trying to give Tokyo my open mind?"

"That's the plan," I say, smiling at last. It's a good plan. Tokyo is amazing. Once Moses sees it, he'll understand. As he holds me, I nuzzle my head against his shoulder, and the excitement I felt after walking out of Everdeen's office trickles back into me. The ring on my hand adds to that excitement. Moses will love Tokyo. He'll move for me. This will work. I'm going to have it all. Success, love, security, a future.

After several minutes, Moses draws away from me. "You ready to head home?"

I rise from the bench, and our hands clasp naturally as we walk back to the restaurant parking lot. We're quieter than usual on the drive back to his place. When he opens his apartment door my hand flies to my throat. Balloons, streamers and a large gold banner that reads 'To our Future Life' greet me. I laugh then step in. Flickering light comes from the living room. I turn the corner. A projector displays photos from our relationship in a slide show. A bouquet of flowers, box of chocolates, and bottle of champagne sit on the coffee table. My laughter mixes with tears as I spin to see Moses standing behind me, looking sheepish but proud. "What if I'd said no?"

He shrugs and a grin bursts through. "Well, then I figured you probably wouldn't be coming back to my place." I run the few steps into his arms and hug him long and hard before melting into the type of kiss that makes my whole body feel alive.

When morning comes, I roll out of Moses' arms and quietly pull my belongings together so as not to wake him. I jot a quick note saying I want to get home before Lori leaves for school so I can tell her the big news. Oddly enough, the news that seems slightly bigger in my mind is the job offer. I justify it by the fact that the job was a complete surprise while I assumed a proposal would come one day. I throw on some sweats and runners, leaving my dress and heels for another day.

Wanting some moments to reflect, I forego a taxi and decide the 40-minute run home is just what I need. It's not often I'm on the streets this early. The city, so quiet and peaceful, seems foreign. The sun, mostly hidden by nearby buildings, casts a hazy light. Life looks so beautiful. And it is. Mine didn't start out that way, but I've turned it into something wonderful. I can't let that change, not when everything I've ever wanted is almost within reach. I turn the corner and smile at another lone jogger, unafraid.

CHAPTER FOUR

Once home, I push open the door to my sister's room and watch her for a few moments. When she's sleeping, I see the little girl she used to be, the baby I raised practically on my own. Sometimes when I look at her like this, it's painful to think how close she is to being a woman and hard not to wonder if this is what motherhood feels like—looking upon another person, feeling they're a part of you, and wanting to provide the best life possible for them. Or, what motherhood is supposed to feel like.

"Lori." I cup my hand to the side of her face, massaging her cheek with my thumb.

"Hmm?" She stretches and yawns, then brings her gaze to focus on me. "What is it? Did I sleep through my—"

"No."

"Is everything okay?"

"It's good." I draw my hand back to my lap.

"Then what…Oh!" Her eyes brighten and she sits up, grabbing my hand. "He did it! He proposed!" She flings her body into hugging me, then pulls back to inspect the ring carefully. "This is awesome. About time." She laughs. "Tell me everything."

"Well," I say, "we went to La Cresida—"

"Wonderful choice."

"Yeah, and he wanted to wait until after, do it along the waterfront, but I had my own exciting news and I guess he wanted both things on the table; so he just did it there, right in the restaurant." She nods, urging me to go on. "I said yes. He jumped up and proclaimed it to the whole room. Everyone cheered."

"When's the wedding? Am I the maid of honour?"

"That's not an appropriate thing to ask." I put on a horrified face. "Really, Lori, I thought I raised you better."

"Oh, please. I am, aren't I?"

"Sure."

Lori opens her big brown eyes wide and smiles her sweet smile. "Who else have you told?"

"You're the first." This makes her smile grow. "But you haven't asked about my other big news."

"What's bigger than that?"

"I got offered a promotion. A big promotion."

Lori leans against the headboard. "More hours? More travelling?"

"Well, yes, but it's—"

"That's great." She glances at the clock and steps out of bed.

"I didn't take it yet."

"You didn't?" She turns back to me.

"No, I'm taking some time to think about it."

"That's not like you."

"What do you mean?"

"So what's the job?" She hastily makes the bed. "Why are you thinking about it?"

I tell her about the meeting with Everdeen, my pride growing with each word.

"Wow," says Lori. "That is pretty big."

"Yeah. It is."

"But you can't take it, right? I mean, Tokyo, and the wedding…that won't work."

"I think I am going to take it."

She's quiet and looks toward the window. "Well, what about me? Will I have to move back in with Pop? He's not in the school district and—"

"No. Not if you don't want to. I wouldn't be living there full time until right around your graduation. I'm sure I could even finagle it so I don't start until after your graduation. Well, I'd try, then you could either come with me—you'd love Tokyo—or stay here and get your own place."

She plops down on the bed. "That might be cool."

"Which one?"

"Getting my own place. If I got into the dance school, maybe I could room with one of the other students."

"Maybe."

"And what about Junior?"

"Junior's a man now. He doesn't need me."

"I know."

We stare at each other. She swallows, not looking in the least bit excited. "Well, congratulations."

Lori rises and grabs a few items before heading into the bathroom. Watching her go, that excitement and peace from this morning dissipates. I expected her to be happy for me, or at least happier. Someone needs to be excited for me. I grab my phone and send out a mass text to several of my girlfriends. *I've got major news. Who's up for drinks after work? 5:30 at Bitter End?* Before I'm dressed, my phone pings several times with confirmations. I can always rely on my girls.

When I walk into my office, I realize my girls aren't the only people I can depend on. James, my manager and one of the people integral in hiring me, follows me through my door and clamps his hand on my shoulder. "I knew you'd be going places," he says.

"Whatever are you talking about?" I ask, playing it coy.

"Oh, come on, you were probably salivating in the big guy's office!"

"Salivating? I'd like to think I have a tad more refinement than that."

"Perhaps." He smiles. "Well, I'm proud of you, my little

protégé. You're taking it, I assume?"

"He told me I have to wait a week before making a decision."

"And?"

"And my decision was made before I left the office." I grin.

"That a girl," says James. "We'll keep it on the down low anyway, until it's official."

"Good idea." He walks out of my office, waving a hand in parting. My stomach clenches: I've betrayed Moses with my words. But I told him I'd take a week to think, so he'd take a week to think. No amount of thinking will change my mind.

I spend the day slogging through a campaign for a large client I secured last week, but don't have my usual focus. The clock seems to go backward, not forward. My thoughts are consumed with what I'll need to do to make the Tokyo office Everdeen's best branch.

When I'm satisfied the campaign is exactly what it needs to be, I grab my gym bag. A quick workout before meeting the girls will clear my mind. In the office fitness room I work up a good sweat on a bike but, as I ride, I can't seem to shake this heavy feeling in my gut. Today should be one of the happiest days of my life—I glance to my hand and smile as the diamonds sparkle in the florescent light—but I keep seeing the look on Moses' face, hearing the tone in his voice. I don't know what bothers me more, that he didn't automatically share in my joy, that he expected this ring would suddenly be more important than my career, or that he may not decide to come with me. I'm not giving up this job. It's not even a consideration, which means he'll have to give up his or I'll have to give up him. I can't let that happen.

The time on the bike zooms by. I stop in time for a quick shower before meeting the girls. On purpose I arrive five minutes late, but only Tracey and Autumn sit in the large booth, talking with animated faces. Half a year ago I would have felt uncomfortable telling Autumn my engagement news, but she's come so far. Though it may bring the loss of her husband Matt in that terrible accident to mind, I know she'll be happy for me.

Before I've even completely made it through the door, Tracey's gaze seeks me out. "Hold out your hand," she almost shouts. I do and she squeals. "I knew it!" She grasps my hand and examines the ring closely.

"Congratulations," says Autumn, standing and giving me a tight side squeeze.

"It's beautiful," says Tracey, bringing her head up. "So how did he do it?"

"Shouldn't we wait?"

"I guess so." She brushes a strand of hair out of her hazel eyes. "I'm so excited for you though!"

I laugh. "This isn't even my most exciting news!"

"You're pregnant!" Tracey squeals again.

"No, I am not pregnant," I say. "Sit down and wait, will you?"

"What's more exciting than an engagement or pregnancy?" Tracey takes her seat.

"Just wait," says Autumn. "She'll tell us."

Tracey gives a little pout, looking like the pixie she must have been in another life.

"Until then, how are you both?" I can't help but glance at the clock, wanting the others to arrive so I can tell the rest of my news and have them agree Moses is being unreasonable for not being more ecstatic, and it's right for me to take this job.

"I started seeing someone," says Tracey. "I wanted to tell you last night but with all those young ears around…" She laughs. "Anyways, he's so sweet. He works at a high school in the next district. We met at a PD conference. We've only been out twice, but it feels like weeks."

"Is that a good thing or a bad thing?" I laugh.

"Oh, it's good," she says. "It's not in a, my gosh he's so boring I feel like I already know everything there is to know about him way. It's a, I feel so comfortable around him way."

"That's great," says Autumn. "You deserve a nice guy after that last creep."

"Don't get me started." Tracey rolls her eyes.

I look to Autumn. "And you?"

"Things are going really well." Her bright smile assures me she means the words. She's not quite the vivacious person she was a couple of years ago, she's more quiet and contemplative, but the joy that was always behind her smile is back. "My mom took a few steps the other day with a walker. It was amazing. Dad, Daniel, and I were all standing around her, cheering her on and she just struggled through it—with such determination, you know?" Her eyes mist. "After the stroke the doctors gave us so little hope, but she was having none of it."

"That's wonderful." I rest my hand over hers. "Before you know it, this will all seem like a bad dream. You'll have your mom back, just like you remember her."

"She'll never be exactly as she was," says Autumn, "but in some ways she may be better, stronger."

"Just like you." We're all quiet for a moment, and I imagine Autumn's thinking of what she went through and how she's come out of it, not unscathed, but more resilient.

"Tell her about your new client," says Tracey, breaking the silence.

"It's not such a big deal."

"It is." Tracey leans forward. "You know the Mayor's right-hand guy, the really sexy one? I can't remember his name."

"Connor," says Autumn.

"Yeah, Connor. He signed on. What was it? Two times a week for three months to start?"

"Three times a week for two months." Autumn rubs a

hand along her throat. "It's really not a big deal."

"It is a big deal," says Tracey. "That's how things get rolling. He's going to know all these other high-profile people with lots of cash to throw away." Tracey's mouth makes a little 'o'. "That's not what I meant—With lots of cash to invest in training. And if he likes you, which of course he will, they'll all start coming your way."

"Maybe," says Autumn. She blushes and raises her hand to her left cheek, covering the scar that's even more pronounced when she's flushed.

"That's really good," I say. "And speaking of sexy men?"

A bigger smile crosses Autumn's face. "He's coming to Nova Scotia next month. Just for a short visit. He'll meet my parents."

"Good." I grin. "So things are progressing?"

"It's kind of hard to progress too much with a whole ocean between us…let's just say we're taking it slow. I've got my business here and he's got the restaurant…" Her voice trails off.

"Are you talking about Jakob? From your European backpacking extravaganza? He's coming to visit you? Are you guys—" Tracey nudges Autumn.

"We're friends," she says. "That's all there really is to say right now. Allison!" Autumn waves to her business partner then extends the wave to Sheila who trails in behind Allison.

"Sorry we're late," says Allison, a bounce to her step. "So what's the big news?"

Tracey grabs my hand and holds it on display in front of the others.

"He finally popped the question." Allison grins and plops into a chair. "It's about time."

"Congratulations." Sheila's thin red lips turn into a smile. "You'll be happy with Moses."

"Of course she'll be happy with Moses." Allison laughs. "Who couldn't be happy with that sweet tank of a man?"

"And just look at the ring," says Tracey, yanking my

hand and whole body with it.

"It's really nice," says Sheila.

"I wonder if he followed the three-month salary rule." Tracey bends to examine the ring. "It looks like he could have."

"Oh, that's ridiculous," says Autumn. "So unnecessary."

"Perhaps," says Sheila.

"I don't think he did," I say. "Not that I'd want him to. It's just a symbol."

"Of course." Tracey releases my hand. "Eloise has other news too, bigger news—" Tracey pauses dramatically. "But she's not pregnant."

"Bigger news," says Allison. "Haven't you been hinting at this proposal since last year?"

"But not in months," I say.

"It has to do with work, doesn't it?" Sheila leans forward.

"It does." I grin. "I got offered a promotion."

"Congratulations. That's awesome. Good job." The girls chorus.

"It's better than that." I take a deep breath. "The head of the company, Lancelot Everdeen, invited me into his office and offered me the position personally. You know I've been travelling to our branches in Korea, England, and Tokyo the past year or so. Well," now I pause dramatically, "he wants to train me to take over the Tokyo branch." My words are met with silent glances. "The Tokyo branch. I'm going to manage it, be at the top. In Tokyo."

"That's amazing." Sheila clasps my shoulder. "You deserve it. No one works harder than you at that company. I'm dead jealous."

"Well," I say, "I don't know about that. Plenty of people have more experience, people who wouldn't need months of training and mentoring, but so many of them are old settled men. I'm basically unattached. And young. Able to be molded." I let out a little laugh. "So, I guess I was the best of that lot. It is pretty amazing."

"Absolutely," says Autumn. "Congratulations."

"But…" Tracey hesitates, glancing among us. "If you're going to be heading up the company in Tokyo, does that mean you'll live there full time? And for how long?"

"That's exactly what it means. I don't know how long. Probably indefinitely. Who knows?" I shrug. "Maybe it'll open new doors, maybe I'll move to another company at some point, but if I'm staying at Everdeen I can't ask for better than this."

"Eloise," says Autumn.

"Wait." Tracey interrupts her. "You're telling us you're moving to Tokyo for good?"

"I'll come back to visit."

"But that's crazy. And what about Moses? He's okay with this? He's going to pick up and move across the world with you? Leave the school? He loves those kids."

"He loves Eloise more," says Allison. "I'm sure Moses would follow you anywhere."

"And he was planning to leave his job anyway when he finished his degree, wasn't he?" asks Sheila. "To get a job as a professor."

"That was the plan," I say.

"So he's okay with it?" asks Autumn.

"Well, he needs some time to think about it. But I'm sure he'll come around." I take a sip of my tea, reliving the chill I got from him last night. "He wasn't as excited about it as I thought he should be. He actually seemed really upset that I decided I wanted to take the job without talking to him about it."

"Just like a man," says Sheila, "to think you need to consult him before making a decision about your career."

"Be fair," says Autumn. "They have a life together, and this is a huge decision, a huge move. It either means he has to pick up and transfer his whole life, or deal with long distance or…"

For the next few minutes the girls ask questions and pose

problems—mostly the same ones Moses and Lori have already presented. I try to sound more convincing than I feel as I answer them. Fed up, I stop them. "I expected you to be happy for me. Excited." I cross my arms. "I need your support right now."

"You have our support," says Sheila, the only one who wasn't posing problems.

"That's right," says Autumn, "we just don't want to see you rush into something and—"

"Kind of like you rushed into fleeing the country?" My mouth drops. "Sorry, I didn't—"

"That was entirely different," says Allison, "and you know it."

"I know, I—"

Autumn waves her hand. "Yes, like that. And if it weren't for you butting into my life and helping me think straight, I would have regretted my actions even more."

"Lets all calm down," says Allison. "We're just saying—"

"You're just saying all the things I've heard already." I lean back in the booth. "This is amazing. This is wonderful. A dream come true. You're my best friends and I want you to be happy for me, is that so much to ask?"

"No, of course not. We are happy for you," says Autumn.

"Completely happy," says Sheila. "This is the opportunity of a lifetime and you'd be crazy not to take it after how hard you worked."

Both Tracey and Autumn give Sheila a look.

Autumn places a hand on my shoulder. "We're also happy for the engagement. You never answered, how did he do it?"

"Oh yes, how did he do it?" Tracey leans in, as if all the tension of the moment has magically disappeared.

I tell the girls about the candlelit proposal, the cheering diners, the set up back at Moses' apartment, and leave out the worry that lingered behind it all. I smile at their gushes and congratulations on what a wonderful guy I've found but am unnerved by their lack of enthusiasm for the job—well, of everyone but Sheila. She seems to think this is the right thing to do. The others though …they don't understand. Tracey loves her students, but the job isn't her life. Autumn and Allison work hard at their business but they work for themselves. Disappointed this impromptu meeting didn't give me the boost of confidence I hoped for, when we stand to depart I place a smile on my face and make plans to meet up with them again this weekend, telling myself they just want what's best for me.

On the walk to my office's parking garage my smile fades. This should be one of the best days of my life—for multiple reasons—but it's not. As I'm approaching the building, the faint sound of my Vivaldi ringtone makes its way to my ears through the cacophony of the world around me. My hand glides into my purse and latches onto the phone.

"Lori, hi. I'm on my way home."

"Oh, good. You didn't answer me about Pop. About Sunday dinner. He called again."

"Why don't you ask him if we can all meet for dinner?"

"He wants us to come home."

I squeeze the phone between my ear and shoulder and scrounge through my purse for the fob to open the parking garage door. "I know Lori. But—"

"Maybe I'll just go. Me and Junior. Pop said Junior is coming. We can take a cab."

I sigh. "You want to go that much?"

"I haven't seen Pop in weeks."

"He could come see us, you know."

"Eloise."

"Lori." Inside the garage, I hit my car's fob this time and slide into the leather seating—safe in my sanctuary. I don't want to think about going to Pop's, but I also don't have the energy to hash this out with Lori right now. "Tell him we'll come."

"That's great. He says he has a surprise too."

"How lovely," I say, trying to sound enthusiastic, while realizing my word choice makes me sound sarcastic. "I'm in the car now. See you at home."

Pulling into the traffic, I close my mind to my father's surprise, to the questions competing for answers in my brain, to the confusions of the past two days, and try to enjoy this moment of solitude. The drive home is usually when I do my best thinking, when problems from the day are suddenly made clear, but it's the day after our engagement and I haven't heard from Moses once.

CHAPTER FIVE

Lori looks up from the kitchen table when I get home, a textbook and binder in front of her. I hang my bag on the rack and walk past her, giving her a quick shoulder hug and kiss on the temple. "Did you call Pop?"

"Yeah. We're going over for three thirty. Dinner's at five. We'll pick Uncle Archie up on the way and Junior will meet us there."

"And what does he want me to make?"

"Nothing. He said he's making Sloppy Joe's."

"Glamorous." I sit at the table across from her.

"Why do you have to do that?" She lifts her head from her textbook, looking so old—a woman almost, not a little girl.

"Do what, Lori?"

"Talk like that about him. Talk like he's a failure or something or…you like Sloppy Joe's."

"Sure, I like Sloppy Joe's. I'm sorry, kid. You know I don't really like going back there. But you're right. It'll be nice." I stand and walk towards the fridge, feeling her gaze on me. I stare at the full shelves, seeing nothing.

"And it's not so bad," she says.

"What isn't?"

"Pop's house. Going there. I know it's not fancy like this," she waves her hand through the air, "but it's nice. I like it."

"You like it, Lori? If you like it so much why are you

here? Why aren't you living with Pop, going to school with the kids you grew up with?"

She puts her head back down. Why did I say that? "Because you wanted me here," she whispers, seeming the little girl all over again.

I hold a glass of water in my hand and ache for the both of us. "I know. I'm sorry."

"I could have gone to school there. It's not such a big deal. You did. Look at how you turned out. All Miss Fancy-pants on the track to CEO." She glances up, a grin creeping through. That's Lori, always able to smooth over any situation. I don't deserve her kindness.

"But you'll do better here." I take a sip of water. "You already are. No worries about getting jumped on your way home from school." I lean against the counter. "What are you studying?"

"Advanced Chemistry."

"And how's it coming?"

"Good."

"Good. I'm going to go lie down and read for a bit."

"Sure." Her voice calls as I head towards the hall. "And Eloise—"

"Yeah."

"I'm sixteen. Not a kid, okay?"

"Yeah." I can't help but grin at her defiant expression. "I know." She's not a kid, not at all. But she also doesn't know what the world is like, not really. She has no idea how hard things can be, how hard I worked to get us here and away from there, how hard I worked to get Junior where he is now. I slip out of my pencil skirt, hose, and blouse and into my favourite fuzzy pants and tank top, pull back the covers of my bed, and crawl in. A glance at my phone reveals I have not missed a message from Moses. The only notifications have to do with my work accounts.

Settling under my covers, I luxuriate in the smooth sheets. Tokyo would not have been my top choice. I'm not eager to leave either. Moses is right, our home is here—our families, our friends. His mother would hate to see him on the other side of the world. But if I don't take this opportunity another one like it may never come.

We have to seize life's moments when we have the chance. That's one thing my mother taught me, by doing the opposite. She didn't seize a single moment. She didn't fight for her future. She gave up on it. My hand trails to the box on my night side table and I flick the lid open, gazing at the delicate heart locket inside. I haven't worn it since the day I saw her lying in the tub. It was supposed to be a reminder of her love. But love wouldn't do that.

Before she passed it along to me, I'd never seen the necklace off of her neck. A gift from her mother, she said it represented a life she'd hoped for—full of beautiful things—but one my mother obviously believed she would never receive.

Letting the chain fall through my fingers, I contemplate why I haven't pawned it by now. I've considered it, but I can't and know I never will. It's the only tangible thing of hers I have. In an odd way, it reminds me of how weak she was…and how I'll never be like her. Thinking these words is cruel, but I think them anyway, like I have so many times before. If only she'd been stronger. The poverty, the pressure, the social stigma surrounding my father's failures, it was too much for her. The life she wanted was not the life she had, and so she let go of life entirely.

She turned me into a person who would never let life do to me what it did to her. If I do well in this job, cement myself as indispensable to Everdeen, my family will never have to worry about money again. I can move Pop out of the old neighbourhood and Uncle Archie into a better facility. The necklace falls from my fingers back into the box, and I think of the words engraved inside. Words I didn't really understand when my Mom read them to me, and words I'm not sure I understand now. Maybe my mother didn't understand the words either. Perhaps my grandmother passed this message along without explaining it and it's been a mystery to us both.

Closing the lid, I pick up my phone again and scroll to Moses' beautiful face. I snapped the picture on our second date, saying I needed to get his image in my phone right away so I wouldn't mix him up with any of my other suitors. He laughed as the photo clicked. Five rings sound before he finally answers.

"Hello, my love." His voice and words wash over me like a warm rain.

"Hi." I answer with a smile.

"I was hoping you'd call. I wasn't sure how much longer I could wait."

"Why were you waiting?"

"Just giving you your space. Your time. I know how you need that sometimes. You've got a lot to think about."

"I thought maybe you were having second thoughts."

"About you? Never."

My mind travels back to last night. My hand trailing over his strong chest, his muscles against my back as his arms wrapped around me. The way he could still be so tender and passionate despite all the questions that must have been racing through his mind. "Good."

"Good? Is that all you have to say?"

I laugh. "Tell me about your day."

Moses tells me about a visit with his mom and how one of his favourite students won a regional award for an essay she wrote. When he's done filling me in, I let him know about the meeting with the girls—leaving out their hesitations—my workout, a couple of humorous moments with clients. "Oh," I add, "also, we're having dinner at my Pop's this Sunday. Do you want to come? We can tell him about the engagement." I hesitate. "If you want. If you don't think it's too soon, what with the other news?"

He laughs, rich and deep, and so much of my fear from

the day melts away. We'll work this out. "What do you take me for?"

"What do you mean?"

"Your dad already knows."

"What?" My voice rises. "You called him? You didn't let me—"

"No, no. Your dad knew before you did. I know he's a traditional sort of man. I asked his blessing last week."

"You what?"

"I asked his blessing. Isn't that the chivalrous thing to—"

"I love you, you know." I glance at the ceiling, shaking my head. "That must have made him feel good."

"I think so." I can almost see his grin. "Anyway," he continues, "I need to take off. I have a big ol' pile of marking to do."

"Yeah," I say. "I have some work and then an early day."

"I love you."

"And I you." A smile flirts across my lips. It used to drive him crazy that I'd always answer this way, afraid to say the words. Now I'm not afraid, but it's our special little goodbye.

"Sleep well." He pauses. "And Eloise."

"Yeah."

"I'm happy you said yes."

I close my eyes, wishing it were as simple as it sounds right now, as I always thought it would be. "I'm happy you gave me the chance to."

ON SUNDAY MORNING I roll over, wanting to stay under the covers a little longer. A glance at the clock reveals I've already stayed under longer than usual. It's ten thirty. Stretching, I mentally prepare myself to go home. It'll be good to see Pop. He doesn't want to come to my part of the city and I don't want to go to his, so the occasional phone call is all the contact we usually have.

I dress in a purple sweater, Pop's favourite colour on me, and leave my hair loose and wild, the way he likes it best. "Lori!" I call through her door. "You want eggs?" She doesn't respond. The door is slightly ajar and I push it open further. "Lori?" Her bed is hastily made, like it always is, but no Lori. "Lori?" I call into the halls, then walk through the living room and into the kitchen. A paper sits on the kitchen counter—tent style—with my name on it.

Hey, Sis. Gone for breakfast with a friend. I'll be back in plenty of time to pick up Uncle Archie.

Hmm. I toss the note into the recycling. Lori out with a friend she doesn't name. A boy perhaps? I'll have to do some prying later on. Seeing as I'm just cooking for myself, I go for cereal over eggs and use the extra time to lie on the couch with a book. One chapter in, my phone rings.

"Tracey, hi."

"Hi." She practically gushes into the phone. "I think I'm in love."

"In love?" I laugh. "The teacher from the next district?"

"Thomas. His name is Thomas."

"And love so fast?"

"It's not fast, Eloise. It's been three weeks."

"My apologies." I smile.

"Don't try to tell me you weren't starting to fall in love with Moses at three weeks."

"Well, starting maybe." I can't help but smile at the memories of those first weeks. "Tell me all."

"He's so handsome." She lets out a little hum. "But it's more than that. He seems so genuine, like when he talks to me I can see into his soul. He's incredibly focused on me too. We went dancing last night and I swear, he didn't even look at another woman."

"Well, that could be a problem. Are you sure he's batting for the right team?"

"Oh, I'm sure." Tracey giggles. "Definitely. There's no problems in that department."

"My, my!"

"He's attentive there too. But seriously, it goes beyond all that. He's so sweet and smart and he loves his students—you should hear him talk about them. He's so concerned about being an example and role model to them he wants us to keep all of this on the down low as far as our coworkers are concerned. Just in the beginning stages, of course, until we know it's really serious, really going somewhere. He doesn't want the students to view him as a playboy or something, get the wrong idea. Isn't that sweet?"

"That's definitely sweet," I say. "It sounds like you've found a good one."

"I think so." She sighs. "It's been so long."

"I know, Trace."

"I started wondering, you know? What's wrong with me, like maybe there's something about me that's repulsive to good and decent guys."

"Impossible."

"You say that, everyone says that. But my reality for the past six years seemed to say differently."

It's hard to know what to tell her. Ever since breaking up with her high school sweetheart a few months after finishing undergrad, Tracey has had poor luck in the love department. "Well, maybe all of that was so you'd be unattached when Thomas came along."

"Maybe." I hear the smile in her voice. "Anyway, how are you? Any wedding planning yet?"

"No, not yet. We need to figure things out with my job first. Once I formally accept it, I can ask about time-lines, hopefully get a better idea of when I'll be here and when I'll be there…that will help with planning."

"Yeah, of course." She hesitates. "So, you're really planning to go ahead with it then?"

"How could I not? This is the opportunity of a lifetime.

For someone my age to be offered an experience like this, it's basically mind blowing."

"Maybe too good to be true?"

"No, it's not. I'm the top representative, I've implemented procedures that have streamlined operations, I'm more educated than many of the men in the top positions, and as Mr. Everdeen says, I'm young enough that he can mold me to represent his company the way he desires." I laugh. "I'm also very modest."

Tracey chuckles. "You're just stating facts. So, do you want to be molded?"

"If this is what it means."

"Okay then, that's awesome, El, really awesome. I'm happy for you."

"Good. Anyway, I'm happy for you too, with Thomas. Keep me updated."

"Will do."

I look at the time. "I better let you go. I need to get some work in before dinner with the fam today."

"Telling them about the engagement?"

"And the job."

"Enjoy, Darling!"

When I hang up the phone, I put my book aside and grab the files I brought home from the office. It's going to take some work to close off or transfer my clients and contracts over to my colleagues before my transition. I'm sure it won't have to be done right away, but anything I can do to speed up the process is probably worthwhile. Several hours later, Lori walks into the apartment humming.

"And what were you up to?" I ask, watching as she removes her sweater, her face looking too flushed for the cool day.

"Just brunch with a friend."

"You said as much. And what's his name?"

"His name?" She looks at me, eyes wide.

"Yeah, his."

I can see she's debating whether to reveal or withhold. "Drake," she says.

"Drake. And what's Drake like?" I try to keep my voice friendly and interested as motherly, protective feelings battle to surface.

"Wonderful," she says, plopping down pretzel style at the other end of the couch. "He's funny and cute and smart, and best of all—he likes me!"

I grin. "Why wouldn't he?"

"No one ever has before," she says, her shyness returning. "Not really, anyway."

"I'm sure they have." I snuggle into the couch, ready for some girl-talk. "They were probably too nervous to say anything. A lot of guys won't make a move with a girl unless they're ninety-nine percent sure she likes him back. You don't strike me as a girl to go chasing after guys. That's probably why."

"You think so?"

"I'm ninety-nine percent sure."

"I didn't chase after Drake either."

"So he's probably one of those guys who's confident enough to take the risk. That's a very good thing."

"I guess," she says. "He told me I'm beautiful and sweet and not like any girl he's ever known before."

"He does sound smart." I give her an approving look, my insides twisting. Lori is sweet…and innocent and inexperienced. This guy could be all she says or could be a sleaze trying to take advantage of her naiveté. I'm her sister, not her mom, but I can't help myself. "Be careful though. Make sure you don't let your emotions run away with you, you know?"

"I won't." She grins like a girl in deep like and squeezes my foot underneath the throw I'm snuggled up in. "You almost ready to head out?"

"Yeah, almost."

She rises from the couch and practically skips down the

hall. I should be happy for her. I am happy for her. Lori deserves someone special in her life. And if he hurts her, I'll kill him.

CHAPTER SIX

Right on time, the doorbell rings and I open the door to see Moses standing with a bouquet of chrysanthemums. "More flowers?" I sniff their rich fragrance.

"They're from my place the other night. I thought you'd like to have them here."

"Oh, you're sure you just didn't want their scent cramping your bachelor style." I wink, taking the bouquet from him.

"I have no interest in being a bachelor." He leans forward and kisses me, then waves to Lori. "How's it going short stuff?"

"Very good." I answer for her. "Isn't it, Lori?"

"Nice ring," says Lori, ignoring me. "You picked a good one."

"What's the scoop my to-be sister?" Moses gestures for her to come for a hug.

"Nothing." She wraps her arms around him then quickly pulls away.

"A boy?" He elbows her.

"Do I ask about your love life?" She grabs her purse, slings it across her body, then walks toward the door.

"You know about my love life," says Moses.

"Well."

"Well."

Lori casts me a look—half smile, half glare. "Are we

ready to go?"

"My car or yours?" says Moses, holding the door open for us.

"Mine." I grab my purse, place the flowers on a table, and usher the two out of the apartment. The drive to Uncle Archie's nursing home is full of Moses grilling Lori on her courses, her dance classes, and the two of them discussing some sitcom they both watch. My thoughts fill with how natural they sound together, how easy Moses is with my family, and the knowledge that this visit to Pop's will be made easier by his presence. I glance at him, smiling back at my sister, looking like he belongs with us. What if he won't move to Tokyo? I draw my gaze back to the road, hands solidly at ten and two. He loves me. I have no doubt about that, and he knows how important my job is to me. But his job is important to him too. So important he's considering staying at it...not moving on to a university position like he'd always planned. I glance again. He seems so natural, so fine, but is his mind racing like mine? We haven't discussed these issues since the night of the engagement. We haven't really discussed anything.

When I pull into the retirement facility, Uncle Archie is waiting inside the lobby doors. "You're three minutes late," are the first words out of his mouth when we push through the doors to greet him.

"Red lights." I step into his open arms.

"You must plan for red lights."

"Then I'd be three minutes early." He cups my head in his hands and I tilt it down for him to kiss my crown.

"I've missed you." He squeezes me to him once more. "And you need to stop growing."

"Will do." We both know it's him who's shrinking.

"And let's see this one." He puts out his arms to Lori, who steps into his embrace. "You're just shooting up."

"I'm five two," she says. "I'd hardly call that—"

"And you used to be five one." Uncle Archie kisses Lori

in the same spot he kissed me then offers a hand to Moses.

"Do you have everything you need? Meds? Anything else?" I ask.

"Listen here, I can take care of myself just fine." He winks at Moses. "Me, I'm just in this joint for easy access to the single ladies."

"Of course." I laugh, helping him down the steps and to the car. "What was I thinking?"

As we drive through the old neighbourhood, my chest tightens. It's stupid, really. This is just a street. It's not even one of the worst streets in this area. And the house is just a house. A house bursting with good memories. Lori took her first steps in that house, said her first words. We were on the front porch when Junior told me he got a full tuition scholarship, the reward for all those hours and hours of helping him study. Lots of good memories.

Lori laughs as Uncle Archie tells a story about swindling another resident to switch rooms, giving Uncle Archie the best view in the place. Uncle Archie can swindle anyone and make them happy he did. I owe my sales skills to him. Pop says Archie could convince a butterfly to give up its wings, and if they spoke the same language, I bet he could.

I manoeuvre the car into the driveway and feel Moses' hand on mine. He gives it a slight squeeze. He knows me.

This feeling of dread is silly. It's stupid. I lived in this house for years after, but now that I don't anymore, it's transformed. Now, every time I pass through the door I feel my mother's presence. I see again, the few drops of blood dripping from the upstairs landing and into the front hall. I stood, watching them, one by one as the drops made their slow descent, creating a small stain on the rug. I remember walking up the stairs, cradling Lori against my chest, full of fear. Of all of us, I'm the only one who saw. I should have been at band practice but a stomach ache brought me home early. I picked up Lori from the sitter's on the way. Junior was at basketball. Uncle Archie was at work. Pop was out looking for work. Mom probably thought he'd be the first one home, the one to find her.

"So what do you think Pop's surprise will be?" Lori asks as we walk to the door.

"With your ol' man," says Uncle Archie, "could be anything. Clearly, it's not a new ride!" He slaps the top of Pop's old clunker with a laugh.

"Maybe he's retiring," says Moses. "He must be nearing that time."

"Pop still has a few years," I say. "Besides, he'll keep working until they force him to stop. I doubt that time is yet."

I get to the door and debate knocking, but before I have a chance the door swings open to reveal my father, a huge grin on his face. He's thinner than I remember, though it's only been a few months since I've seen him last, and his face seems more lined. Despite that, he looks better than I ever remember seeing him. His smile is bright and his eyes seem full of life. "My girls!" He bellows, drawing Lori and me into a tight embrace. I'm taller than him with my heels on, but I always feel tiny in his arms. "It's been too long," he says, kissing Lori and then me, "especially for you."

"I know, Pop. I'm sorry. Work's been crazy."

"It always is."

"You look good," I offer.

"I feel good."

Junior stands a few steps behind Dad, something uncertain hiding beneath his smile.

"You're looking the part," says Moses, gesturing to Junior's attire. In a checked shirt, wool vest, and black-rimmed glasses, I can see what Moses means. "So what is it? Just a few months now and I can head to you for all my legal dealings?"

"Like what?" Junior laughs, stepping forward to give Moses a man-hug. "A prenup?"

"So you heard the news," says Moses, with an

exaggerated eye roll. "She finally convinced me to sign up for the old ball and chain."

I shake my head, "Ha ha," then turn to Junior. "Well, at least maybe when you're a legitimate lawyer you'll stop all your protests and rallies? Fight from the inside."

"Maybe." He grins, looking entirely unconvincing.

"Hopefully," I say, watching Uncle Archie and Pop give each other a hug and a tousle. "So what's your news, Pop? Lori's practically bursting."

"Well," he says, getting an odd, almost shy look on his face, "just wait here a moment."

I look at the others quizzically. My gaze lands on Junior. "You'll never believe it," he says with a pursed smile.

Pop returns with a woman on his arm. She looks to be several years younger than him with curly brown hair, obviously dyed. Her smile is tentative, revealing a row of small white teeth. Her dark brown eyes sparkle as if they're meant for a face much younger. She's petite. Nothing like Mom. But from the smile on Pop's face and the way he grasps her hand I know, at long last, he's found someone to take her place.

"This is Evelyn," he says. "Evelyn Washington, soon to be Grant."

"What?" My mouth falls open.

Lori steps forward. "Pop?"

"Don't worry," says Evelyn, her voice sweet, tender, and nothing like Mom's. "I'll treat him well."

"Does this mean you'll be my mother?" asks Lori. I whip my head towards her, not sure who I feel incensed for, our real mother, or me.

"Only if you want me to." Evelyn smiles. "I can just be your friend. I'd be happy to," she glances at me, "take the role, but I also know you all have done very well over the years."

"Yeah, we're fine," I say, feeling dizzy, which isn't like me at all. But being here, standing here, feet from where

Mom's blood… "Can we go to the living room?"

"That's a great idea," says Pop. "Is anybody thirsty? I made some punch."

A chorus of yeses and sures accompany our movement. "I'll help you," says Moses.

"Wait." Pop reaches for my arm. "I gave a greeting hug, but not a congratulations one." He hugs me again then reaches for Moses, giving him a hug and back slap. "And let's see the ring?" I offer my hand, head still reeling, trying to calculate the worth of this house, the worth of my father—I've seen his savings—it's not likely she's a gold digger. "Very nice," he says, acknowledging my ring and clapping Moses' shoulder again.

"Can I see yours?" Lori looks at Evelyn with what seems to be excitement. As Pop and Moses make their way to the kitchen, Evelyn puts out her hand to display a dainty sapphire ring.

"I already had my diamond," she says. "I wanted something a little different this time around."

"You were married?" I ease myself onto the plastic-covered couch.

"Yes. For twenty-five wonderful years. He died three years ago now."

"I'm sorry," I say.

"It was cancer." She sighs and smiles that sweet, placid smile. "He was suffering. It was a blessing, really, that he went when he did."

"Do you have children?" asks Lori.

"A boy and two girls."

"Just like us." Lori sits beside Evelyn. "How old are they?"

I look to Junior, trying to assess how he's taking the situation. Lori doesn't remember Mom at all but Junior, he remembers, and remembers more of the good than the bad from what he's said. Of course, it was still a long time ago, and it's not like Pop has never dated before. Still, marriage?

Junior catches my eye—he looks a little bewildered, but I can't read anything beyond that.

"Twenty-six, twenty-four, and twenty-one."

"Oh, okay," says Lori, "so one exactly Junior's age. And all out of the house? Will you be moving here or will Pop…is he selling?"

"We haven't quite figured that out" Pop enters the room with a tray of drinks.

"So you might sell the house?" asks Junior.

Uncle Archie leans forward. "Hey now, no one talked to me about that."

"Don't worry," says Pop, "you'd be the first person we'd talk to about that."

Uncle Archie leans back, his arms across his chest, trying to look firm. "Well, all right then."

"How long have you two even known each other?" I turn to Pop. "Why have we never met or even heard of Evelyn before now?"

"You're all so busy," says Pop. "You're hardly around. And Evelyn's children are still sensitive about the idea of her seeing anyone since their Dad's passing. They feel it's too soon. So we decided to keep it quiet until we knew how serious we were."

"And how long is that?"

"Well, we've known each other about four years now," says Pop.

"So before her husband died?"

Evelyn smiles, placing her hand on Pop's knee. "Well, Richard works at the hospital where my husband went for treatment, where he spent his last few months. We recognized each other from church and started chatting."

"You go to church?" Junior stares at Dad, eyebrows raised. "Since when?"

"Since Eloise took Lori to the city." My father shrugs, looking almost sheepish. "I was lonely."

"Pop," I say, battling confusion and guilt. "Why didn't

you…you could have come with us. I told you, you—"

"I'm not going to take charity from my daughter." I try to speak but he raises his hand. "You'd need a bigger place, and I couldn't afford something so fancy. Besides, it's not the way things work. I'd bring you down. Me in one of those swanky high-rises? Sitting in my dirty jumpsuit when your college friends stop in to visit? Come on."

I stare at my father, not knowing what to say. He thinks I'm ashamed of him. He thinks he'd be a burden to me. The worst fact—I can't deny some truth to his words. Not now, but there was a time I would have been embarrassed. It cuts me that he realizes that. "You should have told us you were lonely."

"Well." He smiles and takes Evelyn's hand. "I'm not so lonely anymore."

It's the weirdest sight—my father, genuinely happy.

"So, you've known each other for about four years," says Moses. "When did the romance start to bloom?"

Evelyn looks at Pop, a shy smile on her face. Her expression is one that made sense on Lori this morning. To see it on a woman whose hand is in my father's, a woman I didn't know existed until today, is disconcerting. That's what's bothering me the most about this—not that my father has met a woman and fallen in love, but that he's met this new woman and fallen in love without me knowing a thing about it. For years I took care of him, helped him whenever he needed it—not that I always did it as happily as I should have, and not that I've been keeping up with it lately, he hasn't seemed to need me to. Now I know why.

"Only about a year ago," says Evelyn. "We were friends first. Good friends. And then it turned into something more."

"You've been seeing each other for a year?" Lori's expression falls. "And you never wanted to meet us? Pop, you never thought—"

"I told you," says Pop. "Her children."

"But what does that have to do with us? We don't even remember Mom—" Lori glances from me to Junior. "Well, I don't anyway."

"You remember Lincoln and LaMeia?" Pop turns to Junior.

"Sure, I…oh." He leans back in the armchair he's in, letting it swallow more of his weight. "You're their mom. Mrs. Washington. I still talk to Lincoln from time to time."

"Word gets around," says Pop.

"So they know now?" asks Junior.

"We're going to tell them later tonight." Evelyn folds her hands on her lap and lifts her shoulders slightly, looking nervous but excited. "That's why dinner is so early. We're going to LaMeia's place to meet all three of them for some evening appetizers."

Lori, Junior and I sit silently. Uncle Archie pushes himself up from the rocking chair he's in and takes three long strides over to Pop. He reaches his hand out, pulls Pop up, then clamps an arm around his shoulder, hugging him tightly. "Have we even had congratulations?" he asks in his deep, gravelly voice. "I'm happy for you ol' man."

"Old?" laughs Pop. "I'm thirteen years your junior."

"Ah," says Uncle Archie, his hand on Pop's shoulder. "But you're the one who's settling down to married life. I'm a fresh young bachelor on the prowl till the day I die. So age really is just a number."

The rest of us stand, give congratulations, and exchange hugs with both Pop and Evelyn.

As we sit back down, Moses asks, "Have you decided on a date?"

"Not yet," says Pop, "we didn't want to take any thunder away from you two. We figured we'd do it pretty quietly, maybe after your honeymoon." He grins. "So hopefully you're not going to take too long."

"We are a little eager to start our new lives together," says Evelyn, bringing Pop's hand up to her lips and giving it a quick kiss. As she drops his hand a shocked, embarrassed expression crosses her face. "Not that we mean to rush you."

"Have you chosen a date?" asks Pop.

I look to Moses, then back at my father. "No, I have other news that may put the wedding on hold."

"A baby!" shouts Uncle Archie.

"No." I shake my head. "Why do people keep thinking that? A promotion."

"Oh, a promotion," he says. "Well, that's good too. Congratulations, my sweet. You just keep climbing up that ladder!"

"What kind of promotion?" asks Pop.

Once I've explained it all and answered their initial questions, the room is quiet for several breaths. Pop turns to Moses. "You're okay with this?"

"A decision hasn't been made yet," says Moses, "on whether or not she's taking it for sure, or whether she'll stay on if she does." He shrugs. "We still have things to figure out. Either way, it's an amazing honour that shows all of her hard work has paid off. I'm proud of her."

"We're all proud of her," says Pop.

"Wait, wait." Junior puts his hand up. "Why you? No offence, El, but it seems highly unusual for him to pick you when lots of people must be in a better position to take on that role, people who wouldn't need mentoring and molding. Are you sure this is legit?"

"He explained all that," I say, taking offence anyway. "It's a big move, obviously, and the people in those positions have families, children, are set in their ways. He wants someone young, fresh, who really can be molded, who doesn't have such heavy attachments—"

"You don't think Moses is an attachment?" asks Pop.

"Moses could move." I glance over at him. "We can figure it out."

Both Pop and Junior look to Moses. "I'm trying to keep

an open mind," he says.

"But still," Junior rests his elbows on his knees, "you can't be the only…lightly attached person there."

I list off my accomplishments, ones they should already know. "Besides," I add, "he wants to pass on his knowledge to someone who'll absorb it but also to someone who has her own mind."

"Well, you having your own mind I can believe." Uncle Archie slaps his knee and chuckles. "Now this whole molding business—that Mr. Everdeen may be in for a nasty surprise!"

"I can do what I need to do," I say. "This is the opportunity of a lifetime."

"It sounds it." Pop rubs his hand across his chin. "But Tokyo? You want to move so far away?"

"It's a really big pay raise, Pop. I could come visit probably three or four times a year. It wouldn't be too bad."

"And you'd be there?" He looks to Moses. "To keep her safe?"

"We're still trying to figure things out," says Moses, "we don't know that she's accepting it yet."

"When do you have to decide?" asks Junior.

"Tuesday."

"And the wedding?" says Pop.

"We'll figure it out."

"You've got a lot of figuring to do." Uncle Archie shakes his head.

"We can wait until after I'm established over there before getting married. Lots of people have one to two-year engagements."

Moses turns his gaze to me. "So you have thought about it."

"A bit." I look to Pop. "We certainly wouldn't want you and Evelyn to feel like you had to wait if that was the case."

Pop rubs his chin again. "It's what you've always wanted, I guess. To get far away from here?"

A chill settles over me and seems to coat the room as well. Lori gives me a cutting look. "That's not fair. I didn't know this was coming. I didn't—"

"Well, anyways." Pop rises. "Who's hungry? The scent of the Joe's tempting you yet?"

"I could eat," says Junior.

"Me too." Lori stands and grasps Pop's arm with both hands as she heads to the kitchen. It's an action she started when she was about five years old. It always made me think she held on like that, with both hands, to make sure he didn't disappear too.

CHAPTER SEVEN

After dinner we drop Uncle Archie and Lori off. Moses gets into his car and I drive behind him, yet again, my hands tightly grasping the wheel. Images fight their way into my mind. I manage to block out the worst moment, but others flow freely.

The day Mom left the first time, I came home happy, proud. Her yelling, her frustrations, her anger at not living the life Pop so wanted to give her was commonplace by then. We saw her smiles so infrequently that when she did smile it felt like a gift. The paper in my hand would bring that smile. I was sure of it. For weeks I'd felt a failure each Friday, never winning my class's student of the week award. I embodied what it meant to be a model student—I did extra assignments, helped my classmates whenever I could, volunteered my recesses to help clean up after art class. Yet I never won. This Friday though, Mrs. Vrantis announced a surprise—the student of the month award. And that student was me. I jumped with joy, knowing I'd make my Mom smile.

I tiptoed into my parents' room, my body rigid with excitement. 'Mom. I have a surprise for you.'

'Not now.'

'It will make you happy.' My feet slid across the rough carpet as I inched my way over to her. Her smell, lemon cleaner and bleach, filled my nostrils and made my smile grow.

'I told you I'm busy.' She waved her hand at me, gesturing for me to leave. I stayed and stepped closer. Two suitcases and a duffel lay across the bed. We used them when we moved into Uncle Archie's house several months earlier.

'What are you doing?'

'I'm packing, Eloise.' She spit out my name like it tasted bad in her mouth, like she couldn't wait to be rid of it.

I shuffled closer. 'Are we moving again? I like it here.'

'We're not moving.' She considered each item before placing it in. Her hands moved deftly, the way they had the few times she'd taken me with her to clean houses—years before. Her hair fell in long dark waves across her shoulders. Not curly and kinky like mine, it did whatever she wanted. Her skin was light, like caramel candy, and soft. When I was younger, I loved to rub my cheek against her arm.

'Then why are you packing?'

She looked at me straight on, she smiled, but not the kind I wanted. This kind made me more alone. 'Because I'm going on a trip.' The word 'I'm' came out long and heavy.

'When will you be back?'

'I don't know.' The air hung between us. She stopped folding her clothes and looked at me with an expression that made me think, *she does love me. She's not going anywhere.*

'But when?'

She turned back to the suitcase and continued folding. 'When your father's a millionaire.'

After zippering the final bag she picked up all three and walked past me. I followed her up the hall, down the stairs, and through the living room. Junior sat watching reruns of Duck Tales on our little rabbit-eared TV. She held his head in her hands and kissed the top of it. He smiled up at her, saying nothing, then returned his gaze to the screen. At the front door she hesitated, turned, at last acknowledged me trailing behind her. She waved for me to come toward her and I ran into her embrace, holding on so tight she had to peel my arms away. The door opened and closed. My mom was gone.

Eight and a half months later the door opened again and my mom stepped over the threshold, with Lori in her arms.

I pull into the visitor's parking section at Moses' apartment and turn off the engine. My eyes are dry, but I'm not ready to go upstairs. I've never quite put into words the way it felt when I saw her there again, though God knows the psychologist had me try. Seeing a ghost couldn't have been more shocking, which was odd because every single day I imagined her standing at the threshold, just like she was. When I heard footsteps on the porch, even knowing by the time of day it was Uncle Archie or Pop, my body would tense, my heart quicken in anticipation. In summer, the mailman tended to come at different times of the day—this maddened me. At night I lie in bed going over every moment of that last day, and then of the last week, of moments as far back as I could remember, wondering which exact moment it happened—what exact instant did she know she'd leave. What action or word made her decide Junior and I weren't enough reason to stay. I told no one. I talked about it with no one. Without being asked, I took on my mother's share of the household chores.

Still, as she stood there, holding this squiggling thing in her arms, I was surprised to see my mother. She introduced the baby as Delorita. When Pop asked about the name, Mom looked at him as if he were less than nothing. 'It means pain,' she said, 'sorrows.'

Pop took Lori into his arms. 'I know what it means.' It was the first time he looked at my mother with what seemed like hate. The emotion only lasted an instant. As he pulled away the blanket half masking Lori's features, the look was pure love.

Closing my mind to these moments, I step out of the car and head to the lobby where Moses, who entered through the parking garage, buzzes me in. In the elevator I think the words I've thought over and over through the years. If I could hold these words, they'd be a talisman: I am enough. When I step out of the elevator Moses is standing in the open apartment door, leaning against the support, looking like shelter. And with his eyes on me, those feelings in the elevator don't seem so important anymore. The words seem easy to believe. I am enough.

"That was a day." He opens his arms, inviting me to step into them.

"I'm happy for Pop," I say. "I guess."

"You guess?"

I pull my head back so I'm still tight against him but can see his face. "It's weird, don't you think? After all these years that he now wants to remarry?"

"He's found someone he *wants* to marry. If anything, it's weirder that he didn't want it sooner."

I shrug. "What do you think of her?"

"I think she's great."

"She's nice." I let my hand trail across his waist as I step through the threshold. "What?" I spin around. "No champagne? No flowers?"

"Is that what you expect now?" He moves toward me. "I could do that if you want, every time you come to visit."

"And what about when I stop visiting?" I make my way into the apartment, passing the kitchen and entering the open concept living and dining room. "What about when your home is mine?"

"We'll drink bubbly every night and turn our house into a virtual greenhouse of blossoms."

"Sounds good." He closes the distance between us and lifts me into his arms. I let myself melt into his kiss.

He sets me down on the couch and sits on the other end of it. "I don't really want to, but with all those unanswered questions from today I think it's time we talk about some answers."

I prop myself up against the pillows, my legs across his

lap, and nod my agreement.

"So where are you with all of this?" he asks.

"I want to take the job."

"Have you even considered not taking it?"

"I've considered it…but it's such an amazing opportunity. I know it's a big change, a lot to ask. But I'm confident you'll love Tokyo—and love whatever job you get."

"I love it here. I love my current students."

"And you can grow to love a new place too. It just seems foreign to you, different, but once you're there, it won't." I brush my curls out of my face, situating them so I can lie my head back comfortably. "And your family, I know you'll miss them, but I meant what I said today. We can come back several times a year and with video messaging you can still keep in touch."

He pulls the end of the blanket so it covers my feet and his lap. "Why is this so important? You're successful already and even if you couldn't work your way up at Everdeen without this opportunity, you can always move on to another company."

"I know."

"Don't be mad," he squeezes my toe, "but I've always thought you seemed kind of obsessed with this idea of success, of wealth, of making it to the top." He smiles. "I admire your drive, but there are more important things."

"I know there are more important things." I draw my feet away from him and sit up against the other end of the couch. "If I thought it was the most important thing, I'd go whether you wanted to come with me or not."

"Okay, okay." He grins that placating grin he has. "I said don't get mad."

His ideas about life are simpler than mine. I don't know how to make him understand why it's so important. I don't know that I even fully understand it myself. I just know this is a chance to be secure, and I can't let that chance go. "I'm not mad. I've just worked for this. And this job will let me take care of everyone."

"Who says they need taking care of? Your family seems to be doing all right, El. I know it fell on you to make sure everyone was okay for a long time, but they're all fine now, better than fine."

"Sure." I look at the wall above him. "My father is fifty-three and still breaking his back as a janitor."

"His back looks just fine. And it's not like he'd take anything from you, anyway. You know that."

"Well, he might when he can't work anymore. He doesn't exactly have a retirement fund. And I have ways of helping out without it seeming like charity."

"It'll be all right." Moses pulls my legs back toward him. "I promise. And your brother and sister, you've got them on great paths. They don't need your money."

"Lori still has to get an education—years of tuition fees. And if she actually gets into the Academy? That'll be even more expensive."

"And that's not your responsibility. You worked yourself through school, you paid off the debts you had. She can do the same."

He doesn't get it. I let out a puff of air. "I don't want her to have to. I made it look easy." I look down at the blanket, fingering a loose thread. "But it was hard. Incredibly hard."

"It'll all get figured out. We can help her if need be. With both of our salaries it'd be no problem. And it'd be good for her to work, anyway. Give her more discipline and drive."

"What are you trying to say?"

"Nothing at all. Just that those are good qualities. Besides, El. If Lori needs anything from you at this point in her life, it's your presence."

"You're supposed to be open to this." I lean forward, resting my hand on his shoulder. "Are you?"

He sighs, tilting his head back and forth, then grins. "Yeah, if it's really that important to you, I'm open."

"It is."

"Okay. But you need to be open to giving it up if I can't see myself having a life there. I'll give it my best shot but if I can't be happy there you'll come back—for us?"

"That's not going to happen." I grin. "You'll love Tokyo. It's so vibrant, so full of life. Just like you."

He laughs. "Well, if you love it that much I imagine I'll love it too. I just need to know what's important to you is us. Us figuring out how to make our lives work in the best way possible."

"Absolutely."

"We have other things to talk about too."

"The wedding."

"Yeah. The wedding." He purses his lips. "You say it like it's a burden."

"No, not at all." I make my voice light. "It's a little overwhelming right now. That's all. With my mind so full of this new position, how the logistics are all going to work."

He pauses before he speaks. "We can put it aside. There's no real rush."

"You mean you're not desperate to marry me?"

"I'm desperate to spend my life with you." He wraps his strong arms around me and draws me to his side.

I sigh and snuggle into him. "So you're happy for Pop. You think this is all right?"

"Yeah. Why wouldn't it be? Evelyn seems like a nice lady and your Pop's been alone for so long."

"He has." I let the room go quiet as I stare at the city lights outside his balcony window.

Moses rubs his thumb across the exposed flesh of my shoulder. "You okay?"

"I'm all right."

"I know it's hard for you to go back there. I know—"

"Don't." My hand reaches up to find his and squeezes. "I don't want to think about it." I turn and cast him a smile. "How about we put a movie on. Just cuddle and relax?"

"Sounds good to me."

We select a film and Moses dims the lights. Within minutes, my mind travels back to childhood

'You're a failure!' My mother's voice slams against the wall. 'You're nothing!' Pop stands in the middle of the room, taking in the words, looking like he believes every one of them. Mom picks up one of my schoolbooks and flings it at him. He blocks the book with his raised hands, as if he really needs protection from it. 'You can't provide for me. You can't provide for your children. You're worthless.'

'There were cutbacks. It wasn't personal. I'll get another job.' His voice is so meek. I'm hidden behind the couch but can see his shoulders slump. He looks small. 'We'll be okay.'

'Will we, Richard? Will we?' Her voice is nasty, mocking. Do other mothers sound like this? Do other mothers bristle and pull away when their daughters try to hug them or when their husbands pass by and offer a kiss?

'You said this country would be our freedom,' she continues. 'You said we'd have more money than we knew what to do with, more opportunity. You said it would be wonderful.'

'It will be, Rosie. It will. It takes time.'

'Five years!' Her voice reminds me of nails against a chalkboard. 'Five years of scrubbing other people's floors and toilets. Five years of putting my babies in hand-me-downs, of wearing them myself. Look at my nails.' She steps towards him, walking into my view, and flashes her fingers before his eyes. 'Look at them. Five years of living in a cramped and dirty apartment, living with our children in our room, watching you lose job after job.'

'It wasn't dirty,' says my father. 'It was cozy. And now we're with Archie. It's nice here.'

'It's not ours.'

'He's family, Rosie. It's as good as ours.'

'Your family. And five years since I've seen my family.' I crawl out to get a better view and watch my mother's rage transform to tears.

'We'll see them,' Pop says. 'We will. I just need to save the money to—'

'You said that!' Her voice hits the walls again. 'You said soon, soon, and my father died waiting for your soon.'

'I know.'

She raises her arms to pummel him and he grasps her wrists, showing strength he rarely does. He draws her into his chest, wrapping his arms around her. My father is a small man but, crumpled the way she is, my mother seems tiny against him. 'I'm sorry.' He cries into her hair. I can actually see the tears. I've never seen his tears. Pop's face seems to melt into her hair. 'I'll do better. I'll be better. It's harder than I—'

'When?' She yanks away, separating herself from his touch, as if his failure is contagious. She spits at his feet. 'You are nothing.'

My mother picks up her purse, slips into her shoes, and walks out the door. She doesn't return until after Junior and I are already asleep, entangled in each other's arms in my little bed.

Their murmurs sound through the wall—my father's pleadings, his apologies, the slap of flesh against flesh. Pop would never hit a woman, which means he's letting himself be hit. The next morning he was out early looking for a new job like he said he would be, but my mother didn't wait. The next afternoon I watched her pack.

MY BODY SHAKES GENTLY back and forth, as if I'm in a boat. I open my eyes to see Moses' smile. "I guess you didn't find the movie that captivating."

"It's done?"

"No. I turned it off."

"Why?"

"You were snoring."

"I wasn't." I sit up.

"No." He kisses my nose. "You were whimpering, though. Bad dreams?"

"Yeah." I kick the blanket off of me, annoyed at my body's betrayal.

"Want to talk about it?"

"No." I fold the blanket and extend my hand to him. "Let's go to bed."

His eyes light up and I swat him. "Not that kind of bed."

He grins. "I'm very convincing."

CHAPTER EIGHT

L ori looks up from fixing her breakfast when I return the next morning. She laughs. "You seriously need to keep more clothes at Moses'."

"I have clothes there." I set down my bag and lean against the fridge. "I had some work stuff I didn't think to take. I came back for that."

"When are you two going to move in together, anyway?" She carefully fills each square of her waffle with syrup.

"Those things will kill you—all preservatives and I don't know what else."

"Well, then maybe you should be here to make me fresh ones."

"Maybe." I steal a strawberry from her plate and pop it into my mouth. "In Tokyo I could probably afford a personal maid and chef. If you come, you'll eat like a queen."

"Will Moses live with you there?"

"We haven't talked about it. Mmm, those are good." I steal another strawberry. "I assume so."

"He can live here, you know. Until then. I wouldn't mind." She raises an eyebrow, looking way too comfortable with the subject matter for my liking. "I know what you do at his apartment. It wouldn't make any difference if he were here." She screws up her face. "Unless you're really loud about it. That could be a problem."

"Stop. You're a little girl who knows nothing of these

things."

"I'm not so little." She grins.

"I know." I smooth my hand over her hair, so different from mine, so like Mom's. "I just like to pretend you are."

"So if you go to Tokyo and I don't come…how much would we see each other?"

"I could probably come back a few times a year. And you could visit me. Holidays. The summer break."

"And…I mean I don't think I would, but you'd want me to move with you, if I wanted?"

"Yes. You should think about it." I pour a glass of orange juice and sit across from her at our peninsula. "Tokyo has a lot to offer you. It has excellent universities. One has an acclaimed dance program. On your breaks you could travel Asia."

"And they'd want a foreigner taking a spot? Come on. Besides, I don't even know if I want to go to university."

"Lori, it's important to—"

"I want to go to a dance school, not a school with a program in dance." She looks at her plate and takes a bite. "If that doesn't happen, if that won't be my life," she purses her lips, "then I don't know what I want to do."

"University helps you figure out what you want to do."

"Well, maybe I'd want to travel for a few years first." Her voice speeds up. "I've been looking into these work abroad and travel programs. Drake was saying that—"

"Drake?"

Lori's face goes flush. "Yeah, my friend, Drake."

"Your friend?"

"Oh, stop it." She fidgets with her napkin. "You already know we're more than friends."

"Okay, so go on."

"Drake was saying the way these programs work is that you get to travel and explore as well as live in certain communities while working or volunteering. Some of them even count toward college credit."

"Yeah, I know about them."

"That's not what you did though?"

"Nope, I backpacked the old-fashioned way. Just me and wherever the mood took me, living on a shoestring."

"Blows my mind." She laughs. "Miss have to control everything all the time, going wherever the mood took you."

"Well," I hesitate, "I guess it wasn't entirely like me. But in a way I felt more *me* than maybe ever before. Free, you know? I guess the control factor was that I knew I had the money to do it, and if ever that money got scarce, I had a whole list of places that let travellers work for a few weeks to get some cash."

"I don't know that I'm up for that." She cuts the remainder of her waffle into bite-sized pieces. "I like the idea of really getting to know one place, one people."

"Tokyo is one place, one people."

"That's not what I mean."

"Maybe it's the idea of a certain travelling companion that holds such allure?"

She grins. "Perhaps." Her smile lessens. "What happens if Moses doesn't want to move to Tokyo?"

"That's not going to happen." I try to ignore the immediate tightening of my chest.

"Yeah, but—"

"It won't." I stand up. "I'm sure of it."

⁂

THE OFFICE SEEMS MORE in focus than usual as I walk through it. I notice the pale mint green paint, the way the light shines through the floor to ceiling windows, and how someone has situated the colourful art on the wall to take advantage of that light. Excitement tingles through me. This won't be my office for much longer, so I better soak it in now. It's hard to get through my day knowing I'm leaving while keeping the news secret from my colleagues. My co-worker, Erik, gives me an odd look when I say my workload is packed and pass a new client on to him. While interacting with current clients, I'm mentally trying to figure out who will best suit their needs when I'm no longer on the job.

As I'm packing up to head home, Mr. Everdeen's face appears at my door. He taps the glass. "Please, come in." I stand up straight and watch him glide into the room.

"I'm sorry to disturb you, Eloise."

"It's not a disturbance. What can I do for you?"

Everdeen holds his hands behind his back and paces the room. "Another big mix-up at the Tokyo branch, some cultural faux pas or some such thing." He turns and stops in front of me. "I leave for Tokyo tomorrow. If you have made your decision and your decision is yes, I want you to come with me. It's not likely I'll have another chance to—"

"Yes." I step around the desk in eagerness. "Absolutely, yes."

He steps back, presumably shocked at my interruption, but looks pleased. "And your family, your…" He glances at my left hand, "fiancé? I heard rumours you got engaged. He's okay with this?"

"It's taking him some time to warm up to the idea. But as you know, I can sell just about anything."

He laughs heartily, the laugh of a man who's used to being in control. "That you can, my girl. That you can." He strides towards the door. "Be at the airport for two p.m. tomorrow. I'll have Julie send you all the details and arrange a car." He turns back to me before opening it. "Don't bother coming in. I'm sure you'll have stuff at home to take care of."

"I'll be there." My voice is confident. I am not. Tomorrow? Once Everdeen is out of sight, I suck in my breath and sling my computer bag across my shoulder. This will not be an easy sell.

"Was that Mr. Everdeen," asks Sammy, whose office is

next door to mine. "Yes." I shut the door behind me.

"Well, what was it about? I've only seen him on this floor once."

"I'll be working on a project with him." Of all of my colleagues, Sammy is most definitely my least favourite.

"A project with Everdeen?" She gives an obvious look to my ring. "Aren't you engaged?"

"Yes, I'm engaged." I head down the hall. She trails after me. "It's not that kind of project."

"Uh huh." Her voice drips with snarky disbelief. "Then what is it?"

"I'm sure he'll send out an announcement at some point." I hold in my annoyance at her words. "And thanks for the vote of confidence."

She laughs. "Oh, come on, Eloise. He's like God here. What else would he want with lowly minions like us?"

"Maybe that's why he's not making a visit to your office." I keep my voice as neutral as possible. "If you thought of yourself as more than a lowly minion others may too." I push the down button for the elevator and lean against the wall.

She holds her smile as well. Good for her. "You can't tell me what it is?"

"That's not my prerogative." The elevator doors open and I step in, turning so I look out at her. "I won't be able to make my meeting with the executives at Southlink tomorrow. Would you like to handle the presentation for me?"

"Would I?" Her face glows. "Thanks. That's awe-" The doors shut and I slink into the corner of the enclosed space, glad to be alone. Tomorrow I'll be in Tokyo. Tonight I have to tell Moses. I glance at my watch—6:20—and try to remember whether Moses has basketball on Monday. No. Monday he leads a study group after school then goes to the gym. He won't be home yet, but soon, and he'll be hungry. I dial his favourite Thai place, put in a delivery order, then slip into my car and weave my way into the dying traffic. At a fancy Chocolatier shop, I pick out an assortment of Moses' favourites. Next stop, I hit the liquor store for a bottle of Grand Marnier, hoping all these things will appease him.

As I'm about to buzz my way into Moses' apartment, I meet the Thai delivery man and pay him on the spot, adding the bundle of food to my already full arms. I curse myself for not thinking to change into flats as I balance everything precariously. Without dropping a thing, I make it to the apartment door. Once inside, I lay out the containers of food along the counter, light some candles, set up the chocolate and Grand Marnier in the living room, and wait by the door. Then wait, and wait, and move to the couch to keep waiting. At 8:15 the key turns in the lock. Jumping up from the couch, where I've been sorting through client profiles, I make my way to the counter and stand, arms stretched out like a game show host to display my offering.

His face lights up at the sight of me. "What's this?" He steps forward, scanning the spread, then pulls me in for a kiss. "It smells amazing. I'm starved."

"It's a little cold." I move behind him and wrap my arms around his middle.

"We'll heat it up." He peeks under a few lids. "Some of the kids were having some trouble and there's a big test next week so I stayed late with them, then still hit the gym."

"You softy."

"What can I say?" He turns and reaches for some plates. I let my arms fall from him and lean against the counter. He smiles back at me. "I love those kids."

"And I love you."

"Apparently." He raises an eyebrow. "I would have called if I knew you were waiting. Any special occasion? Some anniversary I'm not aware of?"

"No. I have news."

"Oh." His face drops. "News I'll like or…?"

"It's not bad news. It's just…sooner than expected."

"What is it?" He sets his plate on the counter. "Spit it out."

"Mr. Everdeen came to see me today. He has to head to Tokyo. Suddenly. He asked or…basically told me to come with him."

"You're not even supposed to give your answer until tomorrow!"

"I know."

"And you said yes?"

I shrug.

"And this food is to try to buy me into being okay with it?"

"I'm not trying to buy you into anything. I just wanted to have a nice night with you before I leave."

"Humph."

"I have chocolate and Grand Marnier in the living room, too. Let's just enjoy the—"

"He made you decide on the spot? You couldn't have called me to talk about it first? At least pretend you care about my opinion?"

"Of course I care about your opinion. It's just—"

"It's just that if you've already made up your mind, you've already made up your mind." He leans on the opposite counter, arms crossed, staring me down.

"We agreed that I was going to go to Tokyo. We talked about this."

"I know." He picks his plate back up, fills it, and slides it into the microwave. "I didn't think it'd be so quick."

"Neither did I."

"How long will you be gone?"

"He wasn't sure. Two, maybe three weeks."

"On a day's notice?" He taps his fork on the counter, again and again.

"What difference does it—"

"What if you had kids?"

"I don't have kids. That's one of the reasons he was

interested in me."

"Well, what about when we do have children? Will you take off on a business trip like this then?"

"That's years away." I pick up my own plate and scoop food onto it. "I'll be in a more stable position by then and I already told you I won't be travelling so much when I'm settled in Tokyo."

"Years? How many years?"

"I don't know." I turn to him. "Five. Seven?"

"Five to seven years?" His voice raises. He drops the fork and crosses his arms.

"Once we're established."

"We're established now."

The microwave beeps, making him jump.

I keep my voice even, conversational. "When did you want to start having children?"

"I don't know. A couple of years. Maybe two."

"Two?" Now my voice rises. "We might not even be married in two years."

"Well, when I planned the proposal I thought we could be married in six or seven months."

The reminder beep sounds and he steps to the microwave, yanking open the door, pausing, then gently setting his plate down.

"I don't want to fight." I say.

"Neither do I."

Silence.

I put my plate in the microwave, biding my time before speaking. "I'm not positive I ever want children. Maybe, but—"

"What?"

"I'm not sure." This is the first time we've fought. It takes me back to childhood, to memories I don't need right now. "My mom, you know…" I shake my head, letting my words trail off, hating the way my voice catches when I speak of her, how, even after all this time, my hands sometimes shake. "I don't know that I'll be a good mother."

He steps toward me, sets his hands on my hips, pulls me close. "You'll be an amazing mother. Look at how you were with Junior and Lori. How can you even wonder?"

"They weren't mine."

"Exactly. When it's your child, you'll be that much more phenomenal."

His arms make me seem tiny. Usually I like it, but in this moment it makes me feel fragile. "Do we need to talk about this now?"

"No. But we'll need to talk about it. I want kids, Eloise. That's really important to me. I thought you did too. We've talked about it."

"You've talked about it, and hypothetically." I shift out of his embrace. My stomach growls. "I've entertained the idea. But have I ever actually told you I want children?"

He opens his mouth as if to speak but no sound comes out. His brow furrows. "No," he admits, "not explicitly, but you've implied. I'm sure you've implied."

"Maybe." I shrug. "Sometimes I think I do. Sometimes I don't."

"I think that means you do." He comes behind me as I make my way to the table, trailing his hand across my back.

"If I do have kids, I don't want them yet."

Right in the centre of my back his hand pauses, then drops. He turns so I can see his face, his crinkled brow and clenched jaw. "You're right," he says, and I can't tell if it's anger or sadness in his voice. "Let's not talk about this now. You've had a lot on your mind the last few days, we both have." He smiles, then gives me a quick peck before reaching back for his food, holding it up like he's the game-show host. "And it's never a good idea to have important conversations on an empty stomach."

I allow myself to laugh, then follow him to his little dinette where we eat in near silence.

"A movie?" he asks when we finish. "In my arms?" I

nod and curl up on the couch with him, the chocolate in my lap and our glasses of Grand Marnier beside us. We fall asleep like that. Such a familiar occurrence. When I wake, the clock under the TV flashes. Debating what to do, I watch it change from 2:03 to 2:04. Rather than tiptoeing away from him and heading home to my own bed, like I usually would, I stay in his arms until his alarm wakes us four and a half hours later.

CHAPTER NINE

Later that day I stand outside the door of Autumn and Allison's office, waving. Autumn glances up from a slew of papers in front of her. 'Hey,' she mouths, then motions with her hand for me to come in.

"Something monumental must have brought this on." She walks around her desk to give me a quick hug. "Eloise Grant not at work at ten on a Monday morning. Did you quit?"

"Me?" I laugh. "Never. And it's Tuesday."

"Oh, right." She shakes her head. "I really am overworked. So," she pulls over a chair for me, "tell me what it is."

"I'm going to Tokyo." I slide into the chair and cross one leg over the other.

"I know." She sits. "Well, you hadn't decided for sure but now you have? And Moses is okay with it?"

"Yes." I smile. "But I'm actually going today."

"Today?" She leans back.

"In a few hours. Moses is," I search for the right word, "shocked. We had a bit of a tiff last night. But we still fell asleep in each other's arms. I think it'll be fine."

"I hope so," says Autumn. "He's a good guy. You two are awesome together."

"I know." I watch my ring glint under the office's fluorescent lighting, then draw my attention back to Autumn. "How's the business going?"

"It's steady." Autumn gestures to the files on her desk. "We don't have a full client load yet but every week we're building our list."

"And what type of marketing has been working best for you?"

She stares at me for a moment. "Why are you here, El? Did you come to talk business?"

"No." I pat a hand on my knee. "I guess I wanted to see you before I go, and to ask you a favour."

"Ask away."

I ask Autumn if she'll mind filling in at Aspire for me. She agrees, and we spend the next few minutes going over the topic for my next session. With her schedule she can only commit to two sessions, which should cover until I get back.

"They're amazing girls," I say. "If I'm not back in time, I'll have to find someone else to help out. Think Sheila could put up with teenagers?"

Autumn laughs.

I smile, remembering how excited the girls were, and how great it felt working with them. "I'll make it work."

"You always do. So," she twirls a pen, then taps it on the desk, "is there anything else going on?"

"Did you know my father is getting married?"

"No." She hesitates, her brows furrowing. "Is this good news or…"

"I don't know. It's surprising news. They'll likely be getting married before I do…if I do."

"What do you mean? You're not thinking of leaving Moses? Is it the job?"

"No, no. It's just—" I sigh. "It's part of what the tiff was about. He thought we'd start having kids in the next year or so. I was thinking the next decade, if ever, though I told him five to seven."

"Why'd you say that? If you don't mean it? And you don't want to have children?"

"I don't know. Not yet. It's scary, you know?"

"You're not your mom, Eloise."

"That's not what—"

"You're not your mom."

I look away from Autumn, wishing she didn't know me quite so well. "My mom was all right," I say, "before she wasn't. But it's not just that. Kids in a year or two? With how much I travel—that's impossible. And even when I'm settled in my new position who knows what kind of hours I'll work?"

"So what's more important? Kids or your job?"

"Right now?" I lean back in my chair. "My job. Most definitely. The real question is what's more important, my job or Moses?"

Autumn nods, her face unreadable, and I can read just about anyone. "And?"

"I don't know."

She taps her pen again. "My guess is this is the first time you two have talked about this?"

"Yes."

"Give yourself time to think about it. You've had a lot of sudden things happen. I would think, though, if you're not sure the man you want to be with is more important than your job, there's a very real possibility he's not the man you should be with." She purses her lips. "I would have given up any job, any opportunity, to be with Matt."

I want to tell her it's different…but I don't know that it is. "I don't think I'd give up Moses for my job." I pause. "I wouldn't. But he might give me up if I'm not willing to put kids before my career."

"It works out to the same thing."

"I suppose." I check my watch, more to not have to look into her eyes than to know the time. This is not what I came to talk about. At the same time, I know Autumn can read through my facades like no one else, and I could have just called about the Aspire session. I stand and smile. "Thanks so much for helping me out next week. I'll forward you the info in a couple of hours."

She makes her way around the desk. "Not a problem. It should be fun." She rubs a hand along my upper arm. "Don't stress, okay? Go to Tokyo. Have a great time. Assess the job. Give yourself time to think when you have the chance. It'll work out. Moses loves you. Really loves you. I never thought he'd even consider moving to Tokyo. But he's thinking of it, right?"

"He is." We hug. I step away with a wave, my heels clicking against the tiled floor of her office then sinking into silence on the rubber padding of the studio.

Would Moses give up his dream of children in the near future for me? He's most often the one to compromise in our relationship, so he might. But he wouldn't give up children completely, and I wouldn't want him to. "This isn't something you have to figure out right now," I speak into the space of my car. "Not at all."

On the drive home, I realize I didn't think to call Lori before she left for school this morning. As Moses got ready for work, I crawled into his bed and snuggled under the covers, not waking up until nine. Checking the clock, I see I have time to go home, quickly pack some items for the trip, meet Lori during her lunch, then contact a few key clients before the flight.

"*Hey, Lor,*" I text when I reach our parking lot. "*Need to talk for a minute. Meet me out front at 12:30.*"

"*Everything okay?*" she replies twenty minutes later.

"*Absolutely.*"

The bench I wait at gives me a perfect view of the school's front doors. At precisely twelve thirty Lori appears at the top of the steps among a crowd of other students. She looks so old, like the high school senior she is, her long waves of hair blowing in the breeze. She laughs and smiles at a boy who walks along beside her then reaches forward and kisses him before turning to wave at me. This must be

Drake, kissing my sister on the school steps. She's not the shy little girl I thought she was. Drake grabs her hand and she turns back to him. They exchange a few words. I stand, waiting, smiling, assessing this boy who's looking at Lori like she's not a little girl at all. They continue to talk, clearly arguing about something—not angry, just disagreeing. Watching the exchange gives me time to assess further. He's taller than Lori, nearing six feet. His frame is somewhat lanky but already the shoulders hint at the broadening they'll undergo in the next year or two. He wears his hair in a shaggy mix between an afro and dreads. He's clean shaven, and yes, it's clear he shaves. He grins at Lori in a placating friendly way, a way that would melt any sixteen-year-old girl's heart. It's easy to see it's melting hers. He's winning the argument. They stop talking and he grins, squeezing her into a hug that lifts her off her feet. They walk towards me, his arm slung casually across her shoulders.

"This is Drake," she says, and instantly I see the shy girl I was expecting.

"Her boyfriend." Drake extends a hand. I take it. He has a good shake. Confident. Assured.

"Her boyfriend?" I raise an eyebrow at Lori, fighting the urge to be a mother, not a sister. "Is this a development?"

"Four weeks now," says Drake. "It's nice to finally meet you, Eloise. I wanted to sooner."

"I see." I put my sales smile on, I am the sister, after all. "Well, congratulations, you two. That's great."

"It's not like it was officially official or anything," says Lori. "If it were, I would have said something. It's just how long we've been dating."

Drake looks at Lori, seeming hurt, but he doesn't contradict her. "Anyways," he turns to me, "Lori said you two needed to talk, so I'll take off. I just wanted to say hello to the famous Eloise." He grins, and it's so genuine and open it makes me smile too.

"Famous?" My eyebrow rises again, this time at him.

"Well, you know, Lori talks about you a lot." His smile reminds me of Moses, how he must have looked at this age. "Does she talk about me?"

"She's mentioned you." Without thinking, my voice takes on a teasing tone.

"Good." He wipes his hand across his forehead in overdone relief and adds an exaggerated 'phew.' "So, that means I'm not just one of many. She actually gets my name straight."

"Ha, ha, ha," says Lori, punching him in the arm. "You're one of a dozen." I watch their little interchange, amazed. She loves this boy, or near to it.

"I'm off," he says, jogging backward, and almost tripping over some kid's skateboard. He laughs it off then turns the other way, taking the steps two at a time.

"He's always in a hurry," says Lori with a shake of her head. "Jogging everywhere."

"This is serious." I look at her, keeping my 'sister' smile. "Isn't it?"

"Well," she turns back to me, excited, "I guess it is."

I motion toward the bench and we sit down. "That's really great."

"You think so?"

"Sure."

"I was nervous you'd tell me to keep it light, casual, that I should be focusing on school and boys could come later."

"Well," I tilt my head back and forth but still smile, "I think all that too."

"See."

"But I'm still happy for you. He seems like a nice boy."

"He is. Anyway," she says, "let's not talk about it. It makes me nervous."

"Okay."

"What are you doing here?"

"I accepted the position."

She scrunches up her face, like my words are pointless.

"I know, you said you were going to today."

"Yesterday, actually, and today I'm flying out."

"To Tokyo?"

"Yes."

She pulls away from me "For how long?"

"A week…two, maybe three. I'm not sure yet."

"So this is how it's going to be? Flying off whenever on a moment's notice? My audition is this week. You probably forgot."

"I didn't forget. But what was I supposed to say?"

"You promised your sister you'd be there this time?" She kicks a tuft of grass between the cement's cracks. "This is important. This determines whether I get into the Academy."

"I know. I can get Moses, or…no, he'll be busy. Junior will go. He can tape it for me."

She shakes her head and adjusts the strap of her bag over one shoulder. "It's cool. You don't need to."

"I will. I want to."

"You've been to plenty. What's another? Besides, Pop will be there and Evelyn too."

"Evelyn's coming?"

"Yeah, Evelyn's coming."

"Oh, okay. That's great." Her body is leaned away from me, her gaze directed at a group of students arguing about something. "Well, I don't want to keep you. I just wanted to say goodbye in person. You have the joint credit card—for groceries and such."

"I know." She smiles at me, but it's not a smile I like. "Have a wonderful trip."

"This is good for you," I say. "It'll help you be more independent, handling things on your own."

"Mm-hmm."

"Well, see you." We stand. She accepts my quick hug.

"Love you. Stay away from the boozers."

"Of course." I grin. "Love you too."

She turns away from me and makes her way up the school steps and through the doors. She resents this, I know, the way I take off, the fact that I'm away so much and will be away more. But I don't owe her anything. She's in this great school because of me. She's wearing stylish clothes because of how hard I work. Her dance classes were paid for by this job and it's a job that requires travel. I fish the keys out of my purse. Most of my school outfits were scrounged from second-hand store bins.

Seated in my car, I mentally shake away the guilt that plagues me—I have no reason to feel guilty—and try to envision my upcoming hours and days. First the flight…the incredibly long flight. But that means hours to sit with Everdeen, learning from him. Next will come the inevitable business meetings where half the men will be enraged that I have any authority in the room, half will be terrified that I do, and half of both groups will be imagining me as the star of some exotic sex fantasy—all while I have to avoid getting drunk during the 'nominucation,' Japan's tendency to mix business meetings with copious amounts of alcohol. Staying sober is a task I have mastered, and I'll work to eradicate the drinking tradition from our branch's business meetings as best I can. However, there'll be no avoiding it when we meet with prospective clients. I smile. None of that matters. I will be groomed. I will stand in Mr. Everdeen's shadow knowing soon I can step into the light.

CHAPTER TEN

""Eloise, my girl!" Mr. Everdeen weaves through the crowded terminal and claps his hand on my shoulder. "I thought I'd beat you here."

"I always try to be punctual."

"You're twenty-two minutes early. I'd say that's more than punctual." He waves Julie over, who carries a folder I imagine holds our tickets. "So, what do you think Ms. Grant—Can we handle it from here?"

"Absolutely."

Everdeen thanks Julie, sends her on her way, then turns back to me. "It's been quite awhile since I've done this trip, and beyond the straight numbers I'm not as up-to-date on the status of the office over there as I'd like to be. I can't seem to get a straight answer out of Kamlyn. You've met him. What's your impression?"

"Well—"

"He's American raised, mostly. Completed high school and university in the states, then moved back to Japan after graduation. I thought that would make him relatable..." Everdeen's voice trails off. "Well?"

"Kamlyn-san is very capable."

He laughs and ushers me deeper into the terminal. "That's not exactly a recommendation."

"He's...hesitant." I match my pace to Everdeen's long strides. "He's still an outsider. In some ways more so than you or I would be."

"He's Japanese born for goodness' sake," barks

Everdeen. "How is that possible?"

"He's Japanese born but speaks English better than Japanese. He's lived away. He's heading a foreign company on Japanese soil. A company that doesn't garner the respect Japanese owned companies garner." I contemplate the best way to phrase my words. "He's looked down upon, to a degree. And he's trying to do business in a way that works for the Japanese, without realizing it's not going to work in our situation."

Everdeen stops and stares at me. "You've studied this?"

"And observed. I've been there twice now."

"What do you mean by 'our situation?'"

"I mean the situation of being a foreign PR company in an industry dominated by what we would call old boys' clubs. We're never going to be welcomed into those clubs, but Kamlyn-san seems to want to be."

"Never going to—"

"It's all right. We don't *need* to be. The economy is booming, the interest in the Western World is booming. We have our place. We're just not situated in that place at the moment."

Mr. Everdeen rubs a hand through his hair, looking at something in the distance. I thought he would be the one filling me in. He brings his gaze back to me. "And I presume you have a plan to get us in the place we need to be?"

I nod.

"So tell me about the employee situation. What are your thoughts on why we can't seem to hire quality people, and every time we do get someone who seems to be quality they're stolen away?"

I spend the next two hours—as we travel through security, wait in the lobby for our flight, then finally board and take off—talking about the history of Japanese corporate culture, the plight of the salaryman, and the way that the male-dominated business world puts the company above family (with the justification that company life provides for family life). I talk of respect, social ranking, the career track, and the desire for a secure position in a longstanding and respected Japanese company—for life. This is why the best graduates, male graduates, are not knocking at our doors.

Everdeen knows some of this already, is frustrated by much of it, and only shows excitement when I tell him about the opportunities we do have. The women who want a career, but not one that has them at the office until midnight. Many top-level female graduates go into secretarial roles because they think that's the only option if they want a husband and family.

"And what about our problems securing new clients?" asks Everdeen. "The team seems to scare off half of the contacts they make. You secured more new customers in your three weeks there last time than the team did in the three months prior to your trip!"

This news shocks me, and I wonder how many of those clients I secured have become repeat customers. "I think they're going after the wrong targets," I say, "and in the wrong ways. As we know, not everyone on staff is as qualified as they should be."

"Go on."

"Many of the companies we're trying to engage have consultants and PR specialists they've been working with for fifteen years or more. They have relationships. They have respect. It's going to take a lot to convince them that some new company can do better, and for good reason.

"Most of the current success came from targeting companies who are already looking to try something different, to appeal to a younger, more westernized crowd. That's where we have the opportunity to make a name for ourselves." I shake my head, no, to the stewardess who offers me wine, opting for water. "We don't want to bother with the companies who are happy with their consultants and packages. There's no benefit in stealing away that business."

"But—"

"What we want to do is show how we can complement company's current strategies, to expand their reach. Help them break into a younger market more interested and in touch with the Western World."

Everdeen grins at my words, nodding, and I'm relieved he didn't bristle at me cutting him off.

"That's what we can offer that our competitors can't. If we recruit female workers, young women who want a career and a family, we can use their knowledge to reach women like them, appeal to the newly found buying power they have."

Mr. Everdeen's laugh, a big guffaw that reverberates through the cabin, makes it difficult for me to keep my game face on.

"Is there something—"

"You. You, Ms. Eloise Grant are definitely the right person for the job."

I smile. I've wowed him and couldn't be more thankful for all those extra hours I spent studying and assessing the situation. "There's an added advantage to targeting young women who can enlighten us with their varied experiences of their culture."

"What's that?" He asks, grinning.

"Many of the current staff will resent having a woman in a position above them, or at least resent having to tell their friends about it—a foreign woman no less—whereas it could help the women feel empowered, help them feel more equal in the workplace."

"I can see that," he says, laughing more softly now. "I can certainly see that."

We brainstorm strategies for almost the full first flight to Calgary, then take a break while we eat dinner during our layover. As soon as we get on the next flight, Mr. Everdeen pops in several pills and sleeps through almost the full ten hours to Tokyo. I sleep too, but it's fitful. I'm awakened every time a flight attendant or passenger goes up or down the aisle. I try a movie but lose interest quickly. I open a business book but can't focus. Lori, Moses, Pop and, most of all, Mom flit through my mind. I haven't thought about my mother this intensely in years, but ever since Pop announced his impending nuptials I can't get her out of my mind. And after Lori looked at me this afternoon the way she did, I can't help feeling like maybe I'm more like my mother than I would like—leaving my family for a better life.

It's not the same thing, though. I know it's not. When the pilot announces we're landing, I realize I've slipped into sleep again, but even as I wake, the thoughts persist, just as strong as they were in my half-slumber. But I'm not abandoning my family. I've invited Lori to come with me. I expect Moses to. We'll all reap the rewards of this job. I'll make sure they want for nothing. They won't be left alone.

Everdeen greets Kamlyn with a large smile and fatherly embrace, claps him on the shoulder, the same way he did me, and chats with him about the flight, the touring he plans to get in at last, but nothing regarding the business. He laughs easily and carries himself like a man who's ready to take on the world.

Kamlyn bows to me, a mix of awe and resentment in his eyes, and I bow back, feeling bad for the way I'll have to undermine him in the following days. I'll make the process as painless as I can. I like Kamlyn and know in different circumstances he'd like me too.

On our way to the restaurant, Kamlyn interacts with Everdeen with more presence of mind and thinly veiled flattery than I've ever seen from him. He wears the same tailored suit he always wears—the same make at least. My guess is a dozen identical ones hang in his closet. He's still as lean as ever. With the amount of time they spend in the office and at the bar, it baffles me how so many Japanese salarymen have the figure of top athletes. His hair is styled with pizazz, that little eccentricity that separates the more progressive men of his generation from the men of his father's. What's different is his casualness. He's respectful toward Everdeen while treating him like one of the boys, and like he's one himself. I'm used to a rigid Kamlyn-san, a perpetually serious and somewhat stressed Kamlyn-san. A man who keeps everything below the surface. Who seems trapped between two worlds. This Kamlyn gives the appearance of ease. I like it. This Kamlyn has potential.

We sit at the bar and continue our discussions. Kamlyn enlightens Everdeen with aspects of the political culture I haven't touched upon. Everdeen has a cursory knowledge of the state of the country and Kamlyn, by the way he talks, makes it seem like Everdeen knows much more. It's calculated. And smart.

Everdeen brightens when Kamlyn mentions the Prime Minister's efforts to bring more women into the workforce, in leadership positions especially, and to provide working conditions that are conducive to motherhood. As he says this, he glances at me, a self-satisfied smile on his face. Last time I was here the only women in the company were in clerical positions. "I've just had a new hire," says Kamlyn. "Kuri Kokura." He leans over to Everdeen, like they're old chums. "Miss Kokura is quickly making her talent known. When I saw her amazing qualifications—top of her class in one of the country's most prestigious universities, a real go-getter, that's when it hit me—she is what this company needs."

Interesting. On my last visit I told Kamlyn 'she' was what this company needs. He scoffed.

"Hiring Japanese women," Kamlyn emphasizes the word Japanese, "is how we can make ourselves known in the marketplace, the way we can offer something different while serving the needs of the economy." He glances my way as he says this, revealing a moment of venom. One question I'd been wondering about is answered. Kamlyn-san knows I'm here to usurp him, and he's not going down without a fight.

CHAPTER ELEVEN

For the rest of the meal I concentrate on being as pleasant and engaging as possible, both with Kamlyn and Mr. Everdeen. I laugh, I joke, I add in my theories and suggestions while praising Kamlyn's. He may want a fight, but I'd rather him as my ally than my adversary. He's skilled, most of his staff respect him, and if I earn his respect, it will be better for everyone involved. At the end of the night, we agree to meet at the office at nine a.m. sharp.

Kamlyn arranged a car to take Everdeen and me to our suites and as the driver pulls into traffic, I see Everdeen's age creep in.

He sighs, lounging against the seat. "That Kamlyn impressed me today. He was the man I first hired. It's been a long time since I've seen this side of him." He shakes his head. "He was disappointing me." Mr. Everdeen yawns. "It sounds like he's ready to make a change though, ready to grow. I think he'll be on board with your plans."

"He seems motivated," I say.

Everdeen's eyes drift closed. "Kamlyn's going to find it hard." His whole face seems worn. "I could see he doesn't want to answer to you."

"No."

Mr. Everdeen smiles sleepily and taps my knee, like a father would. "He'll come around. You'll see. He may be on the ball now, but he's had two years to prove himself. It's time he moved over."

I nod and smile at the gentle snores reverberating from Everdeen moments later. For the first time since we've landed, I pull out my personal phone. Three messages await. One from Tracey, giving me a quick update on her most recent date with Mr. Right. One from Autumn, telling me she's all prepped for the after-school program and hopes I have a good trip, and one from Moses, full of love and missing. He doesn't remind me that this is a test run, but he also doesn't respond to my question about when he'd like to come see Tokyo for himself. I close my eyes and hold the phone to my chest. Kamlyn's not the only one I need to convince I'm meant to be here.

WE SPEND THE NEXT week strategizing. On my sixth day there, Everdeen's last, Everdeen, Kamlyn, and Kuri smile and nod as we finish our meeting. I've done good. Really good. We've pinpointed our weakest members of the team—the ones to let go. The strongest members will start recruitment advertising at some of the top universities in the country. Graduation is happening soon. It's perfect. A fresh new force of ready, willing, and eager minds. Kuri has a list of experienced women we can call upon for interviews and the first round of hiring. These new plans mean I'll have to stay in Tokyo several more weeks, missing Christmas and Lori's birthday. The thought sickens me, but sometimes sacrifices have to be made. It's just this once.

As I'm about to leave, Kamlyn stops me in the hall. "Your presentation," he says, "you came up with it all?"

"Yes." I adjust my bag, uncertain of where this is going.

"It was good."

"Thank you."

Kamlyn shifts from foot to foot. "If I had listened to you sooner, you may not be here now."

I nod, still uncertain.

He nods too, obviously having more to say, but not saying it. Our silence becomes awkward. "Well, I should get going." I give a slight bow.

"I'm going to work with you." He grins his charismatic grin. "For now, at least." He gives his own bow.

"Well, good." I walk away, perturbed. Should I be happy or skeptical about this? It's better than outright hostility.

On my way out of the office I slide my phone out of my purse and watch the screen light up. Seven missed calls. I scroll through the list—four from Lori, two from Moses, one from Pop. I step to the side of the hall. My hand shakes as I press Lori's number. This can't be good.

"Eloise, oh my God, where were you?" Her voice gasps through the receiver. I can hear she's been crying.

"I was in a meeting. Lori, what's—"

"Answer your phone. Can't you answer your phone!"

"I am now. Lori," I speak calmly, trying to counter the frenzy in her voice, "are you okay? Is everything okay?"

"It's Junior." She lets out a sob. "Junior!"

I take a deep breath, imagining the worst—a car accident, a shooting, cancer. I place my hand to my chest, feeling the repetitive bang of my heart. "Is he?"

"He's in jail." My lungs collapse in relief. "He's been arrested. Arrested!"

With the knowledge that he's alive pulsing through me, I'm able to maintain calm. "Junior is in jail?" And then, with fear gone, the calm turns to anger. "What happened?" I yell. "What idiot thing could—" and then I stop. I know exactly what idiot thing. "Unlawful protest?"

"It's lawful," she spouts. "People are allowed to express their opinions."

"Not necessarily." I sigh. "How serious is it?"

"He's in jail, Eloise. And you aren't here."

"Junior would have done whatever he did to land himself in jail whether I was there or not."

"But…"

"Lori, it is what it is."

"I want you to come home. Now. You were supposed to leave next week, right? What's a few more days."

"There's nothing I can do for Junior."

"He's going to have to go to trial. This could ruin his whole life." Her sobs come in strained little choking sounds that make me more annoyed than sympathetic. He hasn't killed anyone or participated in grand theft…whatever. This is not the end of the world.

"Lori."

"Eloise!" My name comes out in a long whine. One of the men who won't be working here tomorrow walks by me, staring with a wary look on his face. Rumours of my 'reorganization of assets' must be spreading.

I slip into the ladies' room and into a cubicle, considering Lori's words. She has a point, albeit an exaggerated one. My brother, the soon to graduate law student, with offers of employment from two firms, now has a criminal record. All because he couldn't leave well enough alone, fight his fight the legal way, like I told him.

"You're right, Lori." I say, picturing the way her eyes will widen at my tone, that look she gets when my views don't line up with hers, which, to Lori, is an act of betrayal. "It could ruin his life. It probably won't, but it could. And this job I'm busy working at? The one you're so eager for me to leave? It helped put him through school and what does he do? Risks squandering that, squandering his future. For a protest." The line remains silent, her crying over.

I imagine her standing somewhere in the apartment, shocked, alone. My sympathy returns. This isn't her fault. She's not the one I need to lecture. I soften my voice. "I'm sure it's not going to end up being that big of a deal. Are you even sure he's actually been arrested? Not just detained or something?"

"What's the difference?" Her voice leaks with

resentment and fear.

"There's a difference. Don't worry, okay. I'm sure it will work out. And it may be good for him, teach him a lesson."

"El."

"I'm serious."

"But…"

"What, Lori?"

"Are you coming home or not?"

I let a puff of air stream out of me, feeling the weight of my family like a wooden yoke. "I can't. I was actually going to call you to let you know I have to stay a couple more weeks."

"What?"

"Things are really progressing here." I infuse excitement into my voice in the hopes it will rub off on her. "We're revamping the whole way this company operates. It's important for me to—"

"A couple more weeks? You're going to miss Christmas? My birthday?" She huffs. "We're supposed to have Christmas dinner together. Us and Evelyn's kids."

"I know. And I'm sorry to miss it. This is really important, though. It's a once in a lifetime chance to show I have what it takes. We can video chat on your birthday, Christmas too." I wait for a response, but there is none. "We'll celebrate again when I get home."

She mumbles something.

"What?"

"I said fine. Stay. Whatever."

"Lor—"

"Abandon Junior. Abandon us all."

"What can I do for Junior?" My attempt to keep the exasperation out of my voice fails. In a boardroom, with an ignorant client, I never waver, but with Lori… "If he needs money I'll send it. Okay?"

"What about a visit? Don't you think he's scared? That he needs his big sister?"

"No, I don't. Junior can handle himself. And you can visit him—and Pop, his friends, Moses. Not that it's likely he'll be in there long, anyway. They may just hold him overnight." A male voice says something in the background. "What was that? Where are you?"

"I'm at home."

"Who's with you?"

"No one."

"I heard talking."

"It's the TV." Her voice is accusatory.

"Okay. Look, Lori, it's the middle of the night there. Go to bed. You have school tomorrow."

"I'm not a child."

"I know you're not. I didn't—" I rub my hand over my hair, scrunching the curls, wishing I wasn't having this conversation with a toilet as witness, even if it is one of the most technologically advanced toilets I've ever seen. "Look, send me any information you have, okay? Of course if there's anything I can do, anyone I can contact, I will."

"What if it were me in jail?"

"It's not."

"But what if it were?"

I sigh. "I'd come home."

"Yeah, right."

"Lori, please." Silence. "Lori? Lori?" I stare at the blank screen, missing the days when you could slam a phone into its holder.

I debate calling Moses and my father back but seeing as I don't have my own office yet and it's late anyway, I decide to wait until their morning.

Junior is in jail. My baby brother, behind bars. It's an end result I fought to make sure he didn't have. He could have. At least a handful of his classmates from high school filter in and out of the system. Statistically, it wouldn't be surprising: A young immigrant black man from a low-income community with a dead mother and a father who worked too many hours. He even got teased for his smarts, which put him at risk of no longer trying. I can see him, the little boy he was, walking towards me one day, sheepish as he pulled out the test I demanded to see.

'Don't get mad,' he said. 'The kids always make fun of me. They call me brainiac.'

The bright red C+ shocked me. Junior never got less than an A-.

I shouted, saying the stupid kids who made fun of him would be spending their lives pumping gas and taking out trash. And then Pop walked in. When he wasn't on some construction job, getting paid less than he should have, he spent his nights getting rid of other people's grime, taking out trash and scrubbing toilets.

Pop wasn't who I thought of when I said these words, not specifically. But that didn't matter, and how could I explain?

Pop took the papers out of my grasp and stared at them, his hand quivering. 'Your sister's right,' he said, his voice catching. 'You're smart.' He shook the papers gently. 'You can do better than this.'

We all stood, silent. 'Never be ashamed of how smart you are. Never pretend to be anything less than what you are.' Pop smiled. 'You are brilliant.' He pulled Junior over to him, then put out his arm for me to step close as well. 'You both are. Be better than your old man, okay? Do that for me?' He looked at Junior when he said this. Junior nodded and never threw a test again. I never figured out a way to say I was sorry.

Back at the hotel, exhausted after a ten -our work ay, I decide I'm being over-dramatic in my worries and reminisces, most likely because Lori was. This isn't an end result. Junior isn't going to face a lengthy trial, be incarcerated for years. He wasn't gang-banging. He was being a political activist. Most likely he'll get the equivalent of a slap on the wrist and some community service.

Crossing the room, I slip out of my heels and rub my feet along the plush carpet. Once at the expansive floor to ceiling windows I pull back the curtains and stare at the flashing, neon colours of the city. That's Tokyo, not just a city of lights but a city of colours.

My eyes close and I picture Moses walking up behind me, wrapping his arms around me, proud at the way I've stepped in and am about to transform this branch. Right now it's struggling to break even, but I'll have it doubling its revenue within a year. Tripling within five. I should be proud.

If he were here, we'd take some wine to the living room, sit on the leather couch and light a fire, just because. He'd tell me about his day, how he's reaching through to his new students, how exciting it is to learn from them as they learn from him, and how this city is starting to get into his bones.

Turning from the window, I slip out of my nylons and skirt and into a warm, fluffy robe. Phone in hand, I scroll through the numbers though I know his by heart. I want to see his smile.

The phone rings several times before I hear his groggy voice. "Hi."

"Hi." I whisper into the phone. "How are you?"

"Exhausted." He yawns. "It's been a rough week, and then your brother—oh, you know about your brother, right?"

"I know."

"Good." I can almost see his body relax as he says this. "Lori was trying to get a hold of you for hours. I was over there for a while trying to calm her down. I told her you'd be back next week."

"About that."

"About what?"

"I'm here for a few more weeks." Silence. "Moses, are you there?"

"I'm here."

"I'm sorry, I—"

"This was a demand, a requirement, again not something you could possibly take a moment to discuss with your fiancé?"

"It's needed. We're really making progress here."

"And when a few weeks turn into three or five or ten?"

"It won't. I mean I'll be back and forth, but why don't you come? I can fly you up. It'd be great."

"It's the middle of the school year."

"I know but…well, okay. For Christmas. I'll fly you up for Christmas."

"You know I can't leave my parents on Christmas. We had plans, El. Christmas morning with my folks, Christmas evening with your family."

"I know."

"They're expecting you. Mom is so excited. You haven't even seen them since the engagement."

"I know." I hesitate, knowing he's right, knowing how excited his mother always is to see me. Now that I'll be her daughter-in-law she must be beyond eager. "Maybe I could fly your parents up too. We could do Christmas here."

"We're not flying to the other side of the world for a few days. Besides, you know I have all that prep for finals and then my own dissertation."

"I know, okay, I know. I'm trying here." Again, silence. "We'll talk every day. And when you do come, you're going to love it. I'll be back before then, I'm sure, but you can come on my next trip. I'll make sure it corresponds with March Break."

He makes some guttural noise.

"Moses?"

"We'll see."

"So that was you at my place last night, when I called Lori?" I ask, trying to shift the subject.

"No, she wasn't on the phone when I was there. Have you thought anymore about the wedding? Dates or venues or anything?"

"I've been really busy here. You know that."

"I know." He sighs. "So it's going well, you're making a lot of progress?"

"Absolutely." I smile, recalling how amazing today's planning session went. "It's practically a work of art. I may win awards." I give a happy sigh. "But tell me about what's been going on with you. How's the team? And your dissertation, any progress?"

In the process of filling me in, Moses notices the time and needs to end the call. Putting the phone aside, I slip under the down comforter, switch on the TV, and call for room service. The suite is the perfect temperature, the mattress, like lying on a cloud. When the food arrives it is divine…and where is Junior tonight? In a cold cell with a thin, lumpy mattress as his bed—if he's lucky. Then I remember, it's morning back home. He won't be in bed. He'll be starting his day and one of his lawyer friends will get him out of this mess.

OVER THE NEXT TWO weeks I throw myself into hires and re-branding and training the current staff—Kuri most ardently, so she can train the hires once they come on. I also focus on getting Kamlyn to work with me, not against me. Him arranging some sort of coup while I'm back at the main branch would be less than ideal. With the go ahead from Mr. Everdeen, I make sure Kamlyn will have a new and prestigious title, one that will look good on his business card. The prospect of leaving the Tokyo branch makes me nervous. I know I've set processes in place for our plans to move forward smoothly, provided no one changes them, but I'm not technically in charge yet. For the moment my role is closer to a consultant, but Kamlyn and everyone else realizes Everdeen's intentions to put me in the lead.

More than being scared to leave though, I'm scared to return home. When my flight lands both Lori and Moses are in school so, rather than returning to my apartment for some much-needed rest, I drive to Junior's place. He opens his door with his usual charming grin and swagger, the 'slap on the wrist' he got for his activism not humbling him a bit. "Ah, she has returned."

"I have returned." If he's playing it light, I will too. "Not too roughed up, I see?"

He sweeps his arm majestically, indicating I should enter. "Not at all, my dear. Not at all. Do you intend to inflict some damage?"

"Ha."

"Verbally then?" he asks. "Have you come here to lecture me?"

"I could have lectured you on the phone."

"And you did."

"Barely." I sweep my eyes across his apartment—the dishes are done, no clothes or takeout boxes lay strewn throughout the living room and kitchen. No trash is about to topple out of an overflowing garbage. "You seeing someone?"

"Maybe I've finally learned the importance of cleanliness."

"What's her name?"

"Matilda."

"Matilda? Are you serious?"

"Yes."

"I thought that was a name for eighteenth-century grandmothers and precocious and fictional little girls."

"Like Eloise?"

I grin and ease onto his sofa. "Fair enough. So, she's special?"

He sits down across from me. "She is."

"And what does she think of your recent incarceration?"

"She was impressed."

"Impressed! I'll have to meet this girl."

"You will." He hesitates and gives me the smile I hate. "If you stay around long enough."

"Come on, be fair."

"I am being fair. I'm being practical. You're not likely to meet her if you're not in the country long enough to."

"I was gone for a couple of weeks. It's not a big deal."

"You were gone for four and a half weeks, on one day's notice. You missed Christmas and your sister's birthday."

"It was business."

"She says with a heart of stone."

I send him a glare.

"Have you seen Lori yet?" he asks.

"She's in school. I just got back. I haven't even been home."

"So not your man either?" Junior finally sits, then reclines.

"No."

"Have you met her man?"

"Lori's? Jake, you mean."

"Drake."

"Right. I knew that. You have?"

"I met him at the audition. He seems nice."

"He came to the audition?"

"Yeah." He hesitates. "They seem close."

"They're dating."

"You think we should be worried?"

"I don't know." I shrug, not wanting another thing to worry about. "I gave her the talk years ago and Lori knows school and dance come first."

"Okay." Junior crosses his arms, as if he's sizing me up. "So, what are you doing here, El?"

"I came to see you. To see if you were all right."

He spreads his arms. "I'm marvellous."

Why did I come to see him—my little brother who

towers over me by a good three and a half inches? My little brother who's starting to live like a man, who has passions so strong he'll risk jail for them. Maybe I came just to see for myself that he's okay, and to ensure he's not angry with me too. I stand.

"Come here." He draws me into his arms. "Don't screw up your life."

"You're one to talk," I mumble into his chest.

"My life is wonderful," he says, "no lasting repercussions. Your life on the other hand," Junior pushes me far enough out of his embrace so we can look each other in the eyes. "You're smart, really smart. And also quite stupid." He steps away from me. "I hung out with Moses the other day. He said you two were barely managing an hour's conversation a week?"

"There's a horrible time difference."

"I know. And he doesn't want to move. Not at all. He might, because he loves you that much, but he doesn't want to. And he doesn't like the way you pick up and leave…not just him, but the way you leave everyone—Lori, the girls at the school, family commitments."

"Wasn't it me who was supposed to be here lecturing you?"

"Sorry, Beautiful." He smiles. "You lost your chance. It's my turn now."

"Humph."

"You coming to Pop's this Sunday?"

"Junior, I just got home."

"Exactly. You should get to know our new mother."

"Step-mother. And maybe." I pick up my bag and nearly trip over the edge of the couch. I stand up straight, not wanting Junior to know how much him using that word shakes me.

"Look, El, I was just teasing. I didn't mean—"

"I should get home, shower, change." I grab my coat and struggle for a moment as I get it on. "I'll try to meet Lori at her school."

"She was wonderful, you know."

"What?"

"In that audition. She was a vision."

"I know. You sent me the clip."

He nods and opens the door as I step into my boots. "Have a good day, my dear."

⌘

THE SCENT OF PANCAKES greets me when I push open the apartment door. Pancakes and maple syrup. I set my bag down in the hall and head to the kitchen, thinking leftovers would be wonderful. There aren't any. Instead, a large mixing bowl with dried batter coating the side of it sits on the counter, plops of batter beside it. I sigh. Marble counter tops and she leaves crusty old batter on them. The dirty pans still sit on the stove and two syrupy and crumb filled plates rest on the nook.

Scrounging in my purse, I find my phone and text Moses: *Did you stay at my place last night?* He won't answer for at least an hour, so I step into the shower to wash the travel off of me. By the time I'm done and dressed I have just enough time to get to Lori's school before class lets out. I glance at my phone while heading to the garage. Moses: *No. Why?* I tell him not to worry and I'll meet him at his place for dinner later on. Lori has some explaining to do.

For January, the day is warm. My breath hardly shows. After I spend about ten minutes watching students trail out of the building, Lori emerges. She walks with two of her close friends, girls from dance she's been besties with for almost seven years. I wave and call her name. She glances my way then flips her head back to the girls, her long locks swishing with the motion. She continues to chat with the girls for almost a minute before coming over. "Hi," I chirp.

"Hi."

"I don't even get a hug?" She steps closer to me and we embrace, me holding her tightly, her limply patting my back. "What's going on?"

"What?"

"Come on, Lori."

"Well, you just come back—a day early no less—and what? You expect me to drop whatever I'm doing and go hang out with you?"

"I'm not early."

"But you said…oh, never mind. I probably got the time change thing messed up or something. Anyway, I came over to say hi, but I can't stay with you. I have practice."

"Right now? Isn't it not for another hour?"

"We're going to practise before practice, *okay*?"

"Okay, yeah. That's fine."

Her look says she's disgusted with me. Disappointment I've seen in her eyes before, but disgust? Never. "So, I'm going to go now," she says, though clearly she's waiting for me to dismiss her.

"Sure. Just one thing though. Did one of the girls spend the night last night?"

"I'm not allowed to have friends over now?"

"No, of course you are. I was just wondering. Usually you let me know."

"Well, they didn't. Why?"

"Two pancake plates."

She shakes her head and laughs. "Two days, Eloise. I had extra batter, right?"

"Oh, okay. Sure."

She turns from me and walks away without a glance back. Never before has Lori talked to me like this, looked at me like this, made me feel like this. Usually I'm the wonderful big sister. Sometimes I disappoint her, yes, but that generally ends in sulking, not this dismissive attitude. A student bumps into me and I lose my balance. It's enough to jolt me out of this stupor I've been standing in. I let another puff of air expel before me. A little cloud mists up this time. In those few minutes, the temperature has dropped that much. Rubbing my arms, I make my way back to my warm car and drive to Moses' high school. He has basketball tonight…or is it study room? Something. And if he's really busy, there's always a chance Tracey will still be in her classroom. Either way, I'm sure I'll get a warmer reception there and right about now warm is exactly what I need.

CHAPTER TWELVE

After parking, I slip out of the car and make a dash to the large, suddenly inviting school doors. My heels click on the old tile floor as I head to Moses' classroom. Peeking my head around his door, I'm greeted with an empty room. I make my way up the hall and glance in the teachers' lounge. "Hey, Eloise." Charlise, one of the language teachers, waves. "I hear congratulations are in order."

"Oh," I smile, wanting to get away from her and close to someone I love. "Yes, they are."

"Well, let me see the ring!" She practically skips over to me, an impressive feat considering the seven-month baby bump she looks to be carrying. "Oh, it's lovely. And on a teacher's salary?" She laughs, making her small afro jiggle. "You are one lucky girl."

"I am."

"Moses said you were in Tokyo? For work?"

"Yeah."

"I went to Vietnam once. It was amazing."

"Yes. It is. I love Vietnam." I back out of the room.

"So, what are you doing here?"

"Well, I'm not working there permanently."

"No." She laughs like I'm ridiculous. "What are you doing here, in the teacher's lounge? Are you looking for Tracey? She's still in her classroom, I think."

"I was looking for Moses, actually."

"Moses?" Again she gives me that look like I'm ridiculous. "Moses coaches basketball every Thursday after school. Don't you know that?"

"Yes, of course, I mean…the time changes, the travelling. I got confused."

"Don't you worry." She laughs again. "It happens to the best of us. For me it's baby brain."

"Mm-hmm."

"Whoo! She kicked. You wanna feel?"

"Um, no. I—"

"Don't be shy." She steps toward me and captures my hand, placing it on her belly. All I feel is another woman's stomach and am about to pull away when a little foot kicks my hand, really kicks it.

I laugh and look up at her. "That's the baby?"

"Your first time, huh?"

"Yeah." I pull my hand away, amazed at the grin that's still plastered across my face. "Thank you."

"My pleasure." She rubs her belly. "Now go find that yummy man of yours."

Before heading to the gymnasium, I turn a corner and make my way to Tracey's room. Watching through the window, I see Tracey sitting on her desk, legs crossed, one hand propping herself up while four girls talk excitedly around her. They laugh and cajole. Three of the girls are my fan club from the last session—Sherry, Jolie, and Jayden. I don't recognize the fourth. All five heads turn when I push the door open. "Eloise!" My name is said in a chorus.

My fan club rushes to me with a dozen questions. "Whoa, whoa. One at a time." I laugh.

"We thought you were in Tokyo," says Sherry.

"She was." Jayden rolls her eyes with flare. "And she was gone, like, forever. Is it true you're moving there?"

"That's the plan." I give Tracey a quick hug.

"The plan. So, like, it's not one hundred percent then," says Jayden. "Not written in stone?"

"Is anything ever?"

"True, true." Jayden loops her hair around her finger and tugs on it. Her thinking motion, it seems.

"You should totally stay here. I mean Tokyo is cool and all, or…I imagine it's cool. But you'd miss us way too much."

"It's true," says Sherry, grinning.

"And Mr. Montgomery. You can't leave him. Wait…is that?" Jayden grabs my hand. "Is that a ring?"

"It is a ring."

"Is it an engagement ring?" Jolie steps forward to get a better look.

"It is."

"You and Mr. M? You're getting married?"

"We are."

I step back from the round of squeals.

"Oh, my gosh, you're like so lucky!" says Jayden. "Mr. M is without a doubt the most delicious teacher in this school."

"Delicious?" I ask.

"Oh yes," says Tracey, trying to keep a straight face. "Moses is definitely delicious." Jolie, Sherry, and the girl I've yet to meet all nod, equally straight faced, but without the mirth behind their expressions.

"So…is he leaving then?" asks Jolie. "Is Mr. M moving to Tokyo with you?"

"I hope so." I make my way into the room and perch on a desk across from Tracey's.

"You hope so?" Jayden stands next to me. "But what if he doesn't?"

"We'll cross that bridge if and when we come to it. But oh," I let my eyes go wide, "we haven't had a session on sales technique yet. If we had you'd know I can sell Tokyo to Mr. M."

"He's not a product," says the fourth girl, a tall, thin beauty with large brown eyes shadowed by unbelievably long lashes.

"I know." I turn to her. "I was just joking. I don't think we've met. You are?"

"She's Caitlyn," says Sherry. "Caitlyn, this is Eloise, who we've been talking about."

"Hi," says Caitlyn.

"It's nice to meet you, Caitlyn." I extend my hand.

"Oh." Jayden gives a little jump. "You did it, right there. You used that technique you taught us, for remembering names."

"Good catch."

"But back to this whole Tokyo thing." Jayden hops up beside Tracey, so she's across from me. "Do you really have to go? You're so good at these sessions. One of the ladies talked about finding a mentor the other week and I was going to ask you."

"Really?" I smile. "I would have loved to, Jayden. I can still be available for questions if you want. Emails, web cam from time to time. The world is so close now."

"Yeah," she says. "I guess that'd be cool. Not the same, of course. But still cool."

"So how long are you back for?" asks Jolie.

"Mmm…it depends how smoothly the project I'm working on goes. But probably about three weeks."

"Will you do another session while you're here?" asks Sherry. "Not that the lady who filled in for you wasn't good. Autumn. She was really nice."

"I'll try." I look to Tracey. "Maybe Autumn and I can tag team something."

"We'll figure it out." Tracey glances at the clock. "Wasn't Sherry's mom coming by to pick you up for dance?"

"Oh, yeah!" Sherry hops off the desk she was sitting on. "Thanks. She's probably outside now. We'll see you later Miss Sampson. You too, Eloise."

After a round of goodbyes and a couple of more looks at my ring, the girls traipse down the hall. I look to Tracey. "Do you remember being that young?"

"Yes." Tracey laughs. "I don't remember looking quite that old though. Most of those girls are thirteen. Jolie just turned thirteen last month." She shakes her head. "I thought that's what we looked like when we started university."

"Maybe that means we're getting old. The fact that we can't picture what we looked like." I smile. "Then again, to me you don't look a day older than when I first met you."

"Oh, you flatterer," Tracey says in a mock southern accent while using her hand to fan away an imaginary blush.

"It's true though. It's been a decade, yet I see pictures of us in first year, and for the most part we look the same. But when I see actual first years? They're babies."

"Yet these girls are ancient." Tracey leans forward. "So, how was the trip?"

"It wasn't exactly a trip." I lean back on the desk, propping myself up with my arms the same way Tracey was. "Work, work, work."

"And no fun."

I grin. "Well, work is fun. I am dominating that office."

"Good for you."

I see the hesitation behind her smile. "What is it?"

"Moses mentioned you two were hardly speaking."

"The time zone issue."

"I know…but still. I think he's feeling somewhat rejected or forgotten."

I slide off the desk. "He said that? To you?"

"Not in so many words."

"I'm really busy right now. I'm putting the pieces in place for a complete office revamp. Complete. We've already let nine people go and are in the process of hiring two new people. We have plans to hire at least five more in the next several months."

"And once you do?"

"Once we do, what?"

"Once you do, will you not be so busy?"

"Well," I chuckle, "we'll probably be busier."

"And for how long?"

"Tracey, what is all this about?"

"I'm worried for you, El. I know this is all incredibly important to you. Moving up in the world and all that. But it's not important to Moses…at least not in the same way." She eases off her desk too. "You say you won't be travelling as much but if you have the responsibility of heading up the branch, you'll probably be putting in even more hours than you are now."

"Maybe."

"Maybe?"

"Okay, probably. What's your point?"

"My point is, where will your husband who has moved to the other side of the world for you fit into that?"

"He'll have work. And I'm busy now. We'll figure it out." I look away from her, then back. "Since when has it been your job to analyze my life?"

She steps closer, a softness to her smile. "It's not my job. I'm just…this is a big move. A really big move and it seems like you jumped into it. I don't want you to do something you'll regret. I mean come on," she makes her tone light, "I wouldn't want to see my matchmaking skills fail."

"Tracey."

"And from what I've heard the first year of marriage is tough as it is."

"Well, we're not planning to get married for a couple of years, anyway. Not until things are more settled at the branch. It would be impossible trying to do all that and plan a wedding."

"Impossible? For Eloise Grant? I thought that word wasn't in your vocabulary."

"You're right." I wink. "It's not. But I think both endeavours would go much better if they didn't overlap."

"Fair enough."

"But what about you, my dear? All this talk of me and none of Mr. Thomas Right?"

"Thomas McGivern."

"Oh? I was sure you said he was Mr. Right."

"Ha ha." She seems to study her shoes. "Things are okay."

"What happened?"

She laughs again, more an expulsion of air really, then looks up. "Nothing happened. Technically things are going really well. He's as devastatingly handsome as ever. He's sweet. He's attentive. He makes me laugh…when he's around."

"Trace."

"I'm not being overly demanding or needy or anything. Really. It's just…we can only see each other Tuesday nights and Sunday afternoons. No other time. He says he has commitments."

"Okay…"

"I haven't met any of his friends or his family."

"Haven't you only been seeing each other for a couple of months?"

"Yes. And he says he's private, that he doesn't introduce a woman to the important people in his life until he's confident she's going to become equally important."

"That seems reasonable."

"It does."

"So…"

"I don't know. It doesn't feel right. Especially the whole *only* Tuesday night and Sunday afternoon thing."

"You've never met at another time?"

"Once we spent the weekend together, but even then it was at my place."

"You think he's cheating on you?"

She sighs. "No. I think I'm the one he's using to cheat on someone else. Is that paranoid?"

"It's not paranoid, no. But you may be jumping to conclusions. Not every guy is a scumbag. I know you've been hurt but—"

"I know. I know. Of course not every guy is a scumbag." She smiles. "Your man proves that."

"He does. And I'm sure Thomas only has eyes for you. He's probably busy, like he says. He's a teacher too, right? All the marking, the after-school programs, and then fitting in family and friends on top of that."

"It's just…no." She shakes her head. "You're right. I'm being paranoid. And hey, with your big hold up maybe I'll be getting that double ring on my finger before you do."

I laugh. "Maybe! Anyway, I better go check on my ring giver." I make my way to the door and she follows along. We part ways.

Walking down the empty hall, my heel clicks reverberating off the walls once again, I go back to the earlier part of our conversation. Tracey thinks Moses is feeling neglected. She also thinks I'm in danger of jeopardizing my marriage before it even begins. But she doesn't know Moses and me, not intimately. All she knows is the guys who have hurt her, who have left her. Moses is solid. I place my hands on the glass of the gym. On the far side of the court Moses cheers on his boys. With a man like that by my side, we can get through anything. I watch for several minutes, until finally he sees me. His face lights up into a massive grin and he waves for me to enter. "Water break!" He shouts to the panting teens.

"At last!" shouts a boy who must be a senior. He's as tall as Moses, though only half as broad.

"And then two more." Moses gives the boy a deliciously wicked grin.

A communal moan erupts from the boys.

"That's your lady, right?" says another boy. "You go home, enjoy a nice night with her. Let us rest."

"You think the players across town rest halfway through practice?" he asks in his coach voice as I slip into a side hug. "No way."

"All right, all right." The boy jogs over to his water

bottle.

Moses pulls me into a proper embrace then kisses me deeply—a chorus of shouts and catcalls erupts.

"Moses," I gasp, laughing.

"What?" He grins his little boy grin. "I have to teach these boys how it's done."

"Oh, I'm sure they know."

"Not with a woman like you. Let's give 'em some more." He kisses me again and I melt into it. "All right, water break over," he shouts. "Line up!"

After practice we walk back down the hall and toward the parking lot. Moses holds open the door for me. "How was your flight?"

"It was a flight. Same as usual."

"Did you get much sleep?"

"Do I ever?" I laugh as we get to my car. "I studied of course. Marketing trends, hiring potential."

"Maybe you should be spending some of that time studying wedding dresses, venue locations." He wraps his arms around me and pushes me against the car. "I think that would be a wonderful use of those hours in the air."

I place my hands on his chest, holding off the kiss he's leaning in for. "And have you been spending your off hours to research tuxedos and catering options?"

He takes a step back. "I have actually."

"Oh." My smile drops.

Moses shrugs. "It's important to me. To us, right? Why wouldn't I be doing that?"

"That's great. I'm just surprised. I thought most men avoided wedding planning like the plague."

"Since when am I most men?"

"True."

"I'm excited." His voice holds something unnerving. "I want this to happen. And to happen sooner than later. I want to spend my life with you."

"We will…and we are. The legality just has to wait a little

bit, that's all."

"Legality?"

"Let's talk about this at home, okay?" I smile and squeeze his side. "Your place?"

"Yeah." He pecks my cheek. "See you there."

CHAPTER THIRTEEN

oses' retreating figure seems lonely in the large, empty parking lot. A breeze sends dried and crinkling leaves across his path. It's the perfect setting for a farewell scene in some book or movie. Only this isn't farewell, only see you later, so I don't know why the view makes me so nervous. I check my phone before pulling out of the lot. One missed call from Pop, with a voicemail asking me to come for dinner or at least a quick visit—he has something important to talk to me about. After the last important thing I'm not sure anything but him announcing Evelyn was pregnant could throw me off.

Pulling onto the street and making the short drive to Moses' apartment, I prep myself for the talk we're sure to have. The knowledge that he's been looking at tuxes and caterers brings a smile to my face, quickly followed by a frown. I'm not ready. I haven't done what I needed to do. Not that I think marriage will stop me or hold me back…to a large extent, but it will make the trajectory I'm on more difficult. There will be pressure. But I've never met a better man than Moses. That pressure will be worth it.

When I step through the apartment door Moses greets me with a smile, despite the earlier tension. "What'll it be?" I ask, looking over the array of vegetables he has laid out on his cutting board.

"Stir fry. Just a mix-up."

"And what can I do?"

"Besides stand there looking beautiful?"

"Exactly."

"Make a salad?"

We work in basic silence. Not much more is said than "pass the tomatoes" or "where's the grater?" and when we serve our plates I question, "table or couch?"

"Table." He smiles, though it's smaller than usual.

"It smells delicious."

"Thanks. A team effort."

"Barely. I don't think the salad contributes much to the smell."

"I suppose not."

"Are we okay?" I ask, my first bite perching on the fork mid-air.

His lips pursed, Moses expels a long, steady puff of air through his nostrils, making them flare in a way I'm not used to. "I hope so."

"You hope?"

"Do we want the same things?" He sets his fork down. "Because I'd been thinking we want the same things. I knew you wanted marriage, and I thought that meant you wanted it soon and that you wanted all that comes along with it."

"I do."

"Children. Weekends and evenings home with the kids. Family vacations. Cutting back on work so our family can come first…You've done so much for your own family."

I take a bite, chew through it slowly, then swallow. "I don't know that all of that necessarily has to come along with marriage. Most of them, perhaps. In theory. Well, not in theory, it's just…It scares me—the prospect of my life mapped out like that, especially before my career is solidified. I mean, you know, you've known since you met me, how important my career is."

"You need to be at the top."

"Exactly, I—" My voice cuts off as I register the tone he's said this in. "That's not a bad thing. That means security. It means never having to—"

"We're not your family, Eloise. It's an entirely different situation. They struggled. They really struggled. We're never going to struggle like that. Our children are never going to have to wear clothing two sizes too small with holes in them."

"I know."

"And you're not your mother. It had to be more than the struggle. I know she had it hard but," he pauses, "lots of people have it hard. They don't abandon their families, their children, because of it. They don't take their own life."

"You don't know what it was like for her."

"And neither do you, not really. But I do know she must have had bigger problems, mental instability or depression. That's not us. Your parents' story is not going to be ours."

"I know," I snap. "Don't try to pretend you know my parents or my life."

"El."

"Listen." I take a deep breath. "I'm not stupid. I know my mom had problems. I know her life isn't going to be our life. That's not what this is about, okay? I want a good life, a comfortable life, and that's not a crime. Maybe it has something to do with my childhood but it's also what most of the world wants." He stares at me, waiting, and I almost want him to yell. It'd be easier to be angry if he were angry too. "I'm not satisfied with mediocrity, okay? I want success. I want to be respected. I want to know that I am the best me I can be. And for me, for the path I'm on, that means doing my job to the best of my ability and not shirking my responsibilities. It means getting where I need to get and then staying there."

"So you think not doing that is being mediocre? When I'm at my job, I'm giving it one hundred percent. I'm devoted to those kids. And yes, sometimes I bring that home with me. I have to—marking and such. And to be the best teacher I can be sometimes means going the extra mile outside of work hours. But I also know how to turn it off. I know there are other things that deserve my time and attention."

"And I don't? I practically raised my brother and sister."

"Yes. And now they're raised and you're still providing for them, which is great, which is really admirable, but what they really need from you now is to be a sister. A sister who—"

"I'm there for them. And Lori does need what my job can provide. She needs that apartment I'm paying for. She needs an education that she doesn't have to slave through to afford."

"And we can give her that, without you working seventy hours a week."

"I don't work seventy hours a week."

"Eighty then?" He offers a half grin and the wall I've built these past minutes starts to crumble. "I don't want to fight," he says.

"I think it's too late for that." I offer a weak smile. "But neither do I. Dinner's getting cold."

"It is." We eat then, for several minutes, smiling at each other occasionally, politely. Moses looks up. "You make me scared."

"Scared?"

"Yeah. Scared I'm going to be this pathetic guy who trails behind a wife who loves her job more than she loves him."

"Moses. That's ridiculous."

"Is it?"

"Yes."

"Then give up Tokyo. Or half give it up. Continue this revamp you're working on, be that consultant, and then get the people in place that you need to get in place to make it work from there, without you. Impress Mr. Everdeen through that, but tell him your situation has changed, that you need to be here, where your family is."

"Why is it so easy for you to want me to give up this opportunity but so hard for you to give up your job?" My shoulders tense. "How is it any different? Is your resistance not putting your job above us?"

"Don't speak to me like that. I don't deserve that tone."

"Well?"

"It's not just my job. As much as I don't want to leave my job I would in a heartbeat if that's all it were, if that was best for us. But it's my family. It's your family. It's…" He stops. "It's the fear that I'll move to the other side of the world only to see you for an hour or two before you go to bed. To spend every weekend with you only half present. Tell me the truth—in the past three weeks how many of our scant phone calls did you get through without glancing at numbers or checking some file for work?"

"I—" My voice catches. "I was still listening to you."

"Listening so well that I could tell, huh?"

"It's going to get better. This is a very intensive time right now."

"And what about the next intensive time? What about when you're so successful with that branch that Mr. Everdeen wants you to move again, start a new branch somewhere else? Would you take it?"

A shiver runs through me. Now it's me who doesn't like his tone. Not that it's harsh or angry, but it scares me.

"Eloise?"

Defeat, I realize, his tone is one of defeat. "I don't know." I let my words flow faster than normal. "I don't know what I would do. But you are important to me. *We* are important to me. I had no idea you felt this way, okay? I didn't realize. I will do better. I'll give us the attention I need to give us. You're what I want."

He reaches his hand across the table, squeezes mine. "I hope so."

"You are."

He rubs his thumb across my fingers, making the

diamonds shift and sparkle in the light. "It looks good on you, you know."

I nod. "It does. Very good."

"And we're going to make sure it stays there…forever?"

"We are. Don't even talk like that."

"Like what?"

"Like you think there's a possibility it won't." His eyes tell me there is a possibility, and it's the first time I've seen this. It more than frightens me. It makes my lungs contract. His eyes might as well be saying failure. Worthless. Unlovable. Nothing. These are the words I see and he's not speaking any words to contradict them. "Moses?"

"Not if we work at this. Not if we put each other first."

"And if we don't?"

He stares at our hands. "Then maybe it's better we know now."

"I see." I push my plate away, the food's cold anyway, and pull my hand back in the same motion. I keep my expression cool, even, not letting emotion show through. It's what I do, what I've always done, when it's needed.

"Eloise, don't worry, okay? I didn't mean to imply anything."

I laugh. "You didn't mean to imply anything? Well, here's a news flash. You just implied you think there's a chance we're going to break up."

"No. That's not what I said."

"It sure sounded like it."

"All I said is we're going to have to work at this. We're going to have to communicate more, to think about the other's needs. To put each other first."

"And what you really mean is I have to put you first."

"No. El, come on."

"Come on, what?" I stand, almost knocking my chair over as I do. "You don't want me. If you don't want me the way I am, then that means you don't want me. I'm a workaholic, okay? I'm always going to be a workaholic. I've always been a workaholic. You know this!" I back away from the table, from him. "And yet now that I've got your ring on my finger it's suddenly a problem. You suddenly want me to change?"

He stands. "No, okay. No. I love you, but these last months—"

"I love you—but!" I repeat.

"These last months." He stops. "Almost this last year you haven't been the same woman I fell in love with. The woman I first met was focused on work, yes. She was driven, yes. But she listened to me when I told her about my day. She wasn't thinking of the next work meeting. She took my thoughts into consideration." He opens his arms wide, as if in supplication, then lets them fall. "We talked about our hopes and dreams and plans together. She didn't just throw hers on me and expect me to go along like a lapdog.

"A lapdog?" I sink back into the chair. "You think I treat you like a lapdog?"

He sits as well, offers the slightest smile, which falls away. "Sometimes, yeah. Sometimes I feel like you think you've got me, you know? That you think I love you so much I'll go along with whatever you want, as long as it makes you happy. And I think, well, I led you to believe that because that's what I've been doing." He places both palms on his knees. "I want to make you happy. I do. But if I only think of your happiness and not mine as well, one day I'll resent you for it. That's the last thing I want."

"I didn't mean to treat you like that." I lean against the table, feeling sick. "I never thought of it that way."

"I know."

We stare at each other until I break the silence. "I'm not sure what to say. I'm sorry but…beyond that I don't know what to say."

He sighs. "Let's call it a night. You've had a busy trip and a long flight. I've had a tiring week, a painful couple of weeks."

"Painful?"

"One of my Uni friends, a guy I used to play ball with, he passed away about a week ago. We'd drifted apart over the years but back then he was one of my best—"

"What?"

Moses brushes his hand across the top of his head, rubs his brow. His shoulders slump, a motion I hardly ever see on him. "He had stage four cancer. He was only diagnosed a couple of weeks ago and the doctors…it was past the point of treatment. He would have wasted away. He was already starting to. He took the fast way out."

"He…"

"Overdosed on his meds."

I'm out of my chair and in his lap in one moment, my arms around him, pulling his head to my shoulder. "I'm so sorry." He pushes me away. "Why didn't you tell me?"

"When, El?" His voice cracks. I can almost hear the lump building in his throat as his eyes moisten. I've never seen Moses cry.

"Any time."

"On the phone while you're a world away and we have only five to ten minutes before you need to head to work or look over some numbers?"

"If you'd told me I would have been there for you."

"Really been there for me? Would have come back early for me? Would you have gone to the funeral with me?"

"I…I don't know, but—"

"That's what I wanted. I wanted the woman I love to be standing beside me, holding my hand."

"You could have asked. You could have at least told me."

"I was too scared to ask. You didn't come home when your brother was in jail. And I get that. In reality, there's nothing practical you could have done…besides comfort your terrified sister. But I wanted you. I really wanted you. I just knew there was nothing practical you could do about this either." He shakes his head, then lets it fall. "I was scared to ask because if you said no, well," he pauses, "I really didn't want you to say no."

"I'm so sorry Moses. If I could have…I would have done my best, anyway. At the least I could have taken a few hours, talked to you, listened. Been there for you. You should have told me."

"Yeah." He nods, glances up at me. "Maybe I should have." We both breathe. His eyes close. "I'm probably just worn down, making a bigger deal of things than I should." He eases me off of him. "Why don't you go home. We'll both get a good night's sleep and then we'll see each other tomorrow. Isn't Autumn's new fella in town? I thought you mentioned something about a night out with them."

"Yeah." I stand in front of him, unsure what to do with my hands, my feet, my whole body. "That's tomorrow. But I was planning to stay the night. We haven't seen each other in weeks."

"Lori's been alone in your apartment for weeks. You two should spend some sister time."

"I'm not sure she's my biggest fan right now." I shift back and forth, wishing he'd stand, wishing he'd look at me. Moses and Lori, the two most important people in my life, and as of this moment, neither of them wants to be near me.

"All the more reason." At last he looks up. "You two need some time."

"All right." I step away from him, grab my purse and let it slide onto my shoulder. "You're right. We're clearly tired. I'll see you tomorrow. I'll text you the details once I get them, of where we're meeting and such."

He nods. "Great."

My steps hesitate by the door. He doesn't rise to hug and kiss me goodbye, like he usually would. "Your friend. Was it…uh…someone I knew?"

"It was Danny."

"Danny, uh, snowboarder Danny or Danny who just had

a little girl, Danny?"

He gulps a large breath of air. "Danny who just had a little girl, Danny."

"Oh, Moses."

"Sandy's a wreck." His smile quivers. "Sorry, I…I don't mean to dump this on you." He offers a forced chuckle. "I greeted you today all smiles and everything. It's not fair."

"It's okay," I say fighting the urge to go back to him. "You're not dumping it on me. I want to know."

"Yeah." He looks away again. "Well, bye. I'll see you tomorrow then."

"Bye."

I wait by the door a moment longer. He stands to clear the plates, without glancing over at me, and I slip out the door. It's only seven thirty, Lori won't be back from dance yet. The girls always go for bubble tea afterwards. Rather than get in my car and head to an empty apartment I walk down the circular drive of Moses' building and into the street. I'm blocks away from my old neighbourhood. If I go east, I'll be on the streets I grew up on in minutes. I head east, feeling younger than I have in years. It's as if my whole life is hanging by a tenuous thread, about to unravel. I don't even care that I'm mixing my metaphors. Everything else seems mixed up now, anyway. Moses says he's tired, that he's overwhelmed, worn out from the horrible couple of weeks he kept secret. But keeping them secret in the first place? That's what scares me the most.

The cold night air seeps up my coat sleeves and down my collar, chilling me in a way that almost makes me thankful. Focusing on the cold keeps my mind from completely spiralling into places I don't want to take it. But as my body numbs, my thoughts travel to these places, anyway. Moses thinks I think only of myself…or at least of myself first. He doesn't believe I'll put him above my job. And when it comes down to it, I'm not sure I will. I've worked too hard. I've put the last ten years of my life into getting where I am professionally; I've only put two into our relationship. Our relationship isn't less important but there are times when the job has to take precedence, and this is one of these times.

I walk down a path I haven't walked since high school, and into the park where I had my first kiss. Sitting on the swing where I sat that night, I pump my legs, just as I did then, until I'm soaring so high the seat buckles time and time again, jerking my body. This slight discomfort is worth it. The city lights in the distance are nothing like the lights of Tokyo, but still beautiful.

Just a few months after my mother left us for the second time, I came to this park with a boy three years older than me. He made me laugh. I had forgotten I could do that. He told me how beautiful I was, words my mother should have been here to say. Though I was only twelve, he said my body was a woman's and any woman should know how to kiss, so when he leaned in I leaned in too. It wasn't horrible, as first kisses go.

Afterwards, he said we could go steady if I wanted. I said if he bought me a candy pop ring. He told me he was flat broke and wouldn't spend money on a stupid ring, anyway. It was nothing really. One of many childhood moments, but a moment I always think of when overwhelmed by work, wondering if I really need that next promotion or how important it is to impress some superior. The memory reminds me of the importance of having my own money, my own source of security. I never want to rely on anyone else to get me what I want and need, not like Mom. She slaved and never had enough. I slave too, in a different way, but it gives me everything I want and enough to give my family just about anything they want too. This is important. Incredibly important. Moses has no idea. He's come from a comfortable family. Not rich, but never poor. He never pretended to be sick so he could stay in from recess and steal items from other children's lunch boxes. He doesn't know what it's like to feel forgotten.

I let my legs go limp and wait until my feet trail along the sand. Rising from the swing, I look toward the east. I'm only about fifteen minutes from my Pop's, who wants to see me. But getting there would mean a forty-five-minute walk back to Moses' apartment. I look west. Returning to my car now means I might beat Lori home and Moses is right, we need time. I turn west.

CHAPTER FOURTEEN

The scent of pancakes no longer lingers when I enter the kitchen but the mess, of course, remains. Lori hasn't been home, but still the sight annoys me. Rather than have my annoyance boil I turn on the water and sigh with contentment as I let the heat flow over my hands before filling the sink with suds and scrubbing the mess—several days' worth. I assume these dirty dishes are representative of her annoyance with me. Lori knows I like a clean kitchen, a clean everything, and usually does a good job of her share of the housework. She doesn't care as much as I do, and I've suspected things get messier than I would like while I'm away, but usually the scent of recently sprayed lemon cleaner greets me when I walk through the door.

As I place the dishes in the rack, smiling over my collection of plates, hand-picked to perfectly accent the decor in the dining room, my mind travels to Tokyo and today's interviews: two women with experience in marketing, top of their class eight and ten years ago, bright stars in their respective companies, but who have spent the last several years at home with babies. I imagine them prim but brimming with excitement about this opportunity to return to work in something other than a clerical position, basically the only option open to them in most firms if they don't want the expectation to stay at the office long after their children will be in bed.

Maybe Moses would have liked this new policy I'm

implementing, that the branch will respect work-life balance, provide flexibility for young mothers to be at home with their children in the evenings, and to take sick days to care for feverish babies. However, it's not likely I could show the same respect for that balance. At least not as soon as I'll provide it for employees. But I would, eventually, whether I have children or not. I don't want my whole life to be work, not that it is now, even though that's what Moses and my family seem to think.

With my hands in the warm bubbles, I imagine my life with babies. A part of me wants to want them, just not until I have the time to give them the attention they'll deserve. And not before I've given myself attention, not until I've accomplished the things that matter most to me. There's nothing wrong with that.

The apartment door opens and closes. I hear Lori's boots drop on the shoe rack and the front closet squeak open. Her feet pad up the hall and I set down the last of the mixing bowls on the rack then dry my hands, waiting for her to enter. I wait, and wait, until I hear her bedroom door followed by the sound of music wafting from her iPhone dock.

My ear turned towards the door I knock once, twice, wait, then knock again. "Lori?" The music fades.

"Yeah."

"Can I come in?"

"I'm changing."

"Let me know when you're done." I lean against the door, waiting, then knock again.

"Okay, I'm done."

"How was practice?" Her room is messier than usual. She stands in front of the mirror, swiping at her face with cotton pads. Her flannel pyjama pants are the ones I got for her last year, but this frilly lingerie style chemise I've never seen before.

"It was practice."

"Have you heard anything about the audition?"

"Oh, you remember about that?"

"Of course I remember about that. I know you weren't supposed to hear anything until this week, so I didn't see the point in asking."

"No. Not yet."

I sit on her bed. "I'm sure you will soon."

She turns to me, visually softening. "I hope so."

"You will." I grin at her. "You're amazing. I must have watched that video Junior sent me ten times. It was like magic."

She sets down the cotton pad, her eyes a mix of hope and skepticism. "You think so?"

"Have I ever lied to you?"

She turns back to the mirror and picks up the pad. "Well, you're my sister. You're more than biased."

"I also know talent when I see it."

She shrugs.

"You're going to get in, and if by some freak of nature all of the judges that day were blind, you'll get in somewhere else. You were born to do this, Lori. You are made for it."

"Stop it."

"What?"

She turns back again. "I'm pissed at you. So stop acting so nice, like you haven't done anything wrong."

"What? Missing the audition. Lori, come on. You couldn't expect me to fly back from Tokyo for two hours."

"And Christmas, and my birthday. But it's not just that. You were ready to abandon us all with barely a thought about it. Oh, job opportunity? Oh, promotion? Well, that's more important than anything else! Brother in jail? Sister having one of the most important days of her life? Ah well!"

"We've been over this," I snap, more angry by this foreign tone than the words she's saying, words she's said before. "My job is what pays for all those dance lessons. What paid for the years of schooling that allows Junior to think the way he does."

"I know," she snaps back, an annoying whine to her voice. "I know." She loses the whine. "But you're still abandoning us."

"I invited you to come."

"You invited me to come? What does that even mean? Am I going to go to a prestigious dance school there? Am I going to leave all my friends, the rest of my family, Drake?"

I lean against her pillows, trying not to smirk, surprised at myself for not catching on more quickly. "So that's what this is about? Drake?"

"No, it's not."

"He's a high school sweetheart, you don't make major life decisions around a—"

"Don't condescend to me."

"I'm not, Lor. I'm just saying."

"This is not about Drake. But I know what it's about for you. Money. But money isn't everything."

"I know that. Don't you think I know that?"

"I don't know. You've got your fancy car and your fancy apartment and—"

"It's about security. Money may not be everything but let me tell you, security is important. You don't know what it was like. You're too young to remember what it was like."

"Stop it already!" She screams. "Stop it. Stop it. Stop it! You can't do this anymore."

"What?"

"Lay it on me, poor baby Delorita, child of sorrows who has never known real sorrow in her life and can never possibly understand. I understand that Mom left Pop because he couldn't provide for her, because she had to spend her days on her knees cleaning other people's filth, because Pop couldn't provide for us the way she wanted." Lori plops down on her bed and clenches her pillow. "I also understand I was the reason she came back, because she didn't want to deal with me...the unwanted child...and didn't know what else to do. I understand that because of me you didn't just lose your mother, you saw her take her own life. I understand that deep down you hate me for it."

"Lori." I reach forward, my hands grasping her shoulders. "Don't ever say that again. Don't ever think that. I don't blame you."

"You do, you do." She pulls away. "Okay, maybe not hate. Maybe not that bad. But you resent me. Some part of you blames me."

"I don't."

"Well then I blame me, for how…closed you are."

"Stop. What are you even talking about? This is not your fault."

She sits up straight. "No, you're right. It's not, but that doesn't mean you see that. It's our mother's fault. Our stupid, selfish, cold-hearted mother." She sighs. "She was depressed. She had to be depressed. I've researched it. I get it. She probably had postpartum." Lori pauses. "But if she did, she wouldn't have had it if it weren't for me. Maybe she would have been fine. Maybe she would have even come back one day, once Pop got things together, like he did. But you'll never know because of me."

"Stop," I say, not believing Lori's talking like this, thinking like this, that she thinks about our family in this depth at all. But…why wouldn't she? I do.

Not knowing what aspect to respond to, I go with the simplest. "She wasn't stupid. She was so smart." I settle in beside Lori. "And she could be tender. She could be sweet." I wrap my arm around her. "It's not because of you. She loved you. She just didn't love Pop and the life he gave us. She didn't want to be with him and saw us as a burden only because she couldn't give us the life she wanted to, not because she didn't love us."

"That's crap." Lori's eyes remained dry this whole time, but now they redden and start to water. The sight makes mine mist, but I hold back. I need to be strong. Tears are weak. "She hated me," says Lori. "She hated the sight of me."

"She sang to you." I squeeze her tighter. "She'd sing to you at night, to help you sleep. Sometimes even when you weren't crying, she'd pick you up and sing to you and kiss your head." I can remember less than a handful of these moments, but that doesn't matter. "She loved you."

"Not enough," says Lori, her face going hard. She takes a big breath. "I have homework, okay?"

"What is with people wanting to get rid of me tonight?" I ask, trying to lighten the mood—though my question is legitimate.

"Listen, just—" Lori's expression softens. "Don't go, okay? Tell Mr. Whatever-his-name that you can work for him here."

"It's not that simple."

"Then get a new job." She raises her arms in exasperation and swings her legs off of the bed. "Or don't. Whatever. But I'm not coming."

"You might think differently once you see Tokyo."

"I doubt it."

I stand and make my way around the bed so I'm in front of her, not knowing what to think or feel but needing her touch. "Give me a hug, okay?"

"El."

"Sister's orders." I yank her to me and wrap my arms around her slim frame, glad I still have two to three inches on her and hoping that doesn't change. She's stiff at first but eventually melts into my arms. "I've never blamed you," I whisper. "Not for a second." She mumbles something unintelligible as I hold her tightly, wondering if in some small way my words are a lie.

❧

MY WALK INTO THE OFFICE the next morning is followed with a small entourage of whistles and cheers. "Funny, funny." I wave and give an exaggerated bow.

"The playing field evens out at last," shouts Ron, who is always several clients behind me. "Now the rest of us will have a shot at number one."

I shake my head. "I'm just doing the job." I push open my office door. "Only the job." The light dims as I pull my office blinds shut and then brightens as I open the ones against the window. I lean on my desk, my hands wrapped across my chest, perturbed by the display of envy and admiration that I imagine held hints of mockery with some malice thrown in. We all work hard, but no one as hard as me. This office I'm standing in proves that. I generally thrive on being someone worthy of jealousy, but today, with the people I love loving me less because of this job, it all seems a little hollow.

A sharp knock sounds against the door, making me jump. "Come in."

"You little hustling scamp!" James pushes through the door, closes it firmly behind him, spins a chair around, then slides into it.

"Excuse me?"

"Do you need me to repeat myself? I said, you little hustling scamp."

"I need you to explain yourself." I spin my chair and sit so I'm facing him.

"Lance thinks you, my dear, are the best thing since Viagra."

"James."

"What? The guy's ancient. I'm sure he's older than sliced bread."

"I did my job."

"Your job? From what I understood, your job was to be trained on that trip. From what I *hear*, you were basically the one training the big guy, while you essentially enacted a hostile takeover. So you're what, two steps away from running the whole place."

I cross my legs smoothly and lean back in the chair, my arms lying across the armrests. "Only two?"

"My, my, someone's even cockier than usual."

"Confident, James. You always get those words confused. I'm confident. And it wasn't hostile."

"Mm-hmm. How did you do it?"

"I told you. I was just doing my job."

"Come on. You can tell me. Are you sleeping with him?"

"Ask me something like that again and I'll get my NON-sexual influence to boot you out of this whole company." I maintain a tease to my voice although his suggestion makes me seethe.

"Now that is cocky." He grins. "And if I didn't love you so much, I'd make trouble for you over it. But alas, I do love you," he hesitates, "like my own child of course."

"You'd be a young father."

"Details. And just so you know, I was also asked to take the Tokyo position but knew my wife and kids wouldn't go for it."

My eyebrows raise. "You were?"

"I was, and I highly recommended you in my place."

These words humble me. Not that James isn't amazing, he is, and I've learned a lot from him. I just thought…

"Not that you don't deserve this chance, obviously you do." My face must have betrayed me. He crosses his ankle over his knee and leans forward. "Just tell me, are you really redoing the whole structure of the place?"

"Yes."

"Firing, hiring, the whole lot?"

"I am."

He rubs his chin.

"What?"

"Nothing. That's probably a good move. A smart move for the branch, anyway. How is Kamlyn taking it?"

"I think he wants to stage a coup."

James sighs. "You're not the only one who thinks that."

"Everdeen?"

My chest tightens but, not allowing another betrayal, my face doesn't flinch.

"Yes, Lance isn't ready to let Kamlyn go, but he also doesn't want a battle going on. You're in charge. He thinks everyone should understand that. He thinks that would be hard to accomplish with you on the other side of the world."

"I'm heading back for another three weeks—" I swipe to my phone's calendar "—two weeks from Wednesday. I got an email confirming that from his secretary last night."

"Yeah. He asked me to speak with you. He wants you back within the week, before the next round of interviews. He thinks you should be present for the incoming hires. He understands if you'll have to come back for a week or two once the ball is really rolling—to handle your personal affairs and such. This week he wants you transferring over your clients here, making sure all of those loose strings are tied, and then," James shrugs, his eyes keenly assessing me, "Tokyo full time."

I swallow, nodding as I struggle not to scream. As much as I presented myself as married to the job, this is ridiculous. Everdeen can't think work is my whole life. My mind flashes with images of how the conversations are likely to go—first Lori, then Moses. Lori is my sister. She can be as mad as she likes and nothing will ever change that, but Moses? I finger my ring and continue to nod. He's not going to like it and if last night was about more than grief…I don't let myself finish the thought. "Do you think there's much chance he'll reconsider? I mean I can keep a close eye on things from here. Kuri is impressively open to keeping me in the loop. I can sit in with video conferencing on the interviews and—"

"With the time change? Come on, Eloise."

I nod again. "Okay then. So this is the only option. This is what he wants done?"

"This is it. You told Everdeen you were committed. It's time to prove it."

"All right then." My voice is enthused with energy and drive, tones I can call upon in an instant. "I've got a lot of work to do, calling clients, setting up meetings with the big ones, figuring out who will best fit with whom."

James stands, rests one hand on my shoulder, and looks down on me. "Speaking as your friend, not your boss, you don't have to do this. You pull out now and I'm not sure what Lance would do but you'll always get a shining reference from me. Lots of other firms would count themselves blessed to get someone like you and wouldn't expect your entire life."

"No," I say. "This is what I want." I wink, while ignoring my roiling stomach. "I'll be outranking you soon, old man."

"That you will, love." James pats my shoulder before stepping away. "That you will."

When he walks out of the office, closing the door behind him, I let my head fall in my hands. "This is ridiculous." I mouth into my sleeve. "Keep it together." I am not a person who crumbles. Not a person who lets any situation seem too big for her. This is a change to my plans, at the worst possible moment, but I haven't worked this long and this hard to let a simple scheduling shift mess me up. Moses will have to understand. He loves me. He said it last night. This quick move is out of my hands. That's all. He'll have to understand. I sit up, letting my spine straighten, and look at my schedule for the week. Picking up the phone, I dial one of my bigger clients. It's time to get to work.

CHAPTER FIFTEEN

The following evening I'm the first one at the restaurant for a night out with the girls and their significant others. A particularly special night, it will be the first time everyone else meets Autumn's new fella. I've determined to let work take a rest and enjoy this night, but my enjoyment is hampered by Moses' choice to come separately. It makes sense, he'll be coming directly from work, but it still hurts that he didn't offer to pick me up on the way or have me get him. Less than a minute after I'm seated, Autumn's cousin, Jennifer, walks up with her boyfriend Rajeev. They wave and say, "How's it going?" at the same time, prompting a cute couple moment I would usually find sweet.

"Good, good." I return Jennifer's quick hug. "And you two? How are you?"

"Wonderful," says Rajeev, squeezing Jenn's waist. "Jennifer just sent off her first novel manuscript to a publisher. So it's a night for celebrating!"

"Oh, it's going to get rejected." Jenn slips into the booth. "Or probably, anyway."

"Still, that's great." I smile, happy for her.

"What's really exciting is your news," says Jenn. "Autumn told me. Let's see the ring."

I hold my hand out, trying not to think of the possibility that this particular piece of jewellery could be coming off my finger. "Beautiful." Jenn releases my hand. "Have you picked a date yet?"

"No, not yet." I slide to the back of our large, round booth. This way I can see everyone as they approach. "We figured why rush, right? We have all the time in the world."

"And you've been travelling too, right? You saw the Andrev's again in the UK and…somewhere in Asia?"

"Tokyo." I tell our server I'll take a Pinot Grigio then look back to Jenn. "I'll be moving there, actually. I received a promotion."

"Congratulations! So that's—" Her sentence drops when Autumn and Jakob walk up to the table. The sight of them holding hands takes my mind off my own problems, erasing my crabbiness.

"Hey," says Autumn, a shy but excited look on her face. "Jenn, Rajeev, this is Jakob. Jakob," she spreads her hand to the two, "Jenn and Rajeev."

Jakob tosses his hair in that way he has. It's grown since I've seen him last and curls in a way that makes his already great smile all the more appealing. He shakes hands with the two, greeting them with the accent I'm sure is part of what made Autumn swoon. He turns his gaze to me and grins. "Come on, now. Get out of there. Give me a hug."

I slide around the booth and step into his arms, enjoying the warmth of his embrace. "I'm sorry about Farfar," I say. "He was a sweet, sweet man. How are you doing?"

"Time makes it easier." He links his hand in Autumn's again. "Plus, he's not suffering anymore."

I nod. "And your family?"

"They're good. Very good." As he speaks, I slide back into the seat. Autumn and Jakob follow me. "Emily has started studying again and her doctors seem to have her on the right med cocktail now. Amelia is still having a hard time, but she'll be okay."

"His sisters," says Autumn, addressing Jenn and Rajeev.

"I'm glad," I say to Jakob. "Tell them I say hello."

"Will you be heading to the UK any time soon?"

"No plans."

"Oh." His face lights up. "Probably too busy planning a wedding. I heard. Congrats."

"No." I keep my smile on. "Just taking a different direction at work. I'll be moving to Tokyo, taking over a firm there."

"You *might* be moving to Tokyo, taking on a firm there," says Moses, approaching the table with Tracey beside him. "It's still in the test phase, right?"

"Jakob," I say, "this is Moses, my fiancé. And Tracey."

"Well, hello." Jakob stands and shakes their hands. "I've heard plenty about you both."

Tracey laughs. "You're even better looking than Autumn said. What a lucky girl!"

Jakob blushes but his smile grows. He elbows Autumn in the side. "You didn't tell her how good looking I am?"

"Words couldn't describe." Autumn blushes back, looking somewhat uncomfortable. I'm sure she's thinking of Matt, her late husband, wondering what we're thinking about Jakob being here, filling his place. I squeeze her hand and she looks over at me, smiles, squeezes back.

"Is Thomas on his way?" asks Autumn.

"Oh, uh, no." Tracey takes her seat. "He's not going to make it tonight. Sorry." She does this little head bob and shrug she's known for. "Guess I'll be a seventh wheel tonight. I was sure you wouldn't mind."

"Of course not." Autumn reaches for her menu. "We'll meet him another time."

The waitress comes with Jenn, Rajeev and my drinks and takes the orders for everyone else's. We're not ready to place our dinner orders so let the conversation lull as we study the menu. Moses is two places down from me and I contemplate going to the restroom so I can slide back in beside him, try to tell if he's still upset from the other night, but I can see his face better from where I am.

After we order, the chat around the table is relaxed and

friendly. Jenn talks about her manuscript. Rajeev, a social worker, entertains us with stories of some of the cases he's been working on, and Jakob gets questioned so much I almost feel sorry for the guy, though he takes it well. When asked how he fell for Autumn, he grins like a man more than just a little bit in like. "So Autumn pushed my sister out of the path of this oncoming truck. It was just barrelling down on them." He laughs. "And it was in that moment, seeing the terror and determination on her face, watching her collapse in a heap on top of my sister, that I knew I wanted to be with this girl."

"It was that soon?" Autumn looks incredulous.

He shrugs. "I mean I'm not saying I was in love or anything. Just that," he pauses, smiles at her, "I wanted to make sure you stayed in our lives, mine in particular."

"You never made any moves. You treated me like a sister, you—"

"You seemed fragile." His voice is soft. His words are for her, not us. "You were hiding something behind that tan line. I didn't want to scare you away or encroach on territory that wasn't available."

She looks to the finger where Matt's ring once rested. "Probably smart."

"I'm a smart guy." He winks at her. "So, Moses." Jakob talks at a level the whole group can hear again. "Autumn tells me you're a high school teacher and close to getting your Ph.D.? That you're going to move to the Uni level soon?"

"Partly true." Moses casts me a quick glance. "I actually finished writing my dissertation last week. Just another go through for copy edits then I can hand it in for approval, the defence, all of that. I'm fairly certain I'm going to stay teaching high school though." Moses is looking at Jakob but, I think, talking to me. "I really love the kids, you know? And actually being able to spend my time teaching them, it's great. My doctorate has mostly been by distance, but I spent a couple of months each year on campus in that academic world." He scrunches up his nose, as if he's smelled something bad. "It seems about seventy percent of what most of the profs do is compete for grants, tenure, and the like, teaching is almost an afterthought."

"I definitely felt that way when I was in school," says Tracey. "Half the profs acted like it was an inconvenience when you even went to them. They were so busy writing and researching."

"Exactly," says Moses. "That's not what I want. I want to be there for my students."

"Brilliant." Jakob nods, his hair shaking back and forth. "That's really awesome. I'm sure the world needs more devoted teachers like you."

Moses smiles. "I do my best. The kids add a lot to my life too. It's not all altruistic or something." He avoids my gaze as he says all of this. A part of me sees the man I fell in love with as he speaks: the man who is kind-hearted and passionate, who put his family, and then my family, above all else. The man who I finally let in. The other part of me is seething. He's presenting himself as some saviour for the children, putting a secure job, an income that would be nearly tripled, and our future to the back burner for some idealistic belief. A career is about a lot more than what feels good.

"So, if Eloise's job ends up taking her to Tokyo full time, will you be finding a teaching job over there?" asks Jenn. "They have some really good international schools. I could probably even give you some names of the principals."

"Jenn writes for ESL programs," adds Autumn.

"I don't think we're quite there yet." Moses looks my way. "But it's possible I'll take you up on that." Well, at least he hasn't written Tokyo off entirely.

"That's a big move," says Rajeev. "But an exciting one. Moving across the world turned out to be one of the best things I ever did."

"Because of the career opportunity?" Jenn smiles, a teasing tone to her voice.

"Oh, a little more than that."

After our food arrives our conversation is interspersed with chatting, laughing, and near silent moments of enjoying the meal. When the waitress returns to clear our plates, asking if we'd like the bill or another round of drinks, Autumn, more worried about such things than she used to be, looks out the window and shakes her head. "It's been snowing the last hour or so. We should all get home before any more piles up." Usually part of me would want to counter this, stay out later—partly for the guilt-free break away from work (out with friends is one of the few times I put my notifications on silent, not just vibrate)and partly because I don't like the way Autumn now fears vehicles. But tonight I'm equally anxious for and dreading the chance to get alone with Moses. My hope is he'll calm my fears, say he was just tired and sad and we'll work it out, like we always do.

"You're probably right," I say, before anyone else can put out a different suggestion. "It's sure to be slippery."

We pay our bills and chat some more, first in front of the table, then in the foyer. We hug and the others promise to meet once more before Jakob returns to England. I smile and nod but make no verbal commitment. I won't be here.

"El." Moses turns to me. "I gave Tracey a ride over. Her car was in the shop. Do you mind taking her home?"

From here, Tracey's apartment is on my way home, so that would make sense, if I were going home. "I thought I'd come by your place." I turn to Jenn and Rajeev. "She's not too far out of your way, right?"

"I can always take a cab," says Tracey.

At the same moment Rajeev says, "Sure, we'll take her."

"Oh." Moses purses his lips. "I need to work on those edits, then I have an early morning. It's best you go home."

"Sure, yes." I accept his quick hug and kiss on my

forehead, like this is perfectly normal, like his words don't make me oscillate between heartbreak and rage. "I'll take you, Tracey."

The snow falls in thick clumps. Not flakes, but clusters. The air is warmer than when we entered the restaurant, a phenomenon I've always loved about snowfalls. Jakob laughs and spins in it, kicking his feet through the slush in the parking lot then hopping to what was a grassy knoll a few hours ago and scooping up a handful of the fresh snow, packing it tightly. "We don't get snow like this in England," he shouts with glee.

"We get it all the time." Autumn looks to the sky. "We've had a bit of a warmer spell but you just wait, by tomorrow we'll be looking out the window at a white world."

He tosses the snowball in his hand but, rather than throw it at one of us like I expect, asks, "Who's up for a snowman?"

"When we get home," says Autumn. "We can make a dozen."

"All right." Grinning, he scoops Autumn up in his arms, carrying her threshold style to her car. "Your boots are not fit for this weather."

She laughs in a way I've heard less than a handful of times since Matt.

"It's nice, isn't it?" Tracey sidles up to me. "That she's found love again. I was worried."

"We all were." The others have dispersed to their vehicles and we walk towards mine. "Do you think it's love?"

"If not," says Tracey. "It will be soon."

"But the distance."

"They'll figure something out." Tracey looks so sure. Her face is practically angelic in her knit hat, with snow clusters settling on her lashes. "I can feel it."

We drive in silence, listening to oldies hour on the radio,

lost in our private thoughts, or at least I assume Tracey is lost too. She stares out the passenger window. When I pull into the driveway of her apartment, she turns to me. "Can you park? I'd like to go for a walk."

"Now?" I ask, before noticing the tear that's made a path down her cheek.

"If you would."

I pull the car into a spot and grab my mitts, hat, and scarf from a bag in the back seat. Tracey gestures to a path to the left of the lot and we fall into step, still silent.

"It's a beautiful night," she says.

"Yeah."

"I haven't walked enough this winter. I get nervous, you know? To be out at night by myself and well, in the winter it's always night when I'm not at school."

I nod, waiting for her to continue, wondering if she has a specific reason for this walk. With Tracey, though, she may just want my presence.

As we walk the trail, the silence that surrounds us settles me. The snow muffles the noises we would usually hear— cars in the distance, radios blaring. The longer we walk, the less I wonder what is causing Tracey's pensive mood and the more I sink into my own. I may actually have to choose between Moses and this job. The thought is hard to comprehend.

"It's over between Thomas and me."

I snap my head toward Tracey and link my arm in hers. "I'm sorry."

She laughs. It's a painful sound. "Just me, you know? Being too hopeful. Being too trusting. Stupid."

"No." I squeeze her arm. "You weren't stupid. He seemed like a nice guy."

"Well," she glances at me, "he wasn't."

"Do you want to talk about it?"

She shrugs and sniffs. "I was right. I was actually right. I guess that's something."

"About the weirdness? How he could only see you at certain times?"

"Yep." She brushes her mitt across a tree branch, making the snow tumble down. "He's married."

I stop walking, making Tracey, whose arm is still in mine, stop too. "Oh, Trace." I pull her into a tight embrace. She squeezes back, and whimpers into my shoulder. Pulling away, she also pulls herself together. We turn off the trail and onto a snow-covered sidewalk.

"Four years," she says. "He's been married four years to a beautiful woman. A beautiful woman who is seven months pregnant."

"The bastard."

"My thoughts exactly." We take several steps before she speaks again. "Why does this happen to me, El? What is it about me that says, 'Hey, Dirtbags, come on over. This one's a loser you can certainly take advantage of?'"

"Nothing. This reflects on them, Tracey. Not you. You've just had bad luck."

"You've never had this kind of bad luck. There has to be something about me." Tracey swipes the snow off a bus stop bench and plops down on it. She leans her elbows on her lap, her head in her hands.

"Okay," I say. "Something is different." I think of Lori's words the other night. "I'm closed off. I resist men for anything but a quick fling. I don't let it go deep, or at least I didn't. Who knows how many cheating men I've dated in my time? I just didn't stay around long enough to figure out they were cheaters." I shrug, realizing this is the first time I've expressed that truth in words. "And with Moses…I guess I was lucky. Somehow he worked his way in and he's a good one."

"Incredibly lucky." She looks up at me. "Don't do anything to screw that up, El. You have no idea what you've found. No idea what creeps are actually out there."

"I don't plan to." But I might… "I know I've got a good

one."

"Seriously." Tracey sits up. "He's not happy about this Tokyo thing. He's not happy with how much time you've been spending on work. He's not sure you even really want to be married."

"He talks to you about this? He's told you this?"

"We're close." She shrugs again. "We see each other every day and with you gone so much, I guess he's been lonely. Don't worry. Be glad he's coming to me about this and not some woman who'd be trying to snap him away from you. I'm on your side. I've been telling him this is just a phase, that when you have a new project on the horizon you become obsessed with it sometimes but then after a while you go back to your normal level of workaholism." She chuckles. "Not this turbo state you're in now."

"I'm not that bad."

"No." She rests her hand on my leg. "I'm not saying it's bad. It's just you, how you've always been. You're devoted and passionate and driven. That's part of what I love about you. What we all love about you. I think Moses just feels a little forgotten, you know? I think he expected you to be more excited about the engagement, to put the same type of effort you put into planning everything else into planning your wedding." She gives my thigh a squeeze. "It's just bad timing. I'm sure if this promotion hadn't come up, you'd be all about the wedding and all about him."

"Yeah," I say. "Yeah, yeah. Of course." I turn my gaze to the street. The snow erases some of the tire tracks. "How did you find out about Thomas?"

"I don't need to go into that. Not my finest hour."

"Fair enough."

"I feel a little better though, just telling you about it. I felt weird telling everyone tonight that he couldn't make it, but I didn't want to—"

"I know."

"Let's head back." She chuckles. "My rump is starting to

freeze."

"Mine too."

When we reach Tracey's apartment she hugs me once more. "Thanks, El. Sorry I'm a bit of a mess."

"Hardly."

"Well, thanks anyway. And El?"

"Yeah."

"I'm worried about you. I mean I know this promotion is an amazing opportunity and you've worked incredibly hard for it. I'm proud of you. And I've probably said it before but just…if Moses doesn't agree to go to Tokyo, well, you wouldn't let that…" Her voice trails off.

"He'll agree." I smile at her. "Thanks for your concern, but I'm not worried."

"You're right." She smiles back. "Of course you're right. He's probably just worn down, upset from Danny dying, overworked. That's all. He loves this school, the kids, but he'll love a new school and new kids too. And you know him better than I do. You know how he'll feel once he's doing better."

"You knew Danny too?" I ask as she pushes open the lobby door.

She turns back, seeming surprised by the question. "No, I've never met him."

CHAPTER SIXTEEN

"Call Moses," I tell my car's phone system once I've left Tracey and am behind the wheel. The phone rings, and rings, and rings, and finally goes to voicemail. "Hang up." I drive carefully over the slippery roads, annoyed at how long it takes me to get home, but more annoyed at how unlikely it is that Moses is already asleep. He's screening my call. Or showering. The tension in my shoulders eases. He could be showering. As I'm thinking this, work thoughts push out my worry over Moses. Over a dozen major clients need representation now that I'll be gone, and that representation needs to be a great fit. Transferring some of the smaller gigs to consultants will be simple, anyone on my team can take them. But these big ones…as I make a tight turn, careful to keep my wheels in check, I mentally try to pair my colleagues' strengths with my clients' needs. I remember the applications Kuri sent me this afternoon. I should go over those tonight, let her know my thoughts on the potential candidates. Then there are Kamlyn's suggestions for a campaign with a current client. I need to give it one more look before signing off on it.

I sigh as I pull into my apartment's garage. It's a lot. But I'll handle it, like always. Mr. Everdeen was right, though. This transition will all go much smoother once my work here is completed and I can focus completely on the Tokyo branch. Thinking of Everdeen reminds me of the three meetings he's set up this week—to make sure we're on the same page for the operation in Tokyo. It's 10:23 and, despite how tired I feel, I can put in a couple of hours of work before bed. The more work I get done today the less I'll have to distract me from the talk I need to have with Moses. I want to give him my full attention.

My apartment is dark and quiet when I walk through the hall. A sliver of light shines from under Lori's door. I need to talk to her too. "Lori," I whisper then gently knock. "Lori?" No response. I turn the knob and push open the door. She's curled up under the covers, the lamp on and a book spread open beside her fallen hand. I watch her for a moment, feeling a tug of anxiety at the thought of living so far from her. I practically raised her. It makes sense that she's upset. I'm the only mother she's ever known, and I'm leaving.

I step into the room on tiptoe so as not to wake her. After placing the book on her bedside table, I bend down and kiss her forehead lightly: a butterfly kiss. If I work hard enough at convincing her, find a good dance school, show her all Tokyo has to offer during a visit, she may come with me. Not before graduation though, which I cannot miss. Mr. Everdeen will have to understand I need to come back for that. He knows I have a family. I turn out the lamp and kiss her once more before tiptoeing out of the room.

By the time I turn out my own light I only have five hours until I need to wake again. I crawl into bed, pulling the duvet up around me, wishing it was Moses I was wrapping myself up in. Sleep finds me and I sink into it, slowly, all my worries circling through my head until finally they're lost, for the moment, in oblivion.

"ELOISE!" I OPEN MY eyes to see Lori standing above me, fully dressed, her backpack slung over one shoulder. "Are you okay?"

"What? Yes." I sit up in bed, my eyes adjusting to the dim light. "What time is it?"

"It's eight-fifteen. I didn't even know you were home, but then I saw your wet boots by the door."

"Arghh." I sit up. "And I meant to get to the office early."

Lori stands where she is, shifting back and forth on her feet as I check the clock. I set it for seven-ten, at night. Just great.

"Is everything okay?" she asks.

"Yeah, yes. Go on." I roll out of bed, my head spinning at the memory of the dream I just woke from. All those doors… "Don't be late."

"Yeah, okay." She hesitates a moment then turns from me. A moment later the apartment door opens then closes. I race to get ready, glad everything is where it should be and easy to access. I arrive at the office exactly an hour later, with a growling stomach but only fifteen minutes late. At least in Tokyo my suite is a short walk from the office. None of this battle with rush hour.

The day breezes by with barely a moment to breathe. I have so much to accomplish before seeing Moses tonight. And it will go well. It has to go well. My cell buzzes as I'm about to call a client. *Sorry I missed you last night. I was beat. Slept early. See you tonight. Love you.* Those two final words make so much tension leave my body.

The rest of the day my breathing comes easier. Knowing Moses wants to see me is one concern gone. As I'm leaving, my phone buzzes again. *Sorry, something came up. I'm going to have to break our dinner plans, but you can come over after 8:30.*

I tell him that's fine, adding a smiley face so he knows I'm not pissed, though of course I am. Or disappointed may be the better word. Very, very disappointed, and frustrated. Yes, that too. I sigh, not liking the way my thoughts are so imprecise. It's not like me.

Realizing I have to do it at some point, and sooner than later may be best, I drive through the gruelling traffic to my father's house. His car sits in the driveway and so do I, unable to garner the courage to go in.

As I stare at the house, hardly changed from the first time I saw it, my mind takes me back. I was ten, scared, and excited to be moving again. We'd come to this country two years earlier and lived with another Trinidadian family in a two-bedroom apartment. Uncle Archie visited us twice, so Junior and I knew him, but we'd never seen his house. It looked so big. 'It's just us?' I whispered to Pop as he held open the car door for me. He nodded. Junior had already gotten out of the other side, his hand in Mom's as they walked up the steps where Uncle Archie, who had driven us here, was opening the door.

'And your Uncle Archie of course.'

'I don't want to go there.' My voice sounded small even to me. 'I want to go back home.'

'This is your home. Your new home. Your new life. It's better than the old one.' Pop looked so hopeful, I wanted to cry. I'd seen that look before and knew saying a new life was better didn't make it so.

'I want to go home.'

'My sweet Ellie, that's not home anymore.' He crouched down to my eye-level, his hunched shoulders looking broad in the opening of the door. 'You'll like it here.'

I shook my head, holding onto my stuffed elephant, which I was too big for but refused to give up. Pop motioned for me to crawl out. I squeezed the elephant tighter. He sighed. He smiled. He told me to shove over then crawled in beside me, closing the door with a firm smack. His arms wrapped around me and I was less afraid.

I have a key but knock anyway. Pop opens the door and grins. "I was wondering if you just came to nap in that swanky car of yours."

"You saw me pull up?" I return his hug, noting how the

air smells different in the house, like cinnamon toast. Candles? Evelyn's touch, I imagine.

He nods and waves me in. "I figured you were working. Important call or something?"

"Or something." I step into the hall, the familiar feeling of dread and sadness, anger and fear, spilling over me. Will it ever go away? Turning to my father, I try to focus on him, and not the memories threatening to take over my vision. "You left a message saying you wanted to see me, so I figured I'd swing by."

"I'm glad you did." He makes his way to the living room and sits down heavily, expelling a long breath of air, as if the movement is an effort. Maybe it is. Salt and pepper curls, deep wrinkles around his eyes, his nose, his mouth. A body that's slighter than it used to be. I noticed all of these things the last time I was here, but still they shock me. My father is getting old. He looks at me a moment before speaking. "So, you've yet to set a date?"

"Not yet. Complications, you know, with my work."

"The promotion?"

"Yes."

He nods, as if my words have confirmed something for him. "Well, I think we're going to go ahead with it then. We're thinking next month. In a little over two weeks, actually. A Valentine's wedding."

My mouth drops, and again my chest tightens. "Valentine's?"

"Evelyn thought it would be sweet."

"Sweet." I swallow. "Well, how about next Valentine's? What's the rush?"

"We're old." He chuckles. "We might not be around next Valentine's."

"Pop, come on."

"Well," he folds his hands on his lap, rubbing them, "she might not be. But then again, she might."

"What?"

"Breast cancer." The words come out so matter of fact, like he has to make them devoid of meaning. "The diagnosis came through a couple of weeks ago, while you were away." He stops, a look on his face like he's just witnessed something terrible and can do nothing about it, but his voice doesn't change. "She's going to have them chopped right off. Do some treatment as well. But," his voice wavers now, as if he's choking on the words, "she'd like her natural breasts for our wedding night."

My lips pucker. Part of me wants to chastise him for talking about his wedding night with a woman who's not my mother, but how can I? "I'm sorry, Pop."

His head moves up and down, barely a nod. "I'm sure it'll be all right. The doctors, they're so good these days. And apparently they caught it really soon. She'll be fine. I know she'll be fine. but we...we don't want to wait." He smiles in a way I've never seen before. "I love her." He repeats the words as if they amaze him. "I love her."

I keep silent, offering a tight-lipped smile.

"After your mother, I didn't think I'd ever love again. How could I? The one woman I'd loved, and loved with all my heart, I failed." He looks at his hands. "I wasn't enough. And because of it..." He looks back up. "I know you've never forgiven me. I've never forgiven myself either. Well," he smiles again, "not until Evelyn came along. She made me think, made me believe for the first time, that maybe it wasn't all my fault. Evelyn blooms under my love in a way your mother never did. That means it couldn't have been all me, right? Not entirely that I wasn't enough. She's given me hope." He laughs now. "Despite these old bones, I kind of feel like a young man again."

I swallow, all these years he's thought it was his fault. And all these years... "That's great, Pop. Really. I'm happy for you."

"I hoped you would be." He looks back down at his hands, squeezing the palms together. "I know I've let you carry so much of the load—practically raising your brother and sister when you were only a child yourself." The couch's plastic lining crinkles as he shifts. "Then getting out into the world, providing for them. I don't know if Junior would be getting his law degree if it weren't for you. And Lori, the way she dances? I couldn't have put her in any lessons except those free ones at the Y. It shames me." He looks up again. "But I hope you know how thankful I am."

I manage a nod.

"I…" His voice shakes. "I wasn't the man I should have been. To your brother and sister, but especially to you. You were just so capable. You seemed able to handle everything, so I let you. That was wrong. You didn't get to be a little girl."

"It's okay. Really. I was fine. I am fine."

He shakes his head. "I don't know about that. You've done good. Amazing. But you hold too much on yourself. I don't know." He puts his head in his hands for a moment then rubs his hands over his tight curls. "You didn't have a mother or a father, not really. You didn't seem to think I could be a father. And I know for a while, after your mother died, I couldn't. I was doing better by the time you took Lori away from me, but at that point I didn't know what to say. I knew you'd give her a better life."

"I didn't *take her away* from you," I say, drawing out the words.

"Sure you did." He slides toward me on the couch, making the lining screech. "Look at me though, rambling on like an old fool. I don't mean this to sound like I'm blaming things on you. It's the opposite. What I want, the reason I asked you to come is that I'm about to start a new life. A life I want you to be a part of, all of you. And Evelyn's kids well, they miss their father, but I know they're happy for us. I know they don't feel the way you do. So, I just need to ask. Will you forgive me?"

"Forgive you?" My voice cracks, and immediately I

struggle to put my client face on. Strong. Resolved. Unbreakable.

"Yes. Forgive me for not being your daddy when you needed it most. For making you grow up too fast." His eyes crinkle as he smiles. "It amazes me the woman you turned into and kills me that I had so little to do with it. I…I understand if you can't, but I need to ask if you'll forgive me for it. If you'll let me be a bigger part of your life now, let me be a father again."

"I don't need anything from you." I keep my voice steady. "It's fine. I'm fine."

"I'm not talking about anything you *need*. I'm talking about, I don't know. Just being your family. Being a real part of your life again." He scans the room. "I know you hate coming here."

"It's the house," I say, "not you. It's just the house." My words are only partly true, and when he looks at my face, I know he knows this. There have been moments when I hated him. He should have done more, been more.

"We've talked about it," says Pop. "Evelyn and me, but also with Uncle Archie. We're selling this old house and the memories it holds. Evelyn's going to sell hers too. Get rid of our ghosts."

A wave of relief rushes through me. I'll never have to walk through that door again, stare at the spot on the floor, forever stained in my mind. He's getting rid of this house, this awful, awful house.

"Look at me." His eyes crinkle. "I've become soft in my old age." He laughs. "Evelyn assures me softness is a good thing." He puts both hands on his knees, as if resolved. "You don't have to answer now. You don't have to answer ever. I just needed to ask. I just needed to say I'm sorry."

"You don't need to." I'm baffled as a tear flows down my cheek. I don't cry. But I am. A mix of pity and anger and confusion swirl within me. He's right. He was barely a father. He's right. I lost my childhood. And as much as it's because of Mom, it's also because of him.

But what's the point of letting him know that, how so much of who he is is who I never want to be? There is no point. I say words I'm not sure I believe, but that I want to. "You did the best you could. You've always loved us, we've always known that," and as I say the words, I realize they are true. As much as my father's lack of drive has disappointed and sometimes frustrated me—content to work in menial, labouring jobs his entire life—as much as I've wished he was a different kind of man—a man I could look up to— I've always known he's loved me. I speak the words he's asked for. "I forgive you."

The look on my father's face fills me with guilt for all my unkind thoughts. He reaches forward and pulls me to him, pulling me right out of my chair and onto his lap in a way he hasn't held me since the night Mom died. "My baby girl." His arms grip me so tight it almost hurts. "Thank you."

He holds me like this for several minutes. I only uncoil myself from his grasp when his arms loosen. I scoot my way back to my chair and sit back as he stares at me, his gaze making me want to squirm.

"I was hoping also," he stops, looking shy, "that you'd read at the wedding. You have such a lovely speaking voice. It would mean so much to both of us. We want all our kids to be involved. Evelyn's children are very musical, and they're going to play and sing a song while Lori dances to it. Junior will be the MC at the reception."

"They're going to…you mean you've already asked them?"

"Yes."

"Well, I—" and then it hits me. "I'm sorry, Pop. I won't be here."

"What do you mean? It doesn't conflict with one of your trips to China? I thought you'd be back for a while now."

"It's Japan. Tokyo. But yes, no, I mean. Yes, I'll be in Tokyo but it's not for a trip. I'm moving there now."

"Well, I know. But not for five or six months?"

"Things have changed. I'm moving next week."

"Next?" His voice stops. "What about Lori?"

"She'll be okay. I may even see if Junior wants to move into the apartment. He's got such a dingy little place and—"

"And Moses? You're going to be apart all of that time?"

"I haven't talked to him about it yet, but people do long distance. They make it work."

"Oh, Ellie."

"Don't," I say, hating his childhood name for me. Mom's childhood name for me as well.

He waves his hand in front of him, as if dismissing his words. "But surely you can come back for your father's wedding."

I take a deep breath, unable to believe that yet another complication has arisen. "I'll do my best. My very best." I stand.

He stands too. "Well, I guess that's all I can ask. And if you say you will try, I know you will."

"I have to go, but..." I reach forward and hug him quickly, pulling back before he has a chance to hold me hostage in his arms again. "Congratulations. I'm really happy for you, for both you and Evelyn. And I'm sorry to hear she's sick."

He nods and walks me to the door. "You're going to see Moses?"

"Yes."

"You give that boy my love."

"I will." He hugs me again, and for the briefest of moments I am just a girl in her Daddy's arms. I tug away, kiss his cheek and step out the door.

With two hours to kill before Moses said to come over, I decide to head to the gym, despite the work I should be doing. Contemplating my father's words, his admission of guilt, his request for forgiveness, I feel as if some part of me I've been building up for years is about to collapse. On the treadmill, I turn my mind off as best I can and run down the clock as I await the minute I can turn the lock on Moses' door.

CHAPTER SEVENTEEN

Moses stares at me from the other end of the couch, his expression unreadable. "This will work," I say. "You just have to give Tokyo a chance. I promise you will love it."

"Loving it is not what I'm concerned about." He inhales deeply, making his nostrils flare. "It's you."

"Me?"

"Don't give me that." He almost growls.

I lean away from him, make my voice placating. "Moses, give you what?"

"Don't try to sell me." He pronounces each word separately, with a weighty pause between them.

"I'm not." I'm tempted to growl back but restrain myself. "I'm trying to reason with you."

He laughs. "This is reasoning? Telling me you're leaving. No, excuse me, you're *moving* to Tokyo in less than a week and expect me to be okay with it. That's your definition of reasoning?"

"I don't expect you to be happy about it. I understand it's sudden. But I do expect you to support me."

"Why?"

"What?"

"Why should I support you?" He looks at me like he's looking at a stranger.

"Because you love me."

His face freezes, mouth slightly open. "And what about

your love for me? Don't I matter?"

"Of course you matter." A trickle of sweat runs along my abdomen. My skin feels too tight for my body. "How can you even ask that?"

"Because, Eloise, you didn't even think of discussing this with me. You didn't come here asking what I thought and suggest we try to figure it out together. From the beginning you've told me, 'this is how it is,' and expected me to be okay with it. That's not how a man and wife behave. Everything you're doing tells me the only one who matters to you is you."

"All of this is for my family and for you."

He shifts away from me. "Then why don't you ask me what I want? Why don't you ask your family? They won't say this. You're considering missing your father's wedding for this job? Oh, I know, you said you'd ask Mr. Everdeen if you could get a few days off but if not, oh well, Dad!"

"You're being unreasonable. People have to miss family events for work all the time. It's not as if Pop is giving me months to plan." I look away from him. "I knew this job would involve travelling when I took it, and you knew it when you started dating me."

"You just don't get it." He closes his eyes, as if shutting me out. "It's not the travelling. It's not the job. It's you, Eloise. You."

"I'm the same person I've always been."

"Maybe you are." He sits back, stares at me. "And maybe I just thought you were someone else." His brow creases than relaxes, as if he's made a discovery. "If so, I'm sorry. Really sorry, because if that's the case I think I may have fallen in love with the person I wanted you to be."

I sit back too, feeling like the air has been knocked out of me. "What are you saying?" My voice is quiet, weak. This tone isn't even supposed to come out of me.

"I don't know."

"No." I grasp his hand. "What are you saying?"

He speaks through clenched teeth. "I don't know."

We sit there like that, my hands wrapped around his, his face turned away from me, for what feels like hours. Too soon, he pulls his hand away and stands. In the same moment, my phone buzzes. I glance at the screen, planning to turn it off, but it's Mr. Everdeen. "I have to take this." I step out of the room, my gut twisting.

The conversation is brief, not overly important. He tells me about some meetings he has lined up for me both this week and in Tokyo, where I'll be acting as his representative and that he wants me to send emails tonight, thanking the men for their time and expressing how excited I am to let them know all Everdeen Enterprises can do for their companies. "In case you didn't check your email tonight," says Everdeen, "I thought it best to call."

"Thank you," I say, eager to get back to Moses.

When I return, Moses is standing in the middle of the living room. His smile looks wistful. "You used to put your phone on silent when we spent time together. I always liked that about you." He takes a step towards me, his hands hanging awkwardly at his sides. "I appreciated that."

"I still do," I say. "Sometimes."

"Sometimes."

"I'm working with an international business. The beginning of their day is the end of mine. I need to be available." I take a step, shortening the distance between us. "And we're with each other so much now. It'd be hard to…" My voice trails off—we're not together so much anymore. "I still turn it off when we're out with other people."

He nods, takes a breath. "I don't think we want the same things."

"You said you would consider Tokyo." I step forward again, as he steps back. "How is that changed? I'm going sooner, that's all. You can still come at March break. You can see what it's like there. You can visit some schools.

You'll like Tokyo. You'll see how it can be our home. You'll see that it's not so far away. That we can still come back and visit both of our families."

"And if I don't?"

"You will."

"And if I don't?"

I don't want to lie to him. I want to say I'll give it up. I want to say that we're more important than everything I've been working for.

"And if I don't?" I can't speak. I can't move. "Thank you." He walks towards the dinette area. "Thank you for not telling me what I want to hear, for respecting me at least that much."

"Moses. What's going on? Are we—"

"Let's take some time to think, okay? Both of us. Let's really take some time to think."

"It's different." I follow him. "You can teach anywhere. You'd have an even better position in Tokyo, higher pay. I may never get an opportunity like this again."

"You just don't get it." He smiles, the type of smile you'd give to an uninformed child. I expect him to say more, but he doesn't.

"Are you telling me to leave?"

"Yeah. Go home, think about what really matters to you. Promise me. Do that. Consider what you're willing to give up for this job."

"Why do I have to give up anything?" I sound like a petulant child, and in this moment I hate him for that. "And what are you going to think about?"

"The same thing." He shrugs. "Maybe I am being unreasonable. Maybe if I love you enough, I should be willing to pick up everything, leave the life I've built here, leave my family, my students—all because I love you, because I gave you a ring that's the precursor to a promise. Me and you forever." He looks to the floor. "But that's not even what's really bothering me. It's that you're willing to give everything up."

"I'm not giving anything up! You keep implying I'm abandoning my family. I asked Lori to come with me. Junior is a grown man. I have no responsibility to him."

"You're right. You don't."

"Then what is it?" I'm shouting now, and again, hating that he's brought me to this. I don't shout. I am composed. I am together. Together people don't lose it.

"I don't know." He shakes his head again, shrugs again, looking like he's about to cry. "Maybe it is me. Maybe I am being selfish. Maybe I'm wanting you to be this person I thought you were, instead of..." He steps back until he's against the dinette, so far from me. "You never told me you wanted to have kids soon. I just assumed it. I thought because I did, you did too, because we seemed so lined up in other ways."

"Kids? Is this all about kids?"

"Not all—"

"Is it Danny? I wish you'd told me sooner, when it was happening. I would have—"

He braces his hands on the table. "We need to stop for tonight. I need to think. You need to think."

I close the distance between us and wrap my arms around his waist. "Let's think together."

Moses pushes me away, his hands on my shoulders. He kisses me, hard and fast. Yet again I feel like I'm in a movie—that stoic looking guy from the parking lot is now kissing his woman a final farewell. If we had an audience, I honestly don't know which one of us they'd be rooting for. He walks to the door and opens, actually opens it. It couldn't hurt more if he literally kicked me out. He holds it open, waiting. I walk through, feeling as if I've been thrust into someone else's life. I am not the girl who gets rejected, abandoned...or at least I haven't been for the past seventeen years.

CHAPTER EIGHTEEN

Once the door closes, I stand in the hallway thinking—*he'll change his mind. He'll open the door. He'll realize he was overreacting. He'll realize it's just the grief.* The door doesn't open though, so I check my phone to see if he's called or texted, telling me to come back. He hasn't. I make my way to the elevator. My skin feels as if it's not my own. Inside that tiny box my breath quickens and I have to concentrate—in, out in. It works, and by the time I reach the ground floor my breathing is back to normal. But that's all that's normal. I pass one of Moses' neighbours in the lobby, a sweet, elderly lady, who smiles and says hello as she passes. I hardly see her. What I keep seeing over and over are the two most horrible scenes from my life—my mother packing, and my mother dripping—both instances telling me I am not enough, I am not worthy of love. I've worked so hard to be enough—for everyone. Yes, my job was for me, the status was for me, I'm not blind enough to think it wasn't, but it was also for my family, for the future I wanted to create with Moses, for the children I may have one day. None of it matters. It wasn't enough. I am not enough.

I pass through the lobby doors and into a world covered in white. Everything is beautiful, and pure, and flawless. And then there's me, each step I take sullying the pristine scene. I brush the snow off of my car in long smooth motions, watching the thick clumps fall to the white lot.

Inside, my chilled hands are made even colder as I grip the steering wheel. My leather driving gloves are warm and waiting in my purse, but I want the coldness. I turn the key in the ignition and pull out of my spot. I drive home cautiously knowing this snow, combined with my state of mind, makes me dangerous. I leave the heat off. My body is tense and shivering.

The warmth from my parking garage, the elevator, the hall, warms me. By the time I turn the key in my apartment door I'm only slightly chilled and able to feel again the strength of my fear—I am not enough. My footsteps are the only sound in my still apartment. Lori hasn't come home. Usually I'd send her a text to see where is she, if she's okay, why she's out this late…but what's the point? When I'm in Tokyo, I don't know if she's in or not. Even if she tells me she's safe at home, she could be out anywhere, doing anything.

My bed looks deliciously inviting. I could do work, should do work, but I already decided tonight would be work free. Tonight was supposed to be for Moses. And anyway, the work will be there tomorrow. I snuggle into bed and, with the covers around me, remember the several profiles I didn't look over for new hires. I can leave those to the team. I snuggle in deeper. Everdeen's call comes to my mind, the emails he expects me to send. I crawl out of bed, grab my laptop, and settle down on the couch, the dim glow from the screen my only light. Within minutes my mind is blessedly involved in work, and everything I've been thinking and feeling the past hour drifts away from me. In this one area, I will always be enough.

❧

FOUR DAYS LATER I SIT in the terminal, my bags checked, and hands clasped tightly on my lap. I've only seen Moses once since the night in his apartment. This morning he stopped in for a quick goodbye, told me he didn't know what he thought was best, but he wasn't ready to give up on us. I told him the same. He promised to come to Tokyo for March break, and I promised I'd do my absolute best to come back for my father's wedding, though I know it's highly unlikely I can. Everdeen was sympathetic when I asked but pointed out the hiring schedule I had established and he had signed off on, then reemphasized his belief in the importance of me being on site to establish my authority. I was tempted to tell him the current team could cover the hires and I would be back in time to help train them, but the look in his eyes made me keep quiet, so I also didn't tell him not returning could cost me my engagement.

The screen near the gate flashes, indicating my flight has been delayed again—that's two hours now, due to the raging storm outside, hours I could have spent with Moses. His reasons for not seeing me the past few days were weak. I was busy too, but we've spent plenty of nights working on separate projects while sitting across the table from each other. If he wanted, we could have seen each other every day.

In an effort not to think of him, I congratulate myself on how well I managed the reassignment of all my local clients, savouring the joy and energy from a job well done. However, as I look out at the raging storm, that joy wanes. I recall Lori's eyes, the look of anger and abandonment as I left. Needing a more tangible distraction I stand up, rolling my carry-on behind me. A man watches as I pass by. I'd wondered earlier if it was me he was eyeing. Now I'm sure. I approach a nearby bar and slide onto the stool. "Tequila with lime." I smile at the bartender. "On the rocks."

"Rough day?" The young woman prepares my drink. "Or fear of flying? That's quite the storm."

"Just thirsty."

She nods with a look that says she doesn't believe me.

People don't order tequila because they're thirsty. I pay for the drink, not wanting a scramble if my flight time suddenly changes. Sipping on the cool yet hot liquid, I close my eyes and try to go over the presentation I've prepared for the current employees: my 'plan of action' to turn the company around. Instead, Moses keeps returning to my thoughts— the way he held me this morning, the way his hands felt so strong and tender. 'We need to work this out,' he said. 'Okay?' That last word spoken like a nervous little boy. He's lost faith in me, it said, in us.

The man slips into the seat beside me, orders a drink. "Would you like another?" he asks.

"No." I take a sip from my glass, eyeing him.

"That's not how you drink Tequila."

"Maybe that's how I drink Tequila."

"Where are you travelling?" His smile is confident. His watch is high end, at least a couple thousand. His suit is perfectly tailored. His nails seem manicured, and he has the casual look about him of a man used to luxury. A man like him would understand my focus on work, my propensity to travel. A man like him probably also has a lady waiting in every locale.

"Tokyo." I cast my glance to a couple at the end of the bar. They look happy.

"Me too."

I turn back, my interest piqued. "What business?"

"Pharmaceuticals. You?"

"Marketing and Consulting."

He grins. "You look like a woman who could sell anything."

I throw back the rest of the shot in one gulp, savouring the burn. I've dated this man dozens of times before, or ones like him. Never long term. Never any commitment or deep emotion. I never worried about these men leaving me because I always left them first.

I debate for a moment what it would feel like to lose

myself for a few moments, the thrill of a one-night stand once we land, or if it was really good, indulging for several weeks before deciding to move on. In his eyes, I see he sees I'm considering the possibility.

Only I'm not considering, not really. This man is not the man I want. I've only ever really wanted one man. Meeting Moses showed me I'd been lying to myself for years. I wanted security. I craved it. I was just too afraid I'd never find it.

Moses made me feel secure. With Moses, I allowed myself to look at Bridal magazines and think of a future I didn't have to work alone at creating. And as insecure as I currently feel, that future is still possible. "My fiancé thinks so too." I step from the bar.

The man nods and I imagine his gaze follows me. I return to the waiting area, happy for the reminder of what my life was, and what I don't want it to be again. If seeing that family matters is what Moses needs, I'll prove it to him. Pop's wedding will mean a full three days away, more likely four. But I can do it. I'll reschedule. I'll work it out. Two of those days will be the weekend anyway, and with the environment I want to create at the new office the staff won't be working weekends, so why should I? I'll show Moses I can have both—a family and a career, and when he comes for March break, I'll set up interviews at several schools for him. Everything will be all right. I stretch my hand out, letting the diamonds glimmer in the light.

By the time I board my flight and make it to Japan after two overly long stopovers, twenty-six hours have passed. Rather than having the night of rest I expected, I head straight to the office to finish prepping with Kuri and Kamlyn for their part of the presentation. A united front. That's what I told them we need to present. However, after being in the office for only a few minutes, it's clear the spirit of teamwork I hoped for is not what I walked into. It's also clear I won't make it home for Pop's wedding, not without seriously losing some clout as the leader of this branch.

I see now why Everdeen was so keen on having me over here. Kamlyn ignored a number of my directives and is asserting his authority as much as he can. Kuri, on the other hand, seems torn in her loyalties. "I told him you said to wait," she whispers when Kamlyn goes to answer an important phone call.

"It's okay." My voice is clear and even. I don't want to give the impression I believe in a need for whispers. "I'll talk to him."

"But," she hesitates, "this will affect your whole approach to the presentation tomorrow. The way he did it, it changes everything."

"It's okay." I smile at Kuri. "We'll work it out. It's not your job to worry."

Kamlyn paces in his office, laughing to someone on the phone. I cringe inwardly to think of how I may have to work this situation out. If I let Kamlyn go, I'm not confident Kuri can handle the office on her own. Even if I just demote him and raise her status, could she keep her authority? She's good but…I look at her, sitting across from me, obviously nervous, obviously waiting for me to tell her what to do. No. She's not there yet. "Kamlyn." Ignoring the nagging need for sleep, I present my smoothest smile as he walks back in the room. "Kuri mentioned you already told the staff about the first phase of the roll-out?"

"I did." He stands tall. "Since I'll be taking the lead reaching out to our current clients, letting them know of our revised approach, I didn't see why I shouldn't be the one to tell the staff. The more time they have to prepare the better they'll perform."

I nod slowly, as if I'm considering his words. In reality, I'm processing the fact that he respects my position enough to explain his actions. This is good. "I understand your perspective," I say, arms crossed, tapping a finger to my chin. "I appreciate a 'go get 'em' attitude." A cocky grin flashes across his face before his expression settles back to the cool and confident one he's been wearing. "I don't appreciate you going against my directions." I lower my hand, lean back in my chair, looking relaxed, friendly. "Now, I understand this must be a little uncomfortable and perhaps an unprecedented situation for you. You've been running things around here for quite some time. You're used to taking the lead. I get that. But we need to work as a team. As partners. That will be best for all of us. Give us the best chance of success."

He nods. His body shifts, betraying his wavering confidence.

"Mr. Everdeen has explained to you my role here? That I'm the head of this team?"

"He has."

"Good." I smile broadly. "We understand each other then. What do you say, should we precede with our prep?"

"Of course." He clears his throat. "Now that our whole team is focused on this new marketing plan—"

The next seven hours are some of the longest I've ever spent in an office. My body aches for bed. Promptly at five o'clock I stand, causing Kamlyn and Kuri to look up at me in surprise. "That's enough for today. We'll pick up here tomorrow."

Kuri nods, a look of concern on her face. Kamlyn leans back in his chair. "We're really on a roll. Are you sure you want to lose this momentum?"

"If we're going to advertise this company as promoting work-life balance for the corporate woman, we should be living that ourselves."

"All right." Kamlyn closes his laptop. "If you need the rest."

I do. And I don't care what Kamlyn thinks of it.

※

BY THE NEXT MORNING I'm full of energy and thankful for my youth. Over the next few days I throw myself into meetings, prep and more prep. In the following days my team's excitement grows, and I feel the shift as they begin to view me as their leader, a leader who's going to take this company where it should already be. Even Kamlyn looks at me differently. He's still cocky, but more respectful. He listens to my ideas, presents ones of his own, and supports more than he challenges.

I stay later at the office than I should, not adhering to my initial claims of representing an office focused on work-life balance. At night I work too, so full of ideas and strategy I feel I'll burst. However, once my phone is off and my laptop closed, thoughts of Moses fill my mind. Moses, who may be willing to leave me because I'm not the woman he thought I was, a woman who would happily give up dreams of a career to become a baby factory.

These thoughts aren't fair, though. He's not asking for me to give up my career. He's asking me to have a career that won't always come first. Not so unreasonable I suppose. I don't want to be one of those people who gets to the end of her life and wishes she'd spent more time on family. But it's not just that. I balanced Moses and work before. I could do it again. It's children that are the problem. The idea of them lurks in the silences of every phone call we have, every text message we send, though neither of us have brought the subject up again. Children terrify me or, more accurately, I terrify me when it comes to the thought of having them.

I love Junior and Lori but raising them was consuming. With focusing on grades, my job, and making sure they had everything they needed, I had nothing left for what I wanted. At last I'm at the point where I can focus on me. Even with the demands of my job I have time to take bubble baths and hang out with friends. I can spend my money on anything I want to spend it on. Children would take that freedom away and I fear I'd come to resent it. I never want a child of mine to know what that feels like, to look at your mother and see in her eyes the wish you'd never been born. The only way to ensure that never happens is to never have a child.

It's different for Moses. His parents adore him. Completely. Every moment with him is a precious gift. His Mom thought she'd never conceive then, after years of surgeries and fertility pills, he entered their world, a miracle—their only miracle. He wants a family of his own, and grandkids for his parents to love. Can I even consider refusing him that?

It's my seventh day in Tokyo and I make my way through the crowds of salarymen, ignoring the looks they give me. Who can blame them? A black woman walking like she owns the place, with hair that dances as the breeze blows, is not a sight they see every day. I ignore their glances, excited about my plans for the evening. Tonight is reserved for Cirque du Soleil. It's the first non-work related thing I've done all week. I plan to get lost in the wonder.

I change quickly, then heat up some leftover food. The phone rings in the same moment I open the apartment door. Lori. Odd that she's calling, we generally text, but it'll have to wait. Plus, if I speak to her afterwards, I'll get to tell her all about the show. I grin, thinking how she'll ask technical questions I'll hardly know how to answer.

I slip the phone back into my purse and grab my coat, sliding it on as I make my way to the elevator. The phone buzzes. As I shoot down the forty-five floors, I pull it out.

Answer!!!!

The phone rings again and I pick up. "Hello?"

The line is silent for a moment before Lori's voice spews

into it. "I'm pregnant."

CHAPTER NINETEEN

"What?"

Lori bursts into tears. Or at least I imagine she's burst into tears. Her sobs echo through the receiver. "I'm pregnant."

"How did this happen?" The elevator doors open and I push the number for my floor, watching the doors close again.

She scoffs. "You know how it happens."

"I know. I mean...Drake?"

"Yeah." She sounds so young. And she's so tiny. Could her body even fit a baby? Her voice is barely audible. "Can you come?"

"What do you mean?"

"I need you to come home. I can't go through this alone. I mean, I'm not alone. There's Drake. He's being awesome. But I need my sister."

"I..." My sister. My *baby* sister.

"Are you coming?"

"I'm not sure." I make my way back into my suite and collapse into the desk chair. "What are you going to do?"

She's silent for several breaths. "I'm not sure."

And neither am I. The thought of abortion floats through my mind. I've always been against it. Life is...well...life. But Lori's life? Lori's future? Lori's dreams? Surely they mean more than the life of this baby that isn't even a baby yet. I can't say it though. If she says it...I don't know. I'll support her. I won't try to change her mind…I think. But I can't say it. "Whatever you want is—"

"I'm not having an abortion." She spits out the words. "I won't!" She yells, as if I've tried to pressure her into it.

"Okay," I say, relieved and terrified. "Okay."

"Come home."

"Lori." I imagine her face, can almost see her standing with the phone against her ear, even more terrified than I am. "I can't right now. Maybe in the next two or three weeks, once things are in motion. I couldn't even—"

"Pop's wedding. Come home for Pop's wedding. Then…then we won't have to explain why. That'll be your reason." She goes back to her little girl voice. "I don't want to tell him yet."

For some reason, it's hearing this that puts my practical and annoyed self into gear. She's scared to tell him? She wants me to jeopardize my career because she's scared to tell him?

I want to ask how this happened. She's not stupid. She's not uninformed. I told her if she ever needed birth control I'd pay for it. She knows where the condoms are. But then again, I'm not stupid either. The male voice in the background, two plates of leftover pancakes, teenagers in very deep like—with an apartment all to themselves, Junior's suspicions. I should have known. I should have done something. "Is he there with you?"

"No."

"What's he thinking?"

"He loves me. *All* of me."

"Okay…"

"He's not excited, exactly, but he wants it. He wants us."

"And what do you want?"

Her crying, which has let up, starts all over again. "I can't. I can't abandon my baby. I'm not Mom."

"This isn't the same thing." But in a way it is—an unplanned, unwanted baby—leaving it, allowing someone else to be its mother…but it's also the best option for Lori's life and, as the closest thing she's ever had to a mother, it's what I want for her. Adoption. It's not abandonment. It's brave. It's courageous. It's giving the baby a better life. Except with my money and Lori's love…Drake's too, it seems, we could give this baby a good life. This baby could have a great life. But what kind of life would Lori have?

"I don't want to talk about this on the phone," says Lori. "Promise you'll come. The wedding is in three days."

"I know when the wedding is," I snap.

"I'll tell Pop you're going to read. Okay?"

For a brief second, it flashes through my mind that this is all a plot. Lori's not pregnant. This is their way of getting me back for the wedding. But there's no way, and it's just a few days. The business won't fall apart. Both Kuri and Kamlyn are more than capable.

"Yeah." I lean against the desk, surprised I'm actually saying these words. "Okay."

Lori doesn't say anything. My guess is she's nodding into the phone. I've seen her do this dozens of times. She gives an embarrassed yelp that confirms my assumption was right. "Thank you."

"How far along are you?"

"About two-and-a-half months." My mind travels back to that night I heard the male voice, the night Junior was in jail. Before I can ask, she continues. "I didn't realize. I mean I'm not really that regular, so I didn't know. And El, it was the first time, honest. I was so worried about Junior and Drake was there and then things…started and it was so new and exciting and we didn't think. Every other time we used a condom. I promise."

"Okay." I push the thought from my mind that if I were there, or maybe even if I'd promised to come home that night, my sister's life wouldn't be about to change forever.

"So you're coming?"

"I'm coming."

❧

MOSES' VOICE IS ELATED when I tell him the news. Not the news about Lori, that is her secret to tell when she's ready, but the news I'll be coming home for Pop's wedding. It's like he has hope in me again, in us. Twenty minutes after we hang up, he texts me to say he just looked up a few schools in Tokyo, but he doesn't even know where I work, so could I send him the address. And then he writes: *I really am going to give it a fair chance. People move for work all the time, right? :)*

He wants us, wants me. But I can't even feel happy about it. What will he think when he knows my father isn't the real reason I rescheduled half a dozen meetings, that I am letting Kuri and Kamlyn handle things Mr. Everdeen wanted me to handle, that I suffered Everdeen's wrath in order to come home? Still, I'm coming home for family. That has to count for something.

On the flight I try to put work out of my mind, to put Lori and Moses out of my mind, and think about Pop's wedding instead. My father's face as he talks about his love for Evelyn comes back to me. He deserves happiness. I know having me at the wedding will make the day even happier for him. It's something. Resting my head against the seat, I imagine a happy life for my father, a life where Evelyn's cancer is cured and they grow old together, enjoying their children and their grandchildren. Thinking this, I'm the most at peace I've been in weeks.

After the flight I walk down the stairs leading from customs to the waiting area of the terminal, and the first face I see is Moses'. He wraps his arms around me, hugging me as if I'd been lost and now am found. "Don't worry about the driver," he says, knowing it will be my first question. "I called James."

"Thanks."

He kisses me, the first real kiss we've shared in weeks. Even when I was home last time after weeks of being away, we shared nothing more than a peck. He runs his hand up and down my thigh on the drive home, indicating his desire. I know I need to see Lori but it's been at least six weeks, and how can I explain that seeing Lori is more important without explaining why I am really home. He takes me back to his apartment to make love. I am reluctant at first, feeling guilty for being here, but by the time I'm lying in his arms, our flesh slick and warm, all thoughts of Lori melt away.

"Are you hungry?" His finger trails along my belly.

"Yeah." I roll over to him, happy and spent. "But I promised Lori I'd have dinner with her. She's probably wondering where I am."

"Oh, okay." He sits up in bed, stretching in that languorous way I love. "I'll get dressed."

I put my hand on his chest, still so warm. "I told her it'd be just the two of us."

"Oh." He lies back down. "I'll see you tomorrow then? For the family brunch and rehearsal?"

"Yeah." I go through the room, picking up my scattered articles of clothing. His gaze follows me.

"I'm really glad you decided to come back," he says

"Me too."

"I love you."

I stop, a pile of clothes in my arms, and really look at him, this incredible man who I've just realized I'm terrified of. He has the power to break my heart.

He may not like Tokyo? He's open to it, at last, but open is no guarantee. And we have more to contend with than that. I smile. "I love you too."

❧

LORI PRACTICALLY THROWS herself into my arms when I open the door. "Where were you? You said you'd be here by six-thirty."

"Moses picked me up." I drop my bag to the floor and hug her back. "He surprised me. He wanted some time alone. I couldn't think of a good enough reason why I had to go home immediately without telling him." My voice trails off.

"You can say it." She steps back and smiles, a hand on her flat stomach. "The baby."

I almost laugh, but not quite. "You seem to be doing better."

"I am." She bounces on her toes. "It's going to work out. And now that you're back you can help me. Help us." As she says this, Drake enters from around the living room wall. "We were thinking when the baby was born Drake could move in here with us, and then rather than go to university, he'll go to technical school. The trades are really in demand."

"I thought it was just going to be you and me tonight," I say to Lori after giving Drake a nod of acknowledgement.

"You were almost an hour late." She gives a slight pout. "I was worried, and I'm not supposed to be worried, so Drake came over to take my mind off of it."

"Okay." I head past him to the living room. "Let's sit."

I settle in the armchair and Drake takes the far end of the love seat. Lori cuddles in beside him. My stomach twists with how comfortable she looks in his arms. "I know it's not ideal." Lori stretches out the last word. She takes Drake's hand, stares up at him like she adores him. "But it's going to work out." She inhales deeply then laughs. "I was so scared to tell you."

"I'm glad you did." I watch the way his hand caresses her

arm.

"I'm still scared to tell Pop and Junior."

"They'll get used to the idea."

"Pop has been talking about grandkids, though I think he was hoping they'd come from you. Oh!" She leans forward. "If you and Moses get married soon and get pregnant our kids could be best friends!"

"Lori," I say, thinking, this isn't my sister. My sister is thoughtful, focused. Except when it comes to a new dance movie of course. "What's this about you and Drake moving in here? Drake going to technical school?"

"Exactly that. It sucks we'll have to change our plans." She looks to Drake. "But technical school is good too. For me the worst thing about this is even if I get into the dance school, which is a long shot anyway, I'm due right around the time first semester starts. Not that I think I'll get in anyway, but you never know. Maybe they'd hold my place. Maybe in a year or two."

My heart breaks. A competitive school like that won't be holding spots, especially for someone who could have to leave rehearsal for a sick baby…if she ever ends up taking care of this baby. I speak slowly, as if she's a jittery rabbit easy to frighten away. "I thought it'd be better if you came back to Tokyo with me. You could finish out the year by distance, fly back for graduation. It would be easier for you, and if you have a rough pregnancy I'd be there to help you out."

"Drake will be here to help me. And you too I thought…well, I thought maybe now you'd want to transfer back. Be near me and the baby."

I lean forward on the couch, wishing Drake wasn't here for this conversation. "Are you sure you want to keep the baby, Lori? Like you said, the baby would change everything for dance, and adoption is a great option."

"No," she and Drake say in unison.

"Listen, Eloise," says Drake, looking older than when I

saw him last. "I know this is a shock. I know it's not what you wanted for your sister. It's not what I wanted either. We were stupid." He pauses, shrugs, then smiles the smile that reminds me so much of Moses. "But it happened and now we're going to do what's right. This is our baby and we're keeping it."

"And what do your parents think?" I address Drake for the first time.

He groans, glancing at Lori then back at me. "They're pretty upset."

"What?" Lori looks at him, hurt. "I thought they liked me."

"They do like you, Lori, or they did. A lot. They just—" He pulls his hand across his dreads, making them jiggle. "They said I'd be throwing away my life. But that's ridiculous. How could deciding to take care of a new life be throwing mine away?" He grins.

Lori's eyes mist. "They said you'd be…"

"It'll work out," he says. "We don't need them."

"So, they won't be any kind of support?" I ask.

"No." He draws his gaze from Lori back to me. "They actually said if I can't convince Lori to abort or put the baby up for adoption, if I decide to be this baby's father, they're not paying for my tuition or anything. They haven't kicked me out, though I think my dad was on the verge of it." He shrugs. "The plan was med-school, but that takes years, plus lots of cash. An electrician's course is way shorter and cheaper, something I can swing on my own, and electricians make good money. Really good money."

"That's why you decided to go to technical school?" says Lori. "You made it sound like it was your idea."

"It is my idea."

I glance from Drake to Lori. "Let's not rush into things. If this is what you're sure you want to do, raise the baby—though you don't have to decide now, you have months to make that decision—but if it's what you decide, maybe you and the baby can come live with me." Lori shakes her head. "Drake could go to university, as planned. Perhaps his parents will still help him. You can Skype and Drake can be a part of the baby's life and—"

"We're staying together," says Lori.

I keep my voice light, placating. "You hardly know each other. It's been what, three, four months?"

"We love each other."

"Love?"

"Yes, love."

"Okay, but listen. Drake could still become a doctor. There's no reason both of you should give up your dreams. And when he's far enough along to not need his parents' help anymore, then you two could work it out. Make your lives together."

"I'm not missing my baby's childhood," says Drake. "He or she would be eight by the time I'm done with school, at least."

"And what kind of childhood do you think your child would have? What kind of job could you get to support Lori and the baby when you're in school full time? Babies are expensive."

"I can work," says Lori.

"Not for the first several months you can't and after that, if you did, you'd have to pay for daycare. That is expensive, too." I hate myself as I say the words, knowing I'm trying to bully her into leaving Drake and coming with me. But I'm right, too. Besides, I don't know if I can leave her here alone.

"Maybe Evelyn would watch the baby," says Lori. "She's sweet. And she's raised three of her own children. She's not working anymore."

"I don't think so." I'm surprised Pop told me but not Lori.

"It's worth asking."

"You can ask," I lean back in the armchair, wishing I

could wake up and this would all be a dream, "though that means you have to tell Pop."

"Well, as you said. We have time and I mean," her voice shakes, "you take care of me, right? You were going to cover whatever tuition and expenses my scholarship didn't cover. This is different, I know…but could you help? Maybe even as a loan?"

"Not if I don't have a job, Lori. And my job is in Tokyo."

"Transfer back."

"I've told you it's not that simple." Exasperation leaks into my voice. "They're already training someone for my old job."

"So, they'll take you back in another position or something. Obviously they love you."

"They wouldn't love me so much if I dropped my responsibilities."

"You could get a new job."

"Lori," I snap. "You're asking me to quit my job because you got knocked up?"

She sits back, a look on her face like I've slapped her.

"Listen. I'm sorry, but you're not being reasonable."

"Maybe I'm not," she says, so tiny in Drake's arms. "Yeah. I'm sorry. I just thought—" She looks from me to Drake and back to me again. "But you're right. Don't worry, El. We'll be okay. We'll figure it out. You've done so much for me it's awful for me to ask for more. We'll figure it out."

"Come to Tokyo." I rest my elbow on the armrest, my head in my hand. "Maybe just until Drake is finished his training. You said it's short, right?"

Lori shakes her head. "I didn't have a Mom and Pop was working so much. I want my baby to have both parents all the time."

"You had me."

"I want my baby to have you too."

Both of them stare at me from across the living room.

Drake squeezes his hands together over and over, his nervousness making me tense. His face though, his shoulders, relay confidence, assurance, a man who's not backing down. This part of him makes me a little less afraid. Maybe Lori's right. Maybe he is in love. "We don't have to figure it all out this minute." I stand, feeling weary, and their gazes follow me. "Are you two hungry? How about I order some Vietnamese and I can get to know the father of my niece or nephew a bit better."

Lori smiles her thanks and Drake grins. "Sweet," he says, "Vietnamese rocks."

We spend the next several hours chatting, laughing, and enjoying Vietnamese. I turn off my work phone, deciding any issues will be fine in the hands of Kuri and Kamlyn, and realize this is the first time I've spent this much consecutive time with Lori in months. The job has been taking its toll. As the night goes on, I find myself liking Drake more and more. He's smart, easygoing, treats Lori like she's a royal, without coddling her, and shows excitement about his new child while still realizing it's going to be tough.

After Lori says goodnight to Drake, she turns to me. "Do you like him?"

"I do." I wrap my arms around her. "And I especially like how much he likes you."

"Yeah." She looks up at me. "I think he's smitten."

"And you too?"

"Most definitely." We walk, arms around each other, back to the living room and sit on the loveseat. "Are you disappointed in me?"

I pull her head to my shoulder and answer carefully. "I'm disappointed for you, for the life you won't be able to live. But I know you'll figure it out. You'll still have a wonderful life. It was an accident. We all make mistakes."

"I don't want you, or anyone, to think of my baby as an accident."

"That's not what I meant."

"She might not have been planned, but she's no accident."

"I know." I tilt up her head so I can see her face. "She?"

Lori grins. "I hope it's a she. I mean a he would be great too but," she rubs her stomach, "I feel she's a she. I'd prefer saying she than it."

"Makes sense."

Lori keeps her gaze on her stomach. "I haven't spent much time around babies."

"You'll figure it out. You'll be a natural."

"I want you to be here to help me. I'm scared."

I rub her hair, so soft and long, like Mom's. "Me too. But if you're not coming to Tokyo, I'll visit as much as I can."

"You'll come up for the birth?"

"These things don't always follow a schedule, but I promise I will do my absolute best."

"Do you think Mom loved me, even a little?"

I push her away so she can look at me. "Of course she loved you. Lori, I've told you that."

"But not enough."

"She didn't love anyone enough." I continue to stroke Lori's hair. "She didn't love herself enough."

"Because she was sick."

"Yeah." This is the first time I've admitted it out loud to her, maybe to anyone. I try to believe this was the reason, the whole reason, the only reason, and not Pop, not how he failed her. Not us. "She was very sick."

"Is that kind of thing hereditary?"

"I don't think so."

We're silent for several minutes and I'm sure Lori has fallen asleep when she looks up at me. "I'm going to be such a good Mom, like you were."

I squeeze her to me, tucking my head on top of hers. My eyes close and I wish our own mother were here right now, not as she was, but as she should have been, with her arms around us both.

CHAPTER TWENTY

Sunlight creeps through the blinds, rousing me. It takes me a moment to realize where I am and who is in my arms. I ease off of the couch, setting pillows under Lori's head. She shifts in her sleep, then smiles as she cuddles up under the blanket I situate under her chin. I shower then return to the living room and rub circles on her back until she wakes up. While she's bathing, I make us fruit bowls with real whipped cream, something light to tide us over until brunch. Neither of us speaks of the baby, or of any plans regarding the baby. Lori doesn't ask or remind me not to say a word to our family. It's good to know she trusts I won't.

We help each other with our hair, do each other's nails and, at Lori's request, take a selfie she posts with the caption, "On the way to my FATHER'S wedding rehearsal brunch. Too cool!" In the car on the way to Uncle Archie's, she mentions she's already had forty-five likes. I almost say, 'think of all the likes your baby's pics will get,' but decide against it.

We get out of the car at Uncle Archie's facility in order to help him down the stairs. "Look at my two beautiful girls!" He kisses the top of her head and my cheek. "I'm so glad you decided to come back! You would have regretted it, missing this. I knew my gal would make the right choice." I nod, feeling guilt churn in my belly, and squeeze his arm as if in agreement. "It makes me think." He pulls us both close before letting go to step in the front passenger seat, then turns with a wink. "Maybe there's time for me yet."

Lori laughs. "You should find a lady."

"I'm telling you," he says, "if I dappered myself up a little, the women would fight each other just to get to me."

"Any prospects?" I gesture toward the home.

"Oh." He rubs his little beard. "One or two, one or two. A little old for my liking though. At this age, I think I should grab a woman at least fifteen years my junior, don't you?"

"And why's that?" I make my way around to the driver's side and slip in.

"Well," he waits until I'm seated to answer, "if I've lived my life this long as a confirmed bachelor, I don't want to live out my final days as a widower. Got to make sure there's a *very* good chance she'll outlive me."

"Oh, you'll live to a hundred." I pull out of the driveway with a grin on my face.

"May just do that." He chuckles. "Where's your fella?"

"He's meeting us there."

He turns in his seat. "And what about you, little Miss, do you have a fella yet?"

"Yes." Lori blushes.

"And where is he?"

"He'll be coming tomorrow."

"He will?" I ask, glancing back.

"I told Pop a few weeks ago that I have a boyfriend and he wanted to meet him."

"Well, ain't that grand. And disturbing." Uncle Archie lets out one of his robust laughs. "You make me feel old, my little Delorita. A boyfriend!"

I avoid sending Lori a look in the rear-view mirror, though I'm sure she's looking at me. If Lori having a boyfriend makes Uncle Archie feel old...

Moses pulls me into a kiss and an embrace when we get to the restaurant. Hugs and introductions burst all around us. My father glows. I'm not sure I've ever seen him looking this happy.

As we settle around the long table Lincoln and Junior joke easily, talking about old hijinks and how they're going to be brothers. LaMeia seems hesitant around us, and I suspect, like me, our parents marrying makes her somewhat uncomfortable. Evie, the youngest, looks a little shell-shocked but seems to be trying to have a good time. Do they know about their mother's condition? If so, they're doing an amazing job of acting like everything's okay.

The conversation around the table is a mix of polite, nervous, excited—but for Pop and Evelyn, it's nothing but happy. I find it hard to take my gaze away from them. They look so in love, so eager to start their lives together. Moses and I don't look like that. I glance over at him, having an animated conversation with Uncle Archie. It's not the same though, our wedding isn't a day away, and I haven't had time to be excited about starting our life together. Lately, all I've had time for is making sure our relationship doesn't fall apart. I take his hand and squeeze it. He smiles over at me and squeezes back before continuing his conversation with Uncle Archie, who's laughing so hard (at what I imagine is his own joke) he actually slaps his knee.

Once we've finished our meals Pop clinks his glass. "I'd like to make a toast." He scans the table. "Lincoln, Lori, you both need something in your glass." Lincoln takes the bottle nearest him and pours the Pinot Grigio. Junior lifts a bottle and reaches for Lori's glass.

"No, it's okay." She covers her glass. "I'm underage, remember."

"You've had drinks with us before," says Pop.

"But we're in a restaurant."

"And I'm your father. It's okay."

"I don't want it."

"Lori," says Pop.

"I said no." She spits the words out. Just relax, I want to tell her. Have a sip.

Junior reaches for her glass and she snatches it away. "You're usually begging to get in on the drinks." He laughs. "If I didn't know better, I'd think you were pregnant."

Lori's face pales. She's never had a poker face. I groan inwardly.

"Drake." Junior's voice is a mix between disbelief and anger.

Pop looks from him to her to me. "Lori?"

Tears spring to her eyes. "I didn't want to tell you, Pop, not yet. I didn't want to ruin your wedding. Not that this ruins it." She tries to smile through her tears but it doesn't quite happen. "This is good news. I just…" Her voice trails off.

"Eloise?" Pop glances from Lori back to me. "Did you know about this? Is it true?"

"Well, I haven't seen a test," I say, trying to ease the tension. "But yeah, Lori's going to have a baby."

He speaks his words slowly, staring at me. "How did you let this happen?"

"It's not her fault," says Lori. "It's no one's fault, it just—"

"If she hadn't taken you away, I wouldn't have let you—" Pop drops his head in his hands then looks up at me, stricken. "What am I saying? How often am I home? El, I'm sorry." He turns his gaze to Lori. "You're having it?"

"Yeah," she whispers. "I'm having it and I'm keeping the baby."

"You're a baby yourself."

"It'll be good, Pop, you'll see."

Our father stands and walks around the table to Lori, pulls her up and smothers her in a hug, his body shaking. We're all silent as he pushes her away, keeping his hand on her shoulder, while using the opposite arm to wipe a tear from his cheek with his shirtsleeve, a quick, embarrassed looking movement. "I'll help you, anyway I can," he says. "Anything you need."

I didn't even see her get up, but Evelyn is beside Pop now. She puts her hand on Lori's other shoulder. "We'll both help you."

Lori smiles up at them, shaking a little. I keep my gaze on the trio, nervous to look back and see Moses' face. He'll now know this is the real reason I came home.

"His name's Drake," says Lori, her voice barely audible. "He's coming to the wedding. You'll all meet him tomorrow. He's wonderful and super excited about the baby."

Junior shakes his head and gives me a look that reiterates he tried to warn me. But this is not my fault. "That kid."

"It takes two, Junior." Lori glances around the table. "He's a good guy. He's going to go to school to be an electrician. And he's really smart. He was planning to be a doctor but now he wants to make sure he can provide for the baby and being a doctor takes so long."

"That'll all get figured out," says Pop. "Don't you worry about any of it."

"A baby." Uncle Archie puts a hand to his head. "Now I really feel old."

Silence falls again. Pop, Evelyn and Lori take their seats. Several of us sip our drinks. Lincoln breaks off a roll of bread and smothers it with hot butter as Lori pulls her long strands of hair through her hands, over and over again, her gaze bouncing around the table. A cheer goes up from a group at the other end of the room. Pop smiles at the noise, as if it breaks him out of a trance. He reaches for his drink. "Now we've got two reasons to toast!" His voice shakes a little as he says the words. "To my wife to be, the woman who taught me how to love again and gave me a love I never thought I could have, and to my baby girl, who will be a wonderful mother."

We toast, chat for a few more minutes, then get up from our seats to head to the church rehearsal. "Junior," says Moses. "Why don't you take Lori and Archie in my car. I've hardly had any time with my fiancé these past weeks."

"Sure, no problem." Junior grins. "Sounds great!" Moses tosses him the keys.

We walk to my car and I get in and sit for a moment, my keys in hand. Moses doesn't speak for a good minute, so I turn the ignition and pull out of the lot. "It was a nice dinner," I say. "Evelyn's kids seem pretty likable."

"Lori's why you came home?"

"She made me promise to keep it secret." I turn on the car and pull onto the street. "You can respect that."

"I can."

"It's not like that's the whole reason I came home. I wanted to be at Pop's wedding."

"But would you have come if it wasn't for this?"

"Probably not." I glance away from the road to see his profile. He's looking at the road and not me. "It was really difficult making it work. Mr. Everdeen is livid. But I made it work. For Lori. For family."

"I know." He taps his fingers on his leg, over and over again. "I just thought this represented, I don't know, a change of heart."

I glance over again, tempted to flick his hand: make the tapping stop. "My heart doesn't need to change. Family matters to me. A lot. One of the main things we're working on with the revamp is to ensure work/life balance is a key focus. We're advertising to prospective hires that we believe in women having a family and a career."

"But that's a tactic, right? To help get women, the people who can market to the buyers you're trying to reach?"

"That's part of it. But it doesn't change the premise. I'll be focused on work/life balance too."

"Yet you're still planning to go back when your sister, the sister you raised from an infant, is going to be a single teen mom."

I hesitate before answering. "She's not single. Drake is really supportive. And I'll help her financially—visit when I can. We'll visit."

"She's going to need you."

"I told her she could come live with us. She doesn't want to. She won't leave Drake. They're in love."

"Oh?" He looks over at me. "Your sixteen-year-old sister won't leave the man she loves to move to the other side of the world, even though it makes more financial sense?"

"You're being unreasonable." My hands grip the wheel.

"You told me last year how worried you were that Autumn wasn't going to return home to be with her mother after the stroke, to help her through that hard time. How is this different? Whether Drake is there or not, your sister is going to need a lot of help—"

"And she has a ton of family here who will help her."

"I know her, El, she's going to want that help from you."

I glance back over, frustrated, feeling like I've been saying the same things over and over and he's not hearing me. "I love her. You know I do. But I have to love myself too. I've given Lori so much." I think of the years and years of taking care of her, giving up things I wanted for her, for both Junior and Lori. "You have no idea, Moses. I have to think of me now. It's time." I glance over again, and this time he's staring right at me. "Anyway, I don't see what this has to do with us and our life."

"Okay." His voice is firm, as if he's talking to one of his students. "I see your point. I really do. But you have to tell me, El. Do you want kids?"

"I'm not sure."

"You need to figure that out."

"But I don't know."

"You need to figure it out."

I pull into the church lot, park the car, then stare at my hands, just sitting there on my lap, unable to do anything to make this better. Raising my gaze, I let it settle on his profile, the clench of his jaw, then watch as he turns his head until we're looking straight at each other. "Are you giving me an ultimatum or something?"

His voice and expression soften. "I think so."

"What if I'm barren? What if we try to have kids and we can't?"

"Then that'd be different. We'd do all we could, adopt if that were our last resort."

"And if I decide I never want children, you'll leave me? That's what you're saying?"

He purses his lips.

"You think it's because I care more about work than family. Did you ever think maybe it's because I'm scared I'd be a shitty Mom?"

"Do you think Lori will be a shitty Mom?"

"She wasn't raised by our Mom."

"Yeah. She was raised by you. And you did amazing." He reaches for one of my limp hands. "I'm sorry. It's something I've always wanted. I'll always want. And you've talked about kids before, hypothetically, I know. But it made me think you wanted them."

I sigh. "Hypothetically I do. In reality, I just don't know."

"Maybe we should take a break for a while. This has to be draining on both of us."

I pull my hand away. "What?"

"Take a break."

"You're dumping me the night before my father's wedding? Before Valentine's day?"

"I'm not dumping you." Slight exasperation makes its way to his voice, but mostly what sounds like regret. "But maybe some time apart will help us realize how important we really are to each other, for me, whether being with you means more than my desire for children, for you...I don't know. Whether you think that hypothetical could become a reality. I bet as soon as you see Lori's—"

"Don't." I remove the anger from my voice. "What about March break?"

"I'm not sure." I can see in his eyes he wants to take my hand again; it's killing some part of him to be letting go. "Do you have any idea how long you'd have to be in Tokyo if we did move there? What's the chance we'd be moving back here in a few years? When I think of telling my mother her grandchildren will be in Asia…"

"It would take at least three years to solidify this revamp." My voice is my own again. Solid, in control, work Eloise. "To see that it's meeting its goals, that it's on the right track, three is certainly the minimum." I pause, considering. "After that it's possible Mr. Everdeen would position me back here or give me the recommendation for another company. Even if he didn't, I'd have the success for proof."

"And you'd consider that?"

I smile, touched by the hope in his words when I would have expected skepticism. "It was never my dream to live in Asia. I've always wanted to travel but—" I hesitate, making sure my words are true. "It'd be nice to be close to family." I reach for his hand and he squeezes gently. "We should go in," I whisper.

"Yeah, you're right."

We step out of the car and he looks at me across the roof. "I won't say anything, to anyone. But after tomorrow, let's take some time to think, okay? Some time apart."

"I'll be in Tokyo."

"Really apart. No phone calls…just…Apart."

CHAPTER TWENTY-ONE

The rehearsal goes well. Without a hitch, technically. Everyone gets along, yet the tension seems almost palpable. Moses and me, on the verge of letting go, strive to act like the recently engaged couple we are. Lori's news affects the whole family. Junior sends me looks I don't want to interpret, Pop won't look at me at all, and Lori is unbelievably revved up, most likely trying far too hard to let everyone know she's still the same.

As Junior goes over the various points of his position of MC and debates with several of the others about what guests should need to do to get the couple to kiss, Pop slips out of the church hall.

My thoughts keep travelling from Moses to Mom. Is Pop thinking of her too, or are only Lori and his upcoming wedding on his mind? After Mom he seemed so numb. He wasn't angry. I thought he should be screaming, raging. I wanted to. But he was quiet. For days everyone was quiet. So I was quiet too.

When Pop doesn't return after several minutes, I find him in a dark hallway that leads to the baptismal. "Pop?"

"Oh, Ellie, sorry, I…Did you need me?"

"No." I ignore his use of the name I can't stand. "I was just worried."

"I'm okay." Despite the dim light I can tell he isn't.

"It seems to be a curse of old age." He wipes his eyes. "I've never cried like this before." His eyes have misted, but as far as I can see, no tears have fallen. For him though, I suppose it's crying.

"It's okay." I step toward him. "Lori?"

"She's still a baby," he says. "Just a baby."

"She's not."

He falls against the wall. "I guess you were younger than her when…well, when you…"

"It's going to be okay."

"And your mother…it's like it's all happening again. She was only a couple of years older than Lori. We hadn't planned on kids." He guffaws. "We hadn't even planned on being together. She just got pregnant, and so I married her. I tried to do the right thing, but we never thought…" He looks at me, realizing his words. "Oh, Ellie, I didn't mean—"

I put my hand on his shoulder, the rest of me stiff. "I never thought I was planned," I say. "An eighteen and a twenty-six-year-old. Your anniversary. I did the math."

"From the moment I held you, though, I couldn't have been happier."

"I know, Pop."

"But this, it's stupid you know. When I heard I was so angry at you. If you hadn't left her alone in that apartment…but it's me I'm really angry at. She shouldn't have been living in your apartment. I should have been the one providing for her. But even if I had," he shakes his head, his shoulders slump, "it's not like a whole night is needed for this to happen. Your mother was still under her parents' roof."

I swallow, not knowing what to say.

"You're still leaving?" he asks. I nod. "We'll take her in, of course. We'll have to get a bigger place than we were planning to. And Evelyn…if things don't go well with the surgery…I mean she has money, of course, but depending on how things go it could get expensive. And tiring. She's such a sweet woman. She'll want to do everything for Lori and that baby. And me—" He breathes, a raspy, tired sound.

"You know I haven't been able to do the construction work for years now. The cleaning, it gives me just enough, and with my pension kicking in in a few years, mine and Evelyn's together, I thought I could cut back, stop doing the overtime."

"No one said Lori's going to move in with you. She wants to live with Drake."

"In some shack."

"Didn't you and Mom live in a shack when you had me?"

"And look what happened." He turns his gaze away.

"Lori's not Mom. And they're not going to live in a shack. Shacks don't even exist here." I say this with a smile, hoping it will encourage one in him. It doesn't. "We'll figure something out. All of us, together. I'm getting a big pay raise, remember?"

He nods. "You shouldn't have to keep taking care of the family."

"It's what I'm good at."

"You'll have your own family to take care of."

I flinch at the words. "Let's go inside, Pop. They'll be wondering where we are."

"You're a good girl, Eloise." He pulls himself away from the wall and steps beside me. "Such a good girl. I don't know where you get it from."

"You're a good man," I say.

His head sways from side to side. He opens the door for me. "I've tried."

I hold his arm, thinking of how true his words are and how I've never acknowledged it properly. As hard as life was for me, it wasn't easy for him either. And he tried, he really tried. I think of the day Junior threw the test, the words I never apologized for and so many other little slights over the years. "Pop."

"Yeah?" He lets the door swing closed.

"I'm sorry."

"What?"

"I'm sorry. You have tried, I know you've tried and…well, thank you. You've been a really good dad."

"Honey—"

"I mean it." My eyes mist and I step into his arms. I can't even remember the last time I initiated a hug with him. "And I'm sorry for any time I made you think you weren't." After a moment I look up at him. "I'm happy for you and Evelyn. I hope you have many years together."

He smiles and squeezes me tighter.

When we enter the sanctuary Junior tells me Moses left a few minutes ago, that he said to tell me he'll see me tomorrow. I take this as an indication I'm not to call him and, apparently, so does Junior. "Everything okay in paradise?" he asks.

"It's paradise," I say with a smile. "How could it not be?"

"Crazy news about Lori."

"Mm-hmm."

"Do you think she's going to be all right?"

"She has to be."

He sticks his hands in his pockets, looking completely adorable in his suspenders and black-rimmed glasses. "She can still have a good life, you know. Don't make her feel like she failed you."

"What?"

"Don't make her feel like she failed you."

Along with his words, all the things he doesn't say sink in. "Do you think you could move in with her?" I ask. "Maybe until graduation or until Drake gets a job, that's good enough to—"

"I'm moving in with Matilda in a couple of months."

"Oh." At the front of the church Lori shows Evie some dance move. They laugh. "That's great." I turn my gaze back to Junior. "Until then?"

"I have a lease, El. I can't just…" He's been watching the girls as well but turns to me. "She'll be okay. At this point you being gone doesn't change things…much anyway. I'm sure Drake will be around to help out when she needs it."

"What do you think of him?"

"He's a kid, but I think he's got a good heart and adores her. That's something. He was so excited at her audition." Junior rocks back and forth on his heels and wraps his fists around his suspender straps. "Drake wants her to have a good life. I want to pulverize him for doing that to her, with her, for being so stupid." He lets his hands fall. "But then again, I deflowered a girl or two in high school. And there were one or two times when," he winks, "let's just say I was lucky."

I let myself be enveloped as he wraps his arms around me then pulls back, patting my cheek like he's the big brother. "Now Moses," he says, "is a good guy. I'll see you tomorrow."

Junior walks away from me as Lori comes up the aisle. "I really like Evie," she says. "And she said I can call on her if ever I need a babysitter."

"That's great."

She looks at me, a question on her face as she tries to read mine. I smile, pushing away everything that's making it hard to. "Are you ready to go home?" she asks.

I wave her along and we walk toward the car. I check my work phone when we get back to the apartment—after Moses' comment I'm sure to keep it on silent whenever he's around—then spend about three hours doing what work I can. After that, Lori and I spend the rest of the evening curled up on the couch watching the latest dance movie. She rubs her hand on her belly from time to time and at one point, when the star's dreams seem within grasp, I look over to see the saddest expression on her face. "It's great," she says, "that it's all going to work out for her."

I nod, and turn my face back to the screen, wondering if it's all going to work out for either of us.

❧

POP'S WEDDING IS BEAUTIFUL. Less than forty guests are in attendance, making it the smallest wedding I've ever been to, but it's also one of the nicest. Their vows are simple and sweet and the declarations of love he and Evelyn write for each other leave hardly a dry eye in the place. It's weird. My father, in love.

After they sign their marriage documents LaMeia, Lincoln, Evie, and Lori step up to the front of the church. LaMeia sits behind a cello. She wears a deep, concentrated look on her face. After one line, Lincoln joins in on the piano, followed by Evie singing in a language I can't understand but don't need to. And then it's Lori. She moves as if inspired. It's the first time I've seen her dance in far too long and she brings a depth to it I've never seen from her before. Her moves are graceful, precise, and it's as if her dance also speaks a language I don't understand but don't need to. It is beautiful. My eyes mist for the life she's not going to lead, the one she would be leading if the child inside her weren't about to steal it away.

Moses takes my hand. I can't look over at him, knowing what I know about us, but I'm still thankful. At the reception he holds me in his arms, so close, and I have hope. "Did you rethink…" I let my words trail off.

"This is for appearances," he says. "If we figure things out there's no point in people thinking…whatever they'd be thinking."

If we figure things out.

At the end of the night I hug my father and my new step-mother, step-brother and sisters. Junior and his girlfriend leave early, wanting some time to have their own Valentine celebrations, and Lori leaves with Drake, a Drake who, despite current circumstances, has impressed me. In front of my family he's been humble but talkative, proud of Lori and their new family, but contrite at the way it came about.

"We have to spend the rest of Valentine's together," I say to Moses as we put on our coats. "We're still engaged after all."

He looks hurt by my words, which seems entirely unfair. "Let's not complicate things."

I keep silent as we make our way to the parking lot and he walks me to my car. The familiarity to a scene just weeks ago is unsettling. Before unlocking my door I look up at him. "Are you breaking up with me? Or…well, calling this engagement off?"

"I don't know."

"You don't know." My voice gets sharp. "How am I supposed to work with I don't know?"

He purses his lips and looks so sad.

"Are you still coming in March?"

"I don't know."

"Well, I'd have to buy a ticket."

"I can buy my own ticket, Eloise."

"I know, but."

"Don't worry about that."

I almost ask again if he wants the ring back but am afraid of his answer. "Tell me exactly what this is about."

He leans against the car. "It's about me needing to know that I'm going to come before your work. It's about knowing that you want children. If you don't…and I don't want to pressure you, it's your choice, but if you don't, it's a deal breaker for me."

"You'd leave me over children?"

"I would." He says the words so quietly I barely hear them.

Big thick snowflakes start to fall. I look up, then blink several from my lashes. "I love you."

"I love you too." He holds me and we stand that way for

a long time. I'm not even sure which one of us releases the other first, or if it's a mutual letting go.

"What if I did stay? What if I'm still not sure about kids but I gave up this job?"

"Are you saying you're going to do that?"

"No. I'm just saying…would that be enough?"

He sighs, long and hard. "I don't think so."

So this is most likely the end. Because I'm not giving up my job. And even if I would, I can't say one hundred percent that I want children, ever. And if I do want them, I'm fairly certain I don't want them for years. What I want, instead, is a rest. Not from work, but from being responsible for another person's life. It's not pleasant to admit but a part of me is relieved I'll be in Tokyo and that Lori is set on staying here with Drake because I know if I were here, for the first few years at least, I'd be taking care of Lori and her baby, in more ways than financially.

Moses kisses my forehead and wishes me Happy Valentine's Day and I, the calm, cool, composed Eloise Grant, want to punch him for it. Though whose fault this all is I'm not sure, which may mean it's neither of ours.

I pull into traffic, trying not to think of all the happy couples driving by and hoping that wasn't Moses' and my final farewell. But unless I can give him the answer he wants, an absolute, it may very well be.

Before Lori was born I had dreams of being a dancer, but I let go of that dream and so many others with the hope that she could live hers. I want my own dreams. If I were here, helping her take care of her child, it would hamper that, and if I had my own child, I'd start living for someone else's dreams all over again.

It's Valentine's Day and though recently engaged, I'm technically alone—pretty pathetic—and the last thing I want is to go home to an empty house and be pathetic there. I pull to the side of the road and scroll to the text Autumn sent a few hours ago, wishing me a Happy Valentine's Day, an amazing time at my father's wedding, and saying if I can squeeze in any time before heading to Tokyo she'd love to see me. *Thanks,* I reply. *Something didn't settle well with Moses and he's home asleep and sick. Want to have that visit now?*

She answers yes, with multiple exclamation points, so I turn the car toward her apartment, preparing my game face. The last thing Autumn needs on Valentine's day is me being miserable about the relationship I'm in the process of destroying.

"El!" She practically yanks me through the door and squeezes me. "I can not believe you're moving so soon. Heading to Tokyo on a moment's notice with no idea of how long you'll be gone."

I'm tempted to say, 'sound familiar?' but don't. She beats me to it anyway, the realization apparently hitting her the same time it hits me. "I guess I kind of did the same thing, didn't I, only to Europe."

"That was different."

"Yeah." she says, heading to her living room and curling her legs up under her on the couch. "I was running away."

"But it worked out." I sit in her big blue plush armchair. It feels like a hug.

She tips her head back and forth, a smile growing on her face. "It got me to where I am today." And where she is, is a good place. Each time I see her, she looks more and more like Autumn before the accident. Her hair flows down, with just the hint of a wave. She's regained that amazingly toned, without looking mannish, physique she'd started to lose in the months after Matt, but more than that, when she smiles, almost always, her eyes join in. If it weren't for the scar that runs across her face, I could almost forget the accident. "How was the wedding?" she asks.

"It was good. I wasn't expecting to enjoy it so much, but it was incredible to witness—for the first time in a long time, I think my father is really happy."

"It's amazing," she says, "how that can creep up on

you."

"Happiness?"

"Yeah. Happiness." She stands up. "I have wine and chocolates. You want to indulge with me?"

"Absolutely." I take the glass when she offers it and pick out an array of chocolates. "So, the rest of Jakob's trip?"

Autumn sips her wine. "It was good. Really good. I like him."

"Me too." I wait for her to continue. She doesn't. "And?"

"He's not Matt."

"No."

"And I still love Matt."

"You probably always will."

She twirls her glass. "Jakob seems to understand that. He's okay with that and," she smiles shyly, "he's so patient. We didn't even kiss until his last night here."

"How was it?"

Now she really grins. "Amazing, and weird too. I was really nervous at first but once I got past that? Amazing. It convinced me that I really can move on."

"So what's the problem?"

"Oh you know, a little matter of the Atlantic Ocean."

"Oh, that." I take a long swig of the wine.

"That." She pops a chocolate in her mouth, savouring it, the way Autumn always savours food she deems somewhat sinful. "Though I guess you know all about it. You and Moses will be long distance for a few months, right? But it's not something that can go on forever, you know? And there's no way I can even think of asking him to move here, leaving the restaurant, his family, I wouldn't want him to."

"So…"

"So that leaves me. I have a life here too. My family, my friends, and the business is really picking up. But when it comes down to it, we have people we could bring in to take over my position and I know Allison would forgive me for it. She wants to see me happy."

"And would being with Jakob make you happy?"

Autumn lets a comfortable silence fill the air before replying. "I think so. It's what I want, you know? Love. A family. Children. I want the studio too, but I could start one over there. That was my plan, what, less than a year and a half ago? It could be my plan again. It'd be harder without a partner—Allison is amazing." She holds up the wine bottle. I nod and she tops off my glass then pours some more for herself. "Not exactly the best Valentine's chat, is it? Should we put a rom-com in?"

"No. We should keep talking about this."

She laughs. "It's scary too though, you know? What if I pick up and leave and it doesn't work out with us?"

I shrug. "Then you'll know. Do you think he could be," I hesitate, not wanting to use the term, 'the one,' "someone it could work out with?"

"I don't know. Maybe. There's a good chance." She takes another sip, presumably thinking. "I want to find out."

"Do you think you can find out from here, continuing to deal with the distance?"

She laughs. "It took a year and a half to get to our first kiss. I don't think so."

"It was more complicated than that."

"Oh, I know." We sit for a few minutes more, sipping our wine and enjoying the chocolates. "You think I should do it?"

"I think you've always been one for adventure."

"But leave my job, leave everything I've worked for, just for a chance at love again? Would you do it?"

I smile at her, shaking my head. "I'm not you."

"Good thing Moses is willing." I watch her expression change as she watches mine. "Isn't he?"

"We'll see."

"Eloise." She comes over and perches on the edge of the chair, sinking awkwardly. "What's going on? Is he really sick?"

"I don't want to talk about this. Really. It's Valentine's Day."

"And you're here sitting with me instead of making hot love to your not sick fiancé?"

"I didn't say that."

"Eloise."

"Autumn."

We give each other a little stare down. "You don't always have to be so tough you know. You're always there for others, ready to listen, ready to help, but you seriously need to let others do the same."

"It's not like that," I say. "I don't need help. I'm fine. Really."

She shakes her head, and it strikes me how beautiful she is, despite her scar. In a way it makes her more beautiful, showing her beauty can't be marred by what is technically a disfigurement. Her beauty's more than physical though, she's been through so much and still can be vulnerable, open. She's willing to pick up and move to another continent for a man she's not even sure she loves…whereas I'm not willing to stay for a man I love enough to marry. Of course, he's not willing to move for me either, at least not without questions asked and properly answered. "How serious is this?" she asks.

"I'm still wearing my ring." I hold my hand up and shake it before her face.

"Will he move?"

"I don't want to talk about it."

"Don't give him up for your job, El. Don't."

"I don't want to talk about it."

"Eloise."

"How about that rom-com?"

Autumn makes a noise deep in her throat—it sounds disapproving. She raises herself off of the arm of the chair, flips on the TV and navigates to Netflix, settling on a movie she knows I love.

"More chocolate?" She gives me a smile that says she loves me despite my pigheadedness.

"Please."

CHAPTER TWENTY-TWO

Just past midnight I try to open my apartment door but can't—something is lodged in front of it. I push again then hear whimpers. "Lori?" Shuffles follow next and I try the door again. It swings open and Lori, lit only by the dim light peeking through the door, is curled up on the hall floor. I drop to her side and turn her toward me. Her face is slick and her eyes puffy. *The baby,* I think. "Lori?"

Her words flow out in a long, drawn wail. "I've ruined my life."

"What do you—" She holds out her hand to me; crumpled papers fall into mine.

Before I can reach up to turn on the light, she's speaking again. "I didn't check the mail on Friday. I just didn't think, and I didn't think I had a chance. It's so late. I'd given up. I was supposed to get a yes by last week, but I didn't. And I made it Eloise." Her voice shakes. "I'm in. I made it. They chose me. And…and…" She curls up again. I switch on the light and read the letter. The most prestigious dance school in a thirteen-hour radius has chosen Lori. Not only chosen her. They've offered her a four-year scholarship.

"Maybe they'll—"

"No." She sits up. "No maybes. I said it before but it's not true." She whimpers. "School's like this don't offer holds. Do you know how many people are in line to fill my spot? Hundreds."

"But you never know," I say. Only I do know, and she

knows I know.

"I allowed myself to be happy." Her voice gets steadier, her face looking both older and younger than her age. "I told myself it was okay, that the one thing I've been working toward for the last seven years wasn't going to be mine anyway, and so I would throw all that passion and energy into this baby. But it was mine. It was. And this baby is stealing it away." She collapses forward and I catch her head in my lap, then lean against the wall. We stay there for a long time, her sobbing, me refusing to.

WHEN LORI GOES TO BED, I walk into the bathroom. On purpose, the tiles are a deep blue. Much to the chagrin of my landlord, I insisted on changing them when I moved in. For years I never bathed, only showered. But I bathe now, from time to time. The psychologist insisted it would be good for me and several years after I'd seen him for the last time, when I was a little younger than Lori, I finally did. I sank into the warm water, positioning my body in the tub, just like Mom's was. It was two days after I'd lost my flower, Pop's term for the act, not mine, and the guy who took it walked by me earlier in the day with an arm around his next intended conquest. As I lie there, the worst moment, the one I rarely let myself see, wouldn't be pushed away. After seeing the drips in the hall, after climbing the stairs with a squirming Lori in my arms, I stood at the bathroom door, the foreign splashes of red on the white tile telling me more than I wanted to know. So long I stood, then finally pushed against that door, and there she was. One arm lay hidden in the water, a rich red pool surrounding her body. The other arm draped over the side, a Rorschach on the floor below it. Her eyes were closed, her face was peaceful, as if she were asleep, and that in itself was disturbing. My mother always slept with a furrowed brow.

Yet again, the worst moment won't leave me. Wanting to soak away the past two days—the talks with Pop, with Moses, Lori's announcement and subsequent sorrow—I let the water flow into the tub, testing the warmth of it with my forearm. Did my mother perform this same action, knowing what she'd do to that sensitive flesh minutes later? And that one arm dangling, was it on purpose? Did she consider the mess? Or had she had second thoughts, tried to get out, too weak to lift herself?

Children of successful suicides are three times more likely to commit suicide themselves. After learning this, I resolved to never let myself indulge in misery—not for long, at least. Misery, I decided, was something I could have power over, and so far I have. I am never going to be a statistic. Neither is Junior. Neither is Lori. To achieve this, I've thrown myself into work and into preventing the two things I could pinpoint as possible triggers—Poverty and Pregnancy. I did all I could to prevent the first item for Lori and Junior too. I thought I'd talked to them enough to prevent the second as well.

I slip into the tub, the water around me feeling safe, protective. I view this as a tribute to my strength—I haven't let my mother steal the pleasure of a warm bath. Occasionally, I bathe with barely a thought of her. All my life I've ignored the memory of my mother as best I could. Sometimes because it hurt too much to remember. Sometimes because I hated her and didn't feel she deserved to be remembered. Most times just to cope, because forgetting seems easy…compared to the alternatives. Of course, we're like elephants. So we fool ourselves and hope it fools others too.

Because of her, the fear that security and happiness won't last claws at me, sometimes almost unnoticeable, but there. So I've controlled what I could. I was the top student in my junior high and high school, top five percent in both of my university degrees. I fought my way to get to Everdeen Enterprises and put all my energy into being the best, once there. I use birth control and condoms, always. I left relationships before they could become one—if I leave a man first, he can't leave me. And then came Moses. Moses, who I felt enough for. Moses, whose smile gave me permission to let down my guard. Moses, who I was more scared of living without than of losing, who I thought would never leave. Moses, who allowed me, in at least one area of my life, to become a different person.

When my fingertips prune I rise out of the tub, letting the water, and this moment of indulgence, drip off of me.

IT IS HARD TO LEAVE Lori the next morning. She shakes her head again when I offer for her to come with me. I remind her she can finish high school through distance education. We both know, though, this isn't going to happen. When I close the door to the apartment, more luggage in hand than I've ever taken on a journey, it's not a little girl standing in the hall. It's a young woman. She's had her heart broken, losing a dream she's held for years, and to make it worse, knows she's the one to blame. I smile at her, knowing my sister will never be a child again. Not even close. She's a woman now and, technically, a mother. She stands tall, though I know there'll be days when she'll fall again. She stands resigned, a woman who is determined to make the best of the life she has. I pray, though I'm not sure to who or what I'm praying, that the thing I'm scared of finding in me, that seed of resentment that took our mother away from us, doesn't start to grow in her.

"Anything you need, Lor. Anything at all, I'm only a phone call away."

"And a fourteen-hour flight, if your connections are

seamless."

I smile and shake my head. "That's not fair."

"You're right. It's not." She smiles back, a foreign smile. "But it's true."

"I'll be back around the time of the birth. That I promise. And hopefully, probably, before. For graduation."

She turns before I've closed the door and it hurts but I know her anger isn't directed at me, not really. It's at herself and the world at large. I check my phone on the way to the airport, hoping for a missed call from Moses. When at the airport, I put off going through security as long as I can, scanning the crowds almost frantically, hoping to see him there, saying he's been crazy, saying we mean more than anything else and we'll work it out, somehow. Eventually, I make my way to the terminal.

A little less than a day later I return to the office and throw myself into work. One night during my third week in Tokyo my cell rings—Moses' face lights up the screen. We chat about what's been going on in our lives. Once I've told him every mundane detail I can think of, he tells me he can't handle this limbo anymore and asks if I've made up my mind because he's made up his. He's willing to leave his family, his job, take the chance that I really will put him first. He'll believe it's just been a hectic few months, but only if I can tell him I want to have children with him. It doesn't have to be now. It doesn't have to be next year, but soon, before my age lowers our chances, makes things more difficult.

I can't tell him this. I just don't know. And right now, with the thought of Lori and her baby, remembering how those little creatures consume a life, I'm less sure than ever before. I could say maybe, but maybe is not enough. He deserves the truth. I take a deep breath, knowing my words will change my life forever. "I can't agree to that."

I imagine how much he wishes this wasn't happening over the phone because I wish it just as much. It's at this moment we're supposed to fall into each other's arms, to kiss with the same intensity we had in our first few weeks of dating, to spend the night making love, two, three, maybe even four times, knowing this one night will be the last. We don't have any of that.

"You can't."

"I can't give you a hundred percent answer. The best I can say is maybe…and that maybe is still a far ways away."

"I'm not saying right now."

"But you're saying for sure, you're saying sooner than I can agree to, because I can't agree at all. I don't know for sure." I hear silence for such a long time I pull the phone from my ear to see that the call hasn't dropped. "Should I mail you the ring?"

I can imagine the way his eyes look as I say this, the hurt in them. "No." His sigh makes its way across the distance. "Of course not."

"What am I supposed to do with it?"

"I have no idea."

And neither do I. "Hold on to it in case one of us changes our mind one day?"

"El."

"I'll think of something."

We exchange a few more words. I'm surprised, but neither of us tells the other we love them or we'll keep in touch or we can be friends. I think maybe we could, one day, but probably not. He's going to find a woman, soon, and he's going to have a big family of babies and no way can I be around that, thinking, *if I were a different person that could have been me, should have been me.* And if I do decide I want kids one day, knowing the desire came too late…I don't even want to think of it.

Throwing myself into work even more than I already have is what will save me. I'm sure of this. I can truly, completely, live for myself, like I wanted. Not that I want to be cut off. Over the following months I keep in touch with my family and friends back home but let myself stop feeling obligated to take care of them. So my life is not completely work, I find people here to become new friends, a makeshift family. I search out a foreigner's bar, take an English-speaking hip-hop dance class once our office settles into the work/life balance environment Kamlyn, Kuri, and I have been working around the clock to establish. As work eases more, I throw myself into the new friendships I'm building, I practise hip-hop in the evenings with two girls from the class; I laugh and I smile but none of these new people or activities bring as much fulfilment as I thought they would. Still, when Lori begs me to come home for one of her ultrasounds during our weekly FaceTime chats, I stay in Tokyo. If I go home I know I'll end up in front of Moses' apartment door, which I still have the key for, but what would I do then?

The first time I settle in for that incredibly long flight is for Lori's graduation, almost four and a half months after my last trip. As I travel, something tingles through me. It starts quietly, barely noticeable and then grows stronger and stronger until my body seems to thrum with this new realization—I miss my family. I really miss my family and am desperately anxious to see them. This is a feeling I've never felt before. I've looked forward to seeing them, of course, but never felt this deep missing. As I realize this, it hits me that I've been missing them for weeks.

The plane jerks and bounces, and for a moment I'm terrified. It's just turbulence though. I close my eyes and rather than remaining scared, I let the movement take me back to the afternoon before Mom left us for good. Junior and I had spent hours out with some kids from our street, making go-carts out of shopping carts, speeding down the hill while squealing, racing, living. Looking back, I'm surprised we didn't kill ourselves. I don't know if that afternoon really was so different from others like it, or if it just feels unique and wonderful because of the contrast to what came after. In my mind, a happy, nostalgic, warm sepia glow coats the scene. In my mind, it is perfect. I never had an afternoon like that one again: completely free, completely light, completely happy. My brother was never my brother in the same way, nor my sister my sister. Instead, they were my responsibilities.

The plane settles into a smooth motion once again and I try to let my mind settle along with it. These months away have affirmed I don't need to be responsible for my family anymore. They've been fine. Junior will start his first paid position at a well-known law office in a few weeks, no longer an intern. He's moved in with Matilda and is so busy and so in love with life he's barely contacted me more than a handful of times since Pop's wedding. Lori is scared and nervous and sad and excited and deliriously in love with the life inside her. Once the baby is old enough, Lori will have a job teaching dance with one of her old instructors—at the school where my Aspire fan club goes, actually—not the dream but if she does well at it, a life. She's planning to go to university part-time while Drake takes his electrician's course. The baby will spend three days a week with Evelyn, two at a home daycare so Evelyn, whose surgery went wonderfully, can have some time off. Everything is lining up, without me. My family can survive without me.

I'm resolving to do no work on this one-week trip, none at all, except of course respond to urgent calls or emails. It's nerve-wracking but justified. I want to focus on my friends and family. Besides, the revamp is going fabulously. It's the word Kuri and Kamlyn have attached themselves to, and now I find myself using it as well. Fabulously. We have five new hires, with five more we plan to hire in the next few months. They're savvy and smart and best of all, incredibly motivated. We have eight new clients. Some minor, but two the kind of clients that garner respect and put a business on the map. The branch couldn't be going better, yet a near-constant hollow feeling exists at the back of my throat, and I can't seem to swallow it away.

"El!" I've seen Lori through video-chat at least once a week every week. She's turned and preened and let me 'Ooo' and 'Ahh' over her growing belly each time. But seeing her in person, my petite little sister with what looks like a volleyball under her tank top, makes her pregnancy real.

"How can you move?" I hug her, not able to squeeze her full body against mine like I usually would. Instead, it's her belly that's squeezed and then kicks me in the hip.

"She recognizes your voice!" Lori grins. "Isn't that awesome?"

"It's amazing."

"How was the flight?" Lori asks as Drake, who I'm only just noticing, takes my bag and extends a hand to me. I shake it and smile but address Lori.

"Just your average flight. Nothing noteworthy."

"Says the world traveller!" Lori rolls her eyes at Drake, instead of me. It's odd. She is full of chatter in the car, Drake's jeep actually, which they're going to trade in for a sedan in the next couple of weeks. She insists I sit in the front seat. When we get to the apartment, she pops an already prepared chicken in the oven, like she's done this every day, and turns on the pre-filled rice-cooker to make a warm quinoa salad. "I'm learning to be domestic." She smiles proudly.

"It took her five hours." Drake laughs.

"It'll be amazing. I'm sure," I say. We all stand a moment in the kitchen, staring at each other. Drake should be the outsider in my kitchen but, with his arm casually around Lori's, it's clear I am.

"It's so good to see you!" Lori launches herself toward me and hugs me again. "This belly. It's not the best for hugging." Her laughter is so light.

"When's Pop coming? And Junior?"

"And Matilda, and Evelyn." Lori smiles. "You have to

remember, we're not the only women in their lives anymore." I remember. It makes me the seventh wheel. Perhaps this is what Tracey felt like. "They'll be here in around an hour."

I excuse myself to lie down, blaming the long flight, the weeks of work, and am asleep in moments. My dreams are a tangled mess of Mom, and Lori as a baby, and Lori now, and Lori's baby, and Moses with a new wife and baby, and Pop, and Junior, and me far from them all.

CHAPTER TWENTY-THREE

At dinner my family engages in the usual catching up, though it seems like they're all more familiar with each other's lives than I'm used to. They seem happy together, comfortable. They seem like a family and mention plans for next week and the week after. I can't help but think of what I'll be doing on those days—marketing agendas and scanning through hiring portfolios and never delegating enough. I'll be side by side with people who look at me like I'm so separate from them: some fear me, some despise me. At least they all respect me, and that's what should matter. The life I'm living is the life I've worked for, sacrificed for, for years. With the exception of having a man beside me, I have everything I've ever wanted. I've made it. So why does none of 'it' look or feel as shiny or wonderful as I thought it would? Why am I wishing I could be here next week for Pop and Evelyn's church picnic?

Evie breaks me out of my thoughts by asking a question about the revamp of the division, and I make it sound great, speaking to my family and their significant others with confidence and excitement as I describe the strides the branch has made under my direction, the people I've been meeting in Tokyo, and the lushness of my technologically advanced apartment there.

"Any idea yet how long you'll stay?" asks Evelyn.

"Three years, isn't it?" says Pop. "That's the time-line for the revamp, and then after that's settled you'll be coming home?”

"Well," I hesitate, "Mr. Everdeen is actually so impressed with what I've done there and how I've been molding the staff he's considering partnering me up with another one of his top players to start a branch in Busan."

"Busan?" asks Pop.

"In Korea."

"And that would be…" Lori's voice trails off.

"Another three years."

"Well, good for you!" Junior leans forward and winks, "So you're not just playing up how fabulously you're doing." He emphasizes the word fabulously, and I realize I must have been emphasizing it myself. "You actually are that good."

I shrug and smile back. "I guess I am that good."

"Makes sense." He rests an arm across the back of Matilda's chair. "You've always given up your life for the pursuit of recognition."

"What?"

"Had to have the best grades, get the most sought after scholarships, be the top intern, the top sales rep, consultant, PR guru, and now this. I'm just saying you excel. That's what you do."

"Junior." Matilda hisses his name, this woman who doesn't even know me.

"That's right," I say. "Is anything wrong with that?"

"No," says Junior. "I wouldn't be where I am if you weren't where you are, big Sis. You kept my head to the grindstone. You helped me through." He shrugs. "I just want to make sure you're happy, that the price of all these goals of yours isn't too much."

"Don't I sound happy?"

"Perfectly so."

"So what cost is it then?" I add a joke to my voice. "Not having to see your ugly mug all the time?"

"Moses."

The word is like a lightning bolt through the room, seemingly shocking everyone. "You don't know anything about Moses," I say.

Junior gets this look, like he doesn't want to hurt me, but he's going to anyway. "It was just coincidence that the engagement broke off when you decided you were moving across the world no matter what?"

"Yes. It was." I keep my gaze on Junior's.

"El."

"It got us talking about some other things." My voice doesn't waver. "Things we hadn't talked about before that we both want out of life. We discovered those things didn't line up."

He raises his hands, as if in surrender. Lori jumps up to get a pie she baked that turns out to be barely edible. Everyone else relaxes as they joke over how awful it is.

When everyone leaves and Lori heads to bed, exhausted from the day, I scan through my texts and smile at the ones from my gals. I'll meet with them tomorrow night after the graduation. My phone buzzes as I'm holding it. Tracey: *No, not tomorrow. Sorry. Eloise is in town. But the next day for sure. We'll crack open some bubbly and have a grand old time after all this marking is finally done. Woohoo!*

I laugh then text her back. *Hmm? A grand old time? Bubbly? And is this mutual marking that will finally be done? You seeing another teacher? I'll have to get all the details tomorrow!*

My phone buzzes almost immediately. She apologizes, says no, it's just a friend and nothing more. Odd for Tracey. Generally she's ready and willing to gush about a potential man. Once I've replied to the rest of the texts, I lie on my bed and gaze at the ceiling. I'm itching to do some work. And that itch, in and of itself, makes me sad. I'm supposed to be relaxing yet Junior's words keep replaying in my mind: I've given up my life in the pursuit of recognition. This isn't true, though. I've had an awesome life. An amazing life. On paper, I have a life to be envious of and a lot of what I gave up was not in pursuit of recognition, but in pursuit of a better life for him and Lori. I don't regret that.

My thoughts travel to Moses, the fear I have of being a mother. Next they hop to Tokyo and the revamp and Everdeen and how hard it was to convince him it was absolutely necessary I return for Lori's graduation, even though it meant missing an important company conference. Working would still these running thoughts, but I don't get up. I lie in bed and keep staring until I'm not staring anymore and the alarm rouses me.

The next day Lori walks across the stage like she owns it, her belly on display for all to see. She grins as she accepts her diploma. When she and her friends pose for pictures, she lets her gown split open in the front so her baby belly is captured, a hand resting lovingly atop it. Part of me is worried for this, thinking, she has no idea what's in store for her. The other part says she'll figure it out and to start with this determined love and optimism is not a bad start at all.

CHAPTER TWENTY-FOUR

After the graduation pictures, Drake waves my family over to a man and woman who look austere in their grey suits. The woman's hair is pulled tight against her scalp and arranged in an elegant bun. The man stands tall with thick lips pursed tightly together. Beside them is a girl who looks to be around thirteen. She doesn't match the adults, wearing a hot pink skirt and knee socks. Her tight, curly brown hair flies as free and wild as my own.

"These are my parents," says Drake. "Dr. Reginald Parker, Mrs. Louise Parker and my sister, Tilly."

"It's nice to meet you," says Pop, surprising me with the eagerness with which he reaches for the Doctor's hand. "Quite the situation our kids got themselves in!"

"Yes," says Mrs. Parker. "Quite."

"But they're good kids," says Pop. "And they're going to be fine." He squeezes his arm around Lori's shoulders, pulling her into him. "Just fine."

The Parkers are silent for a moment then Tilly grins. "I'm so excited to be an Aunt! I'm going to be the youngest in my class."

Dr. Parker looks at his little girl, the line between his lips creeping up at the edges. Drake goes through the rest of the introductions. Evelyn mentions how wonderful it will be to have a baby's gurgles in the home again and how beautiful the child is destined to be with these two as parents. Uncle Archie cracks a joke about Lori's ugly mug, said with such love no compliment could have been sweeter. As the conversation progresses, Dr. and Mrs. Parker relax more and more, their whole body language changing. When we say our goodbyes, Dr. Parker lets a large smile shine through. "Call me Reg," he says to Pop, then hesitates. "It's nice to know the kids have your support." He gives Drake a solid hug and tells him he's proud of him. Watching the interaction, I think Drake won't be as abandoned as he fears.

Shortly after the Parkers walk away, our family disperses: Lori and Drake off with their friends, Junior and Matilda to who knows where, Pop, Evelyn and Uncle Archie to some event of Evie's, and me to my girls.

Allison plops down in the seat beside me. "So Tokyo suits you."

"It does." I laugh, surprised at her presence and shocked she's the first one here. "And working with hot sweaty men seems to suit you."

"You bet it does." She grins then waves to Sheila whose heels click across the restaurant's floor.

"Eloise," she croons, hugging me tightly as I rise to greet her. "It is good to see you." She draws out the words in a way that makes me smile. Sheila may be just who I need right now. Sheila who gets me, who supported my academic focus through university, because hers were the same, and who never once has made a comment or had a tone regarding my work ethic or the way I let my job dictate my life. One conversation with her and I'm sure I'd let go of all concerns prompted by Junior's words the other night. Sheila works just as hard as I do, evidenced by the sharp business suit she's wearing on a Saturday evening.

"Coming from the office?" Allison asks with a laugh.

"Yes," says Sheila, either not picking up on or disregarding Allison's tone. She glides into her seat. "My paralegal has been so scatterbrained lately. She's really pulling the team down. We may have to let her go."

"That must be as sweet as Christmas for you!"

"What?" Sheila turns to Allison with a sharp look.

"Well, I thought you liked sucking the fun out of things," says Allison with a mock sheepish expression. "No?"

Sheila rolls her eyes. "I do what needs to be done. You should know that. And weren't you thankful for my ruthlessness when it came to dealing with that lax building manager of yours?"

Allison sits up and smiles. "Absolutely." She puts a hand on Sheila's shoulder. "I love your cold-heartedness."

Sheila laughs.

"I just have to rib you for it every now and then, make sure you don't take yourself too seriously. I need to do it to El from time to time too, isn't that right? The gang's resident workaholics. Well, I guess El's not resident anymore, but you know."

"She's still a part of the group," says Sheila. "And look at where her workaholism, as you call it, has gotten her. I swear," she turns to me, "in the next five years you're going to be in magazines. Maybe sooner."

"That's a stretch." I laugh, feeling uncomfortable at her words, whereas just months ago I would have been thrilled, wondering if it was true and what I could do to up my chances at that kind of recognition.

When Tracey and Autumn arrive, I'm welcomed into another round of hugs and soak in the easy laughter as we put in our orders and sip our drinks. "It's so good to have you back," says Autumn, "even if it's only for a few days."

"And then you'll be gone," says Tracey, addressing Autumn. "Our little group is falling apart."

"Not for another, what," Autumn pauses, "two-and-a-half months."

"Oh, come on." Allison laughs. "Like you had to think about how long it is. I'm telling you, this girl has Jakob and London on the brain 24/7. I'm surprised she hasn't killed a client yet with her daydreaming."

Autumn blushes and smiles. "Well, there's a lot to think about."

"I think it's amazing," says Tracey. "Travelling across the world for love."

"I don't know if I'd call it love yet," says Autumn. "Really big like."

"Well, to discover if it can be love," says Tracey.

"Yeah," says Autumn. "That's more like it."

"I still can't believe it though," says Sheila. "The business is doing so well right now, right? New clients every week, and you're going to walk away?"

"It's just a job," says Autumn. "I can start again." She looks to me. "El helped me see that when I was in the throes of trying to figure it out a few months ago."

"El?" Sheila glances at me. "Who left everything for her career, which I completely support by the way, told you that?" She lets her gaze rest on Autumn. "Honestly, though, I'm worried about this. Are you keeping any legal stake in this business? You've invested nearly the last two years of your life in it and thanks to that politician, Connor, it's boomed in a way start-ups almost never do. What if things don't work out with Jakob? What happens then?"

"Don't try to dissuade her," hisses Allison. "More money for me." She rubs her hands together and puts on what we call her fiendish villain face. "Good riddance." She adds a little cackle.

"You don't mean that," says Tracey. "You're sad to see her go."

"Of course I'm sad to see her go." Allison puts a hand on Autumn's shoulder. "This gal is a money maker. The clients love her, she's organized, and handles all the minutia I can't seem to keep track of. I was actually terrified the place would self-combust a week after she left, but she's secured *three* people to cover the load. Three!"

"So," Autumn smiles at Allison's little rant then looks to Sheila, "I'm signing over the company to Allison. Selling out my portion to have money to start things up in England."

"Do you think that's wise?" asks Sheila.

"I don't want ties." Autumn leans back in her seat. "If things get rough, ties will make it too easy to run back home. We all know I have a tendency to run." She chuckles.

"I wouldn't call once a tendency," I say.

"And as far as the new staff," says Autumn, "two of them aren't full time. They're just handling certain aspects of the business and the other will be taking on my client load."

"Yes," continues Allison, "your full-time client load, which you handled as well as all that other junk. Maybe we have a third workaholic on our hands."

"I have no desire to get that title." Autumn smiles. "This was a short-term thing while we were trying to get started. That is all."

"And will it continue once you try to get things started there?" I ask.

"I hope not." Autumn takes a sip of her drink. "I think I'll start a lot smaller and slower. Perhaps try to get a grant so I can hire someone early on to handle the books, giving me more time for other things."

"For Jakob," says Tracey. "You can say it. That's why you're going."

"It just sounds weird." Autumn runs a finger around the rim of her glass. "I know it shouldn't. But it does, especially with you four."

"You can talk about that weirdness with us," I say. "That's what we're here for, right? We all know why it feels weird."

"I know." Autumn sighs. "I know. Anyway." She gives her head a little shake, making the hair swoosh across her shoulders. "Speaking of what we're all here for, as far as I know nobody's heard much about how you're doing, El."

All eyes turn to me.

"I'm great." I smile. "More than great. The branch is seeing better numbers this quarter than it's ever seen, and

I'm really settling into life over there. It was a little lonely at first, just having work, being away from my family, from you all, for such an extended time, but I've made some good friends."

"You know that's not what she means," says Tracey.

"I know." I say. "But I don't talk about it because I don't need to talk about it. I'm steel, you know that."

Autumn gives me a look. "You broke up with your fiancé the same week you moved to the other side of the world. That ought to make anyone a little fragile."

"I'm not fragile." I put on my best smile, unsure if they can read through it. "Moses and I didn't work out. We loved each other, but when it came down to it, we wanted different things. The move just pointed that out. It's for the best."

"You'll find someone more suited to you," says Sheila, "who understands your drive and vision."

"Oh, come on." Allison slaps a hand on the table. "Not fragile my ass. And finding someone better than Moses? I mean I'm not the sensitive type, but we all know how in love you two were. It's like you were made for each other."

"Allison," Sheila and Autumn snap simultaneously.

"Well—"

"We weren't," I say, cutting Allison off, my words a surprise even to me. All four women turn their focus my way. "I think maybe we were more in love with who we thought the other person was than who we actually were."

"That's bull," says Allison. "Back me up here, Trace. Aren't you the one who's always proclaiming love over all, love can find a way, and all that?"

"I don't know," says Tracey. "I mean it happens, right? People get infatuated. They blind themselves to the other's flaws." She flusters a moment. "Or not flaws necessarily, I'm not saying you two had flaws and that's why you couldn't work. That's me who usually doesn't see a man's flaws. But you blind yourselves to aspects of a person's character. That can happen. And if it does, and then you realize it, maybe it's not so hard to move on?"

"Yeah," I say, a little stupefied. "That sounds right."

Allison raises an eyebrow. "Tracey, I never thought words like that would come from you."

Tracey shrugs. The conversation is cut off by the arrival of our food. I take several bites of my stuffed chicken and salad, barely tasting it. Why do I feel it's so important for Autumn to open up, but am so unwilling to open up myself?

Saying what I just said, about me and Moses, was shocking and unnerving. Since coming home, he's been on my mind even more than usual. It takes all of my resolve not to show up at his apartment, or even to call. I keep going over and over how we could have missed this pivotal difference between us. How neither of us realized sooner…although I know how he didn't, because I didn't let him. I didn't want to let go of how well he fit into my life in every other way: Smart, sensitive, sexy beyond belief, on the road to becoming a university professor. He socialized beautifully at work functions and, best of all, my family loved him. We were both career minded people, driven people, who would climb our respective ladders, never wanting for anything. Then maybe one day, if it all lined up, if we both felt it's what we wanted, we would have children. A big maybe. I saw how much he wanted kids the first time we talked about it but allowed myself to believe I'd be more important. By that point I was falling in love, a new experience for me, and the last thing I wanted to do was walk away.

I nod at something Sheila says then laugh at Allison's response, not really hearing either comment. I feel drained, hollow, and struggle to keep track of the conversation around me. It must be the jet lag. With focus, I draw my attention back to my friends.

"There's no one," says Tracey, "really. I'm trying to be patient, you know? Focus on friendship. Not pursue every guy who makes me feel special. I'm trying to focus on making myself feel special."

"Oh, yeah?" Allison elbows her.

"Not like that." A flush rises up Tracey's neck and into her face. "Just doing things that matter to me, not trying to impress men or get their attention."

"But friendship?" says Sheila. "I wish you luck, my dear. Men and women cannot be friends."

"Of course they can," say Tracey and Autumn at the same time.

"Every man who has ever been friends with either of you has wanted to sleep with you, even if he hasn't acted on it."

Autumn rolls her eyes. Tracey shakes her head. "You got that from some movie," she says.

Sheila smiles her self-satisfied smile. "Whether I did or not, it's true."

Allison lets out an exasperated puff of air at Sheila and waves a hand in dismissal. She turns to Tracey. "What things to make you special then?" She laughs. "I could probably do with feeling special pretty soon. I thought with working around men all the time, it'd be a bit easier to meet someone!"

"The Aspire club, for one thing," says Tracey. "I've been focusing on making it the best it can be. The sessions are amazing, thank you gals again for that, and the girls are so eager. They've grown so much." Tracey's face lights up as she's talking. "They were really upset the sessions wouldn't continue through the summer, and one of the mothers said it should be a year-round, established program, open to more than our little group of fifteen. Hearing things like that," Tracey laughs, "makes searching for Mr. Right behind every handsome smile or pair of broad shoulders seem far less important."

"That's wonderful." Sheila pulls out her phone and presses some buttons. "Good for you."

"So the girls are good?" I ask.

"So good," says Tracey. "Their grades have improved. Their attendance too. It makes me wonder what these types of sessions could do on a larger scale, like the mom said. I've been applying for funding and grants to expand it. If we could hire someone to coordinate and organize, set up speakers, etc., it'd be perfect. The other teachers just don't have extra time." She pauses. "If you have any tips, El, that would be great. I know you're insanely busy, but—"

"No, no." I say. "I'd love to see what your plans are, see if I can streamline anything or cut corners to make it as effective as possible. I mean that's what I do now."

"I know." Tracey sighs. "There was this presentation awhile back for a huge grant that would have let me take the girls to a national conference. I had to do this live pitch. I didn't totally flop it, but I bet if we'd had you here to work your magic, we could have got it."

"Well, I don't know about that—"

"Anyway," says Tracey. "There'll be others. And if ever you could find a spare minute, that would be amazing."

"Send me your ideas," I say. "It's so important young girls feel empowered, and the younger the better. Some of the women I'm working with in Japan, they're crazy smart, insanely able, but they don't always see it in themselves, you know?" I look away, thinking of it, and how good it feels when I see the new hires realizing they can take control over their own lives. "They're still trapped in certain roles and I don't want that for these girls. I mean, how many fourteen-year-olds think they'll ever be a CEO or a master welder? But they can."

"You just lit up!" says Allison, looking at me with an amazed expression. "That's the most Eloise I've seen you all night."

"The most Eloise?" I ask.

"Yeah," says Allison. "Excited. Passionate. On fire. You've been, like, snuffed or something."

"Oh," I say, feeling on display. "Must be the travelling."

The waiter brings our bills and the conversation transitions yet again. A sense of belonging overwhelms me as we partake in what we all agree is a pretty cheesy group hug. We don't know when we'll all be together again, and this thought makes me beyond sad.

§

SEVERAL HOURS LATER I'm sitting on the couch, flipping through the channels when Lori comes through the door, Drake beside her.

"Ah," he says. "It's your last night, right?" I nod. He looks to Lori and smiles like a man in love. "Shall I leave you to the care of your sister then, or would you like me to stay?"

"My sister," says Lori. "You go back to the party."

"It won't be as fun without you."

"Go anyway."

He kisses her. "I'll text you when I get home."

"I'll be asleep. But do it anyway."

"You're quite the couple," I observe once Drake walks out of the room.

"What do you mean?" Lori lowers herself into the armchair and thrusts her noticeably swollen feet onto the ottoman.

"You seem really comfortable, really suited to each other."

"And you think?"

I smile. "It's a good thing. Really good. You picked a nice guy, one who genuinely cares about you."

"He loves me," she says.

I watch her for a moment. "And you him?"

"Yeah. He's great." She sighs. "Really great. We fight sometimes. Not much or anything. I'm just not sure though, if he's my forever guy. No one expects to meet their forever

241

guy in high school, despite what all the gushy romances lead us to believe." She rubs her belly. "He's going to be forever in one way though."

"You don't have to make any decisions about anything else though."

"He thinks we should."

"Hmm?"

"He thinks we should get married. That's what a lot of the fights have been about lately. He'd like to get married before the baby is born."

"Oh," I say, trying to remain calm. "And what do you think?"

She shrugs, looking hidden behind her large belly. "I don't see what the one has to with the other. I mean I *see* what it has to do with it, because of society and stuff, but if I wasn't pregnant, there is no way he'd be proposing. We're high school students who hardly even knew each other before last year. And I like him. I probably love him. But I'm so young. I'm supposed to love a bunch of people before I get married, right?"

"Right." I lean back into the couch, hoping I'm saying the right thing. "Or at least maybe." But what is the right thing? "You should have the chance if you want it."

She rubs her feet on the ottoman. "I might want it. I want the chance to want it at least."

"You want me to massage them?" I ask, proud of her, and wishing we could go back to a time when her biggest concerns were what to wear to school the next day.

"Would you?"

I nod and sit on the edge of the ottoman, her feet in my lap.

"I danced as hard as I would have even without this baby in me." She leans her head against the chair and closes her eyes, smiling. "So hard."

"You did good." I continue rubbing as I gaze at Lori, thinking of how she wanted me here through all of this—

seeing her face light up at her first ultrasound, holding her hair back as she endured days of morning sickness, placing my hand on her belly and feeling those first few kicks, helping her pick out a crib and stroller and car seat. I missed it all.

She opens her eyes. "What's going to happen when the baby's born? I've been meaning to ask you." She closes her eyes again, clearly exhausted. "I just assumed but…will you be keeping the apartment? Can Drake and I—"

"We'll figure it out." I give her feet one final squeeze, gently move her legs so her feet rest on the floor, and extend my hand to help her up. "Don't you worry. It's time for sleep."

CHAPTER TWENTY-FIVE

Back in Tokyo, I work even harder than I had before, yet the excitement and passion I once felt has disappeared. This position is starting to feel easy for me, I tell myself, that's why. Only it's not easy. It's still challenging, and I'm rising to the challenge, I'm just not caring like I used to. Once I pull this off, and Busan too, I'll have proof behind me. If I wanted, I could leave Everdeen, move to a much larger company, get a top position somewhere with real prestige, or go back home. There's nowhere with more prestige at home, but I'd be home…and employed. If I left now?

My thoughts keep travelling back to my family, how close they seem now, how they're thriving, without my help. It's silly to feel this way. I should be happy. They're doing well. Even Lori. On paper she may be a statistic but she finished high school, she's registered for university, she has a plan, a future, and it's not entirely without my help. The scholarship she's getting for teen moms doesn't even cover half of her tuition.

I have no reason to feel the way I'm feeling. I am the youngest branch manager of Everdeen's four branches. Of our competitor organizations, I'm the youngest as well. I have worth. I am respected, and this, more than feeling lonely from time to time, is what really matters. This is why I should be happy. I am enough.

I have worth. I am enough. They're positive words,

technically, but today is the first day I see how sad they really are. A person who believes those words deep down in her core would have no reason to turn them into a mantra.

Gazing into the mirror, my vision blurs. I stare past my own reflection to see my mother packing her bags, looking at me like I am everything that went wrong with her life. I see her form as I trailed behind her, trying to make sense of what was happening. I couldn't imagine any of my friends' mothers packing like this, though several of them, like us, lived in houses that never had fresh paint or nice furniture. We weren't the only children to wear clothing too small and full of holes. Still, I couldn't imagine any of those mothers looking at their children the way she looked at me.

With a deep breath my focus comes back and I see my own reflection. I shake my head, loving the way my curls dance around my face, loving this part of me that's vivacious and free, that gives the impression I'm a woman who loves life, who knows how to relax and party and embrace her own diversity. The woman in the mirror looks happy and fulfilled, which I am…or should be.

As the days pile on, despite my efforts to continue with determined focus, to think of increasing our client pool, establishing new relationships, creating a team under me that is one of the best in the industry, I keep thinking of home. I love training new staff but once I've fully trained Kuri, coached her past her insecurities, I'm confident she can train the new recruits as well as me, better even. The women respond to her, whereas with me I sense hesitation, perhaps a little fear of my foreignness. In sessions, I find myself thinking of the girls from Tracey's class, how I felt so appreciated with them, certain I was exactly who they wanted. How their excitement, successes, and genuine affection made me feel like I was doing something important in the world. Not that employing these women, helping them market to their peers, empowering them with purchasing power isn't important—our branch is making a difference in these women's lives. It's just that now that we've come this far, I know the difference can be made without me.

Kamlyn and Kuri could take the lead from here. Everdeen sees this too. It's why he wants me to head up Busan next. I'm an innovator. I see where improvements can be made, and I come up with a plan to improve them. It's who I am. I need to know I'm needed. All that's left in the Tokyo branch for the near future is proper management of the systems and best practices I've established. Without my family, my friends, and Moses, I need more in my work-life than maintaining the status quo. I need something fulfilling enough to justify missing Lori's baby shower and Junior's swearing in. This job doesn't seem a good enough reason to miss Autumn's goodbye party and drinks with the gang to celebrate Sheila winning the case she's been slaving over for months.

The friends I've made here give me the feeling they like me because I'm a novelty, exotic, or simply because I'm a foreigner, like them. We talk about work, movies, politics, world news, and western and eastern stereotypes—last week's big topic: the growing propensity for weekend plastic surgery among Asian women. I know only tidbits of these people's lives.

In the hot summer sun I walk the fifteen minutes to work among the crowds, my head held high. When I enter the office, my smile is strong and confident, as always. While I hunch over this month's numbers with Kamlyn by my side, the words I spoke to Autumn come back to me. 'I'm not fragile.' I thought I'd been telling the truth but after these past weeks, I now know I wasn't.

It takes a bit of explaining to convince Mr. Everdeen I absolutely have to go home when my sister gives birth, how she is more like a daughter. I'm the only mother she's ever known, after-all. He agrees I can leave on a moment's notice when I get the call, but if I'm needed for any conference calls or meetings, I must make myself available. On the outside, I work with the same energy and authority and drive as I always have, but I can't help hoping for an early delivery.

I'm in the middle of a client meeting when Drake's text comes in—*She's started!!!* Kuri sits beside me and I reach my hand under the table to squeeze her knee, the signal we've worked out to mean 'excuse yourself to book me the quickest ticket.' She glances over at me, a broad grin of surprise and delight on her face. Lori is two weeks early. I nod and she slips out of her chair, giving a pleasant bow before leaving the room. When she comes back, she places a sticky note in front of me. *Three hours. What luck! Be at the airport in two.* I answer all of the clients' questions the same way I always would, but the moment they walk through our office doors I gather up my things and flee to my apartment, where I have my travel bag ready.

Six hours after the birth I'm at the hospital. Amazing, as I expected to arrive a day or more behind. Though not lucky for Lori. I know from calling Junior that I'll be the only visitor. He, Pop, Evelyn and Matilda were in the waiting room throughout the long labour and went home to rest after seeing the baby. The hospital corridor is brighter than I expect, with jungle animals and vibrant colours adorning the walls. Lori's door is a happy green. Outside of it, I take a deep breath, then push. Lori looks exhausted and radiant. A bundle barely large enough to contain a human is nestled in her arms. Drake rises from the seat beside her, takes three steps across the room, and hugs me.

"Guess we're family now." He laughs.

"Guess so." I hug him back, briefly. My focus is elsewhere.

"I'll give you two or, uh, three a moment," he says.

I nod to Drake and step towards Lori, able to see the little face now. *Her* face now. "You okay?"

"I made it," she says, looking tiny and young.

"I heard you were a superstar."

"I'd say I'm never doing that again—it was hours, El, hours of—" She laughs. "It's worse than the movies." She tips her arms towards me. "But look."

"I see." I get closer, taking the seat Drake left. My chest does something I've never quite felt before. Welling, perhaps. Yes, that's it. My chest is welling up. I feel a rush, it's instantaneous: Love.

"You want to hold her?"

My arms stretch forward without thought and Lori passes me her baby. Love. That's what I'm feeling. It hits me in a way that's baffling and so very good. "What's her name?" The words come out in a whisper.

"Beatrisa. It means—"

My smile broadens. "I know what it means."

"I thought seeing as…well, after Mom…"

"It's perfect." I stare at Beatrisa, whose mouth opens in a yawn. "Perfect. She is definitely a bringer of joy." I look back to Lori. "Not that you're—"

"Mom didn't name me well." Lori's eyes droop from tiredness, but her smile is pure joy. She doesn't look quite as young as I thought. "So I wanted to make sure my daughter's name suited her."

"You did well."

"We'll call her Trisa. Drake thought Bea would make more sense."

"Trisa. I like that." I rub my thumb along her cheek and she turns her head to it.

"That's what you do to tell them to suck," says Lori.

"What?"

"It's like a…an instinct." Lori yawns. "She's hungry again. Pass her back."

I do and Lori goes through the motions of nursing her child. It's alarming, to me at least, that she does this so naturally. "How do you know how to—"

"They showed me. And Trisa caught on really fast. They

don't always."

I nod. Amazed.

"It's really weird." She laughs. "So weird. Like, she's eating out of my body." Lori looks down at Trisa. "But I like it."

"That's so good, Lori." My eyes water and I wipe them self-consciously, wishing I'd been here for the first time, wishing—

"You okay, El?"

"I'm fine. I'm good." I feel a smile appear, along with the thought: *This is where I need to be.* "Just a little overwhelmed," I say. "And happy. So happy. For you, and that I could be here."

"Me too. You get to see her fresh." She looks back at Trisa, talking at her but to me. "And you'll see her every week on FaceTime. We'll make sure next time you visit she'll still know you, and it'll be like you never left."

"I'm not leaving."

"What?" Lori draws her attention back to me.

"I…" I stammer, not sure who's more surprised at the words that just came out of my mouth—Lori, or me. "I'm not going back. I'm going to stay here."

Lori's face lights up. "When did you decide this?"

I laugh. "I think right now."

Her face is skeptical. "Uh…"

"No," I say, shaking my head. "Not just right now. For the last couple of months, ever since I went back after your graduation I just…it's not where I want to be. Here's where I want to be."

"Can you get your job back?"

"No."

"Wait." Lori pushes herself up higher on the bed. Trisa gives a little gurgle of protest then settles back into sucking. "So, you're just quitting. You're just…you're not even going to go back and ease out or…Isn't Mr. Everdeen like, already annoyed with you or something or—"

I laugh. A trickle of sweat works its way down my back. My throat goes dry. "I don't know. I mean maybe I should go back for a little bit and ease out. If I leave now…no. There's no way I'm working anywhere in the company again. Or at least I think there's no way. I don't know. I don't know if I even want to."

"What'll you do?"

"I don't know."

Lori shakes her head and laughs; a big Lori laugh that reminds me of the little girl she used to be. "This is crazy. Me, a mom and you not knowing what you're going to do?"

"It is." I laugh with her, almost hysterically. "I always know what I'm going to do."

"And what everyone else is going to do!"

I shrug then look up as the door opens again and our laughter subsides. "Sorry," says Drake, wearing a sheepish grin. "I miss them. Plus," he steps into the room, "I have news."

Lori looks to him, expectant.

"Tilly texted," he says. "Mom and Dad are coming. They want to see the baby."

"I told you they would," says Lori, as he takes her hand. "And once they see her, they'll be hooked."

Drake nods, his excitement like a little boy's. We chat for the next hour. The sight of Drake so excited and nervous, and the sight of Lori, seeming more at ease than I could ever have imagined her, makes me feel things I can't quite explain.

As Drake is changing Trisa, displaying his skills and bragging that he practised on his sister's old dolls, I crawl into bed with Lori for a quick cuddle. "I'm proud of you, Sis."

"Really?" she whispers. "Even though as far as everyone is concerned, I ruined my life?"

"Who says that?" I scoff, squeezing her tighter. I kiss her temple then crawl back out of bed when Drake walks over. I kiss Trisa too and let them know I'll be back for another visit later on. I step into the hall. Walking past those happy animals—a swinging monkey, a smiling snake, a mischievous-looking elephant—I feel as if I'm walking in a dream. I've said it out loud now so I can't take it back, not that I want to. I'm quitting my job. I'm coming back home. I'm terrified, but I'm also resolved.

Mr. Everdeen will be beyond furious. He'll be disappointed in me. He'll lose respect for me. I'm supposed to be his protégé. It's not that I think he'll think it's so horrible to want to be close to one's family, to require a job that allows you to be there for the moments that matter. Many of his top people are those type of people and he respects them, but he chose me for another reason. He chose me because he thought I was like him, more committed to the job than to anything else. That's not the person I want to be. I walk faster through the hospital corridors, leaving the colourful walls and bursting into a lobby full of people. Everdeen wanted me to take care of his Tokyo baby, but that's not the kind of baby I want. I pull out my phone and call a cab, wishing I hadn't sold my car on my last trip home.

Before I have a chance to think about it, I tell the driver where I'm going then wait the interminable amount of time before we pull up to the door. *It's early on a Saturday morning, so chances are good he'll be here.* I still have the key on my ring, something that probably should have been given back a long time ago but as I knock, I think, *Maybe now I can keep it.* I wait at the door, wondering why I didn't prepare something to say. I try to come up with something, anything. After about a minute I knock again, louder this time, then wait. Deflated, I'm about to turn and leave but knock once more.

CHAPTER TWENTY-SIX

As the door opens, I'm struck with the madness of being here. I could bolt. I should bolt, then there he is. Moses, handsome as ever, tall as ever, *him* as ever, complete with the intoxicating scent of the body wash I've always loved. Somewhere in the back of my mind it registers that I bought him the undershirt he has on, and this makes me feel a smidgen less insane for standing here.

"Hi." His mouth hangs open a little as I scan him, taking in every aspect and remembering so much. "I was in the shower," he says. "I heard some knocking, but I thought I was too late then…then I wasn't."

"Lori had her baby last night."

"Oh, uh, wow, uh, congratulations. It's a couple of weeks early, right?"

"Yeah. Yeah it is."

"You got back fast."

"I did." He nods and I try to smile. I can talk to heads of multi-million dollar corporations without breaking a sweat. I can pitch a PR campaign worth enough to buy a jet, but this—"I'm not going back to Tokyo."

"Oh."

"I just decided. Well maybe I've been deciding for a while now, but I just finally decided it's not the life I want. I thought it was and there are aspects of it I love but there…there are other things that are more important."

He stares at me, looking as uncomfortable as I feel, most

likely surprised at my rambling. I don't ramble. "That's good, then. I guess. I mean, it is. I'm happy for you."

"I want a family." The words hang between us for a moment. "I was scared. Really scared. And selfish, I think. I wanted time to myself and didn't want the responsibility of another life but it's not about the responsibility, you know? It's about the love and Lori's baby." I pause. "Trisa is her name. Beatrisa but Trisa for short."

"That's pretty."

"Yeah. It is and Moses, well, it was amazing. I held her and just knew all my fears and all my ideas about wanting a life free from responsibility…I was really wrong." I take a breath and stare at my feet, not caring how my words are coming out but determined that they do. "I'm not my mom. I'm not going to suddenly turn into something and someone else when I have a child—this resentful, bitter person who doesn't know how to be a mother. It's stupid, I know, that I thought that, but I did think it, on some level." I look up.

He smiles at me, a sympathetic smile. It terrifies me and warms me all at once, at least it's a smile.

"I saw Lori." I keep my eyes focused on his. "And it was so natural for her, so right, and I know she's never going to be our mother and it freed something in me. I don't ever have to be her either."

"El, that's all great. It is. I just—"

"I know this is crazy. It's crazy, right? But maybe it's not. I mean that's what—" I stop, seeing something in his eyes I don't want to see. "Is there a chance?"

He backs away from the threshold and motions for me to enter. I step over it, thinking it would be better if I were still standing outside the door. I know him enough to know if he still wanted me, wanted us, I'd be in his arms right now. My jaw quivers and I shake my head, blink my eyes. He gestures for me to sit at the dinette then sits across from me. "I grieved us."

"I know, but—"

"No." He offers the slightest smile. "I'm touched and I'm really happy for you. It's good you're realizing all of these things about yourself." He reaches for my hand but I pull it away. He can't touch me as he says this. "I've moved on."

"It's only been six months. You're completely over me in six months?" I push out a laugh. "Seems quick."

"Of course I'm not completely over you." He makes the sound he makes when he's facing a situation he doesn't want to face and it amazes me how this is exactly the same person who proposed to me, who I know the mannerisms of inside and out, who wanted to spend his life with me. "I just…I'm moving on. You can't expect me to pick up where we left off."

"I don't!" I spew the words then take a breath, speaking more slowly. "I don't know what I expected. I just knew when I knew these things about myself I had to come see you, to tell you."

"I'm glad you told me."

"But you don't want me." I try not to let the familiar feelings of worthlessness creep over me—of being unwanted, of being never enough. That is not what this means.

"I always wanted you, from the first moment I saw you."

"But not now? We could go on a date," I say, feeling pathetic. "Get to know each other again."

"I don't think so." He averts his gaze.

"Is there someone else?"

He looks up, a little sad, but happy too. "No, not yet, but there might be. We're kind of exploring the possibility."

"I see." I stand, letting the air deflate out of me in one long smooth breath. Refilling myself, I put on my work smile. "This was silly of me, ridiculous, really. I'm embarrassed. Racing over like this? What you must think."

He stands and grasps my arm as I turn toward the door. "It wasn't silly. I'm really…I don't know. It means a lot. I wish I could, but I can't. It's too late."

"It's fine." I wave my hand casually. "I'm happy for you. You deserve so much happiness. I hope she's everything you want."

He smiles again and, as cliché as it feels, it's as if that smile cuts through my heart. "She might be. But that doesn't mean you couldn't have been. I wanted…" He hesitates. I pull open the door and step into the hall, hoping to get to the elevator before he can say anything else. As the doors slide open, he calls to me. "For what it's worth, if the timing were different, if…well…it would have been you, El. I wanted it to be you."

As the doors close on his words, again I feel like I'm in some movie. I won't let it continue like that though. I won't turn into a sobbing mess in the elevator. I won't make the door open and run back into his arms. And he won't follow me. I keep my work face on for as long as I can, cool, collected, in control. When the doors open on the ground floor, I want my car more than anything. I don't cry over men. I won't cry in front of a cab driver. But I find I can't not cry. So, with my luggage in tow I walk the hour and a half to my apartment. By the time I get there I've been drained dry and think, what's the point of tears?

My apartment doesn't really seem like mine anymore. The den has been transformed into a baby's room. Baby paraphernalia and the evidence of a boy living here make it foreign. Clearly, Drake has moved in. Entering my room, I'm relieved to find it untouched. I have the urge to call Autumn, but she's in England and while I could still talk to her, I want more than a phone to my ear. Sheila won't understand. She may try to, but she won't. Allison, with good intentions, would crack some jokes I don't want to hear or trivialize the situation. Of all my friends still here Tracey is the best when you need comfort and understanding, but how well will she understand the real reason Moses and I ended things—that I put my career above children and a family? Those are things she wants more than anything. If made to choose, she'd drop her career in a moment.

After five rings I'm about to hang up when Tracey's voice comes through the line.

"Hi." She sounds breathless. "Sorry, I was on the other line."

"It's okay. Should I call you back?"

"No, no. It's fine. I said goodbye."

"Okay."

"So congratulations are in order? You're an aunt!"

"How do you know?"

She stammers. "You're home, right? You never call when you're in Tokyo. It's always online."

"Yeah. Right. You busy?"

"Right now? Uh, no. Not really. Just about to head home from the gym."

We agree to meet at her place in thirty minutes. When I arrive she looks genuinely happy to see me. When I tell her I've decided to move home, she doesn't seem shocked. She nods and tells me that's really great. She's sympathetic when I say there's next to no chance I'll get a job with Everdeen again. "But maybe I'll try another industry, not just another company."

"Any ideas?" she asks.

"Not really. It's weird. I always know the next step. I always make calculated decisions, and this one..."

"This one was from the heart." Tracey smiles in that way she has that tells you she loves you and she believes in you and the world in general.

"I guess so."

"It's exciting, really. You can do anything now."

"Like check my investments? See if I have enough to get me through months and months of unemployment?"

"Like figure out what you're passionate about? What will make you happy."

"I was happy."

"Well," she takes a sip of the iced tea infused with fresh fruit she served us. "Apparently not as happy as you thought. You'll find something that will make you really happy. Something with balance. And you will not be unemployed for long."

"Balance." I groan. "Work/life balance. It's practically been our mantra for the past several months. I'm kinda sick of the term."

"Okay," she says, "something that feels connected then. Work you view as part of your life, not this separate entity that steals away from life."

"Is that how you feel about teaching?"

"Yeah." She leans back, as if enjoying the thought. "It is. Not because of the job, specifically, but because of the connection with the students. And while you're figuring things out," she grins, "maybe you could help us with the granting process for the Aspire group. Your proposal helped get us to the second round. Now it's in person presentations."

"I could do that," I say, brightening. "That would be great."

Her smile broadens, and for some reason this triggers me.

"Moses and I broke up because I wasn't sure I wanted children."

Her smile drops. "Oh?"

"Yes. There was more to it as well. He didn't like how focused I was on work, how I made decisions about it without him, and I get that. I see now how it wasn't right. But the big thing, the thing we couldn't get past, was having kids."

She nods and takes a sip of her tea.

"You must think I'm crazy. I know that's something you want so much."

"People are different. It's not crazy that you don't want

kids. With your mom," she takes a breath, "and your siblings. You kind of raised them, right?"

"Yeah. It was that. Selfishness too, I guess. I didn't want to be responsible for another life. With Junior and Lori grown up, I felt like I'd be free from that burden, you know? Not that it was all burden. I love them." I wrap my hands around my glass, enjoying the bright fuchsia colour of the tea. "But it felt like I was finally free to live for me, thinking of my future and I what I wanted to do with it, and then the idea of being responsible for someone else all over again?" I shrug. "To be honest, I think that may even be part of why I didn't discuss the job and move with Moses either. I didn't like the idea of having to be responsible to him."

"That's understandable." She shifts in her chair. "You had so much responsibility so young. It's not selfish to want to live your own life."

"No. I was wrong." I lean forward. "These last few months with Lori figuring things out on her own, managing without me, with Junior just…not needing me at all. I missed that. I missed being needed. I missed Moses, so much, and even seeing the joy some of our new recruits had, the way they talked about their children, how it seemed to make their lives so much fuller…deep down, I wondered, and finally holding Trisa—I want that. I want all of it."

Tracey nods.

"I went to Moses' before I came here, just showed up at his door. I told him I wanted another chance." My voice cracks. "But he said it's too late. He said there's someone else."

Her face pales. Her mouth opens slightly. I inhale, understanding, and with this understanding my body tingles, like I've literally been shocked. "Eloise." Tracey reaches her hands to grasp mine, but I pull away. "I didn't plan it. I'm sorry! So sorry. I swear. We just see each other so much. We've always been friends and—"

"Stop." I stand and step away, finding it hard to catch my breath. "It's you. You've been seeing Moses. Of course it's you." I turn back. "You're the reason?"

"No. No. I'm not seeing him." She stands too. "I swear. It's not that. I mean we spend a lot of time together, but it's not official. We kissed once and, well, I pulled back, because of you, of course. We see each other every day though, there are feelings." Her voice wavers. "But I'll try harder. I'll get out of the way. I told him that when he called. I told him he should give you two another chance and—"

"You knew I went there this morning. You knew, and you just sat here and—"

"I didn't know what to say!" She intercepts my pacing. "You are my friend first, but Moses and I, we've grown close. He was heartbroken when you two called it off. He needed a friend."

"He called it off, Tracey. Him. I was the one who was heartbroken. I was the one who needed a friend."

"And I tried to be there for you." She puts her hand on my shoulder and I jerk away. "You wouldn't talk, you didn't—"

"No, no, of course," I say. "It makes sense. He needed a friend. And you thought, well, I can't find my own man, so I'll just take Eloise's."

"That's not fair." Tracey couldn't look more hurt if I slapped her.

We stare at each other, just breathing, and I try not to see it in my mind—her and him, arms wrapped around each other, lips—I shake away the thought. "What happened?"

"It's like I told you. We were both lonely and we've always been good friends. You know that." She clasps her hands, as if she's begging. "I guess when two people spend that much time together…and we already had such a strong base." She raises her hand, as if she's about to grasp my shoulder again, then lets it fall. "But it's not official, you know? It's just, it's nothing really. I'm going to back off. I already have. If you two think you can make it work, I'm out of the picture. Honest."

I plop back down on the couch. "He doesn't want that." I let my head fall. "He already said." He's already moved on.

"I know." She sits down across from me. "But I'll put a firm stop to it, and maybe he'll think things through and realize…he's such a good guy, you know? He probably feels he owes me something, but he doesn't. You're the one he loves."

"Loved."

"What?"

"I saw it today." I look at her and force a smile. "The way he talked about you. The hope there. I'm the one he loved. You're the one—" I can't say it. "He wants you."

"No, Eloise. It doesn't matter. If this is going to hurt you and me, then no. Friends come first."

I shake my head. "Friends come before casual guys. Not before love."

"But it's not—"

"Do you love him?"

"I don't know." She stammers. "As I said, it's only been one kiss."

"Tracey."

"I could. I love him as a friend. I care so much about him, but it's been confusing. I love you too. Even though you were gone I didn't know if it was right and I didn't want to hurt you."

"But if I weren't a consideration?"

She smiles sadly. "I'd think I found the man of my dreams."

"Okay." I nod, feeling myself accept this.

"But you are a consideration."

"No," I say. "It makes sense. You two want all of the same things. You're so much alike."

"Yes, but—"

"You'd even get summer's off together with the kids, a

whole handful of them I bet."

"I didn't plan this. Neither of us did."

"I know." I stand again.

"I mean it, Eloise. Say the word and I'll tell him any chance of something between us is over."

"I know you would." I grab my purse, and as I sling it over my shoulder, my whole body feels heavy with the weight of this news. "And that's exactly why I can't ask you to. Besides," I laugh, "what chance would I have with him if he knows I'm the reason you said that?"

"Don't leave."

"I need some time."

"Are we going to be okay?" Tracey follows me to the door. "I don't want to lose you."

"You won't." I smile. "I may not want to hang out with the two of you any time soon but, I don't know, I guess you have my blessing? Or at least I'm not going to hate you, okay? Either of you."

"Are you sure?"

"I'm not sure right now, but I will be. I promise."

She hugs me, something Tracey always does when she says goodbye. At first I'm stiff and resistant, but as she holds on I melt into her embrace. My life feels like it's collapsing around me, so I might as well take love where I can find it.

Again, rather than taking a cab I walk home from Tracey's and think, *I can change my mind.* I can go back to Tokyo, as planned. I can throw myself into my job and kill it, like I always do, then move onto Korea and who knows where else next. But I can't actually change my mind, not after seeing Trisa, after telling Lori, or Moses or Tracey. I'd be running away. It's more than that, though. I don't feel responsible to be here for Lori; I *want* to be here for her, in any way I can. I want to know the woman Junior is probably going to marry, before he marries her. I want Uncle Archie to know one of his favourite gals will be around every week to visit. I don't want my father to get old and one day slip away from this world while I arrive just in time to make his funeral. If I have to find a new company, maybe even a whole new career, I will. I'll be okay. I'll make it.

CHAPTER TWENTY-SEVEN

Several weeks later, I find myself sitting on the edge of my bed, staring at the jewellery box that holds only one item. There is no turning back now. I, Eloise Grant, am officially unemployed. The belongings I left in Tokyo are somewhere in transit back to me. Everdeen fumed and ranted but eventually we parted with a handshake. He even offered me a position in the managing department at the local branch, which I turned down. He said I wasn't who he thought I was but, with a sigh, told me it was probably for the best; he has three ex-wives and four children he only sees every other holiday and when, at long last, he has to stop ruling his empire he feels certain he'll wish he hadn't sacrificed so much.

I, Eloise Grant, am also without the man I thought I'd spend the rest of my life with, and I'm okay with that. When the visit with Tracey didn't turn out to be quite what I expected, I called Autumn. The conversation was enlightening. She knows what it is to have loved and lost and assured me life goes on. Part of me wants Moses back. I still love him. But I think part of that love is tied up in what he represents: the life I'm ready to have. A life I'll have with someone else. I'll just have to be patient, not try to control the outcome, because I can't. For the first time in a long time, that doesn't terrify me.

From what she's said, Moses and Tracey are not going to be anything more than friends. I can't say I'm sorry, though

I want each of them to be happy. Over drinks a couple of weeks ago, Tracey told me she couldn't be a consolation prize. She knew he cared about her but couldn't trust those feelings so soon after me. She said, trying to encourage me, he still gets a certain look in his eyes whenever my name is mentioned and that she'll be happy for us if we ever decide we can make it work after all.

That won't happen. It's the elephant thing. The past can't be forgotten. It can be overcome, but not erased. Moses would always wonder if one day I'd turn into the work crazed woman I was becoming, and I would always feel as if his dream of children meant more than his dream of us. We both deserve more than that.

Outside of spending time with Lori and my new niece, I've been throwing my energy into the Aspire group. Rather than act as the occasional guest speaker I'm helping Tracey facilitate and plan the meetings. Two times a week I head to my old high school to coach a handful of the girls for the grant presentation. If the grant comes through, I'll take on the coordination and expansion of the program full time. First, we'll develop the original program, then we'll lobby for government funding to expand it into some sister schools.

We'll most likely be scraping to get by initially, but with my contacts in marketing that will soon change. I definitely have some favours I can pull in. I grin just thinking of it, the way life preps us for things we'd never imagine. I won't have prestige. I won't make much money. But I think I'll be happy. Lori, Drake and I are moving out of my current apartment to one in a less expensive area of the city next month. Even with the significant pay cut, even if I had no job, my savings and investments would allow me to stay in my current place another year, but who knows? I may need those funds one day. They'd be the perfect nest egg to start a family or a great down payment to buy a house.

I open the box and hold up the necklace. Light glints off

of it and I smooth my thumb over the cool metal, then clasp my hand around the small heart. I think of Trisa, how she changes and grows every day, how Lori changes and grows with her. I flip open the locket and read the words, so delicately engraved: *"We are shaped and fashioned by what we love."* A quote by Goethe.

One day I'm going to give this necklace to that baby girl and tell her about her grandmother. A woman who, when it came down to it, didn't know how to love the way her children deserved to be loved, who put security and money before her family, but who was beautiful and passionate and debilitatingly sad. I'll tell Trisa her grandmother wasn't always like that, though: she could be tender. Once when I was sick with the chickenpox, she stayed home from work for three days, rubbing my arms and legs, bringing me soup, and putting her cool hand on my forehead. Another time, when I was crying after falling off the monkey bars, she picked me up, cradled me in her arms, and said, 'Sometimes in life we fall, but then we get up again, and suddenly the fall isn't so important.' Lastly, I'll tell her the most important thing her grandma taught me, the hardest lesson: we should never give up on life and never give up on the people we love. There are a lot of things we can love in life, but people are the most important. They shape who we are. Trisa will know the meaning of the words she'll wear around her neck.

My mother gave up. She became so obsessed with the idea of the life she wanted and didn't have that she couldn't see the life right in front of her. She was shaped and ruined by her love of a life she didn't have. And those truths don't say anything about my father or Junior or Lori or even me. They say something about her. She was sick, and because of that sickness, because she didn't or couldn't find the help she needed, she missed out on so much good, so much joy. I'll tell Trisa I came close to missing out on joy as well, that I put my love of my job and my pursuit of success and recognition above what really mattered, and I hope she'll wear the necklace as a reminder to never let that happen to her.

For the first time since I found my mother lying in that tub, I walk to the mirror and put on the necklace. Seeing it hang around my neck, the way it falls just between my clavicles, the same way it did on her, I picture my mother's face. How, without fail, she put this on every day. One of the fights between her and my father, just weeks before we moved to this country, was about the necklace. He said she needed to sell it so we could buy warmer clothes. She said he could wrap us up in blankets, but she wasn't letting go of the one good thing she had.

And yet, just a couple of years later, she gave it to me. They'd had another one of their screaming matches—well, Mom screamed, Pop barely ever raised his voice—and Mom found me curled up on the floor, my hands over my ears. 'I don't need pretty things,' she whispered, 'working on my hands and knees like a slave, but maybe one day you'll have a life where this makes sense.'

Thinking of her, how she could be tender, even in her misery, I place my hand over the locket and hold it there a moment.

Turning from the mirror, I grab my bag and open the door. "You ready?" I ask Lori, who stands in the hall jostling Trisa in her arms.

"She won't stop fussing."

"Pass her over." I smile, my arms outstretched. I squeeze Trisa against my chest as her head curls into the nook of my shoulder. She gurgles. I breathe in her scent.

Lori looks at me, exasperated. "You're so good with her."

"So are you." I grin. "You're just nervous to take her out in front of everyone. She's probably picking up on that."

Lori shakes her head. "I hate the way people look at me, like I'm some cheap, stupid teen mom."

"We all know you're not. You know you're not. That's

what matters."

"You're right, I know you're right." Lori grabs her diaper bag, which looks more like a massive purse. "I don't know why this is so important to Pop. None of us were dedicated or blessed or whatever this is." She scans the room then gives a dismissive shake. "Let's go."

We make it to the car and buckle Trisa in. "She's going to do great," I say. "You're going to do great. And there's no harm in having Pop's church friends wish her a good life, promise they'll be there to help her out if needed."

"I know, I know." Lori leans against the headrest. "And everyone's *dying* to see her."

"That's right."

"Eloise?"

"Yeah?"

"I know I said I was fine, but you being back," her voice cracks, "I don't know what I would have done without you."

I pull the car into traffic and consider my life. Here I am with no fiancé. If that grant doesn't come through, no job. Yet I have people in my life who help make life worth living: people I've admitted I need. I turn to my sister knowing, whatever happens, I'll be just fine. "I could say the same to you."

A NOTE FROM THE AUTHOR

Dear Reader,

Thank you so much for taking the time to read *By What We Love*. I hope you enjoyed it. Did it make you think, laugh, cry, or take you out of your life for a few hours? If so, wonderful!

It would mean so much if you took a moment to write a short, honest review on either your favourite online bookstore or Goodreads (or both!). Reviews are incredibly important. They encourage readers to give a book a chance, which means your review could be the one to help a fellow booklover find their new favourite read!

On the following pages, find a description of the next book in the series, *Forever In My Heart*. It follows the story of Tracey as she struggles to realize she is worthy and enough, just as she is.

To learn about future books, if you haven't already, feel free to sign up for my newsletter at charlenecarr.com. For a limited time, you'll also get a free novella, *Before I Knew You*.

Don't worry, I won't flood your inbox. I rarely send newsletters more than twice a month.

You can also learn about my new books and promotions by following me on Bookbub. And if you've read *By What We Love* as part of a book club, you can visit my website for a Book Club Discussion Guide

Turn the page to learn about the rest of the books in the *A New Start Series*.

Read on, my friend,

Charlene Carr

When Comes The Joy
Book 1

Jennifer's not perfect. Not even close. But she may just capture your heart.

At 27, Jennifer's out of work, her mom just died, and despite stellar qualifications, every job interview ends in rejection.
Haunted by the teasing, taunts, and fat jokes that defined her childhood, Jennifer blames her unhappiness on her ever-growing waistband.
And she's ready for change.
Messy and real.
Beautiful and harsh.
When Comes The Joy (previously titled *Skinny Me*) explores one woman's journey along the road of forgiveness, healing, and strength.

Forever In My Heart
Book 4

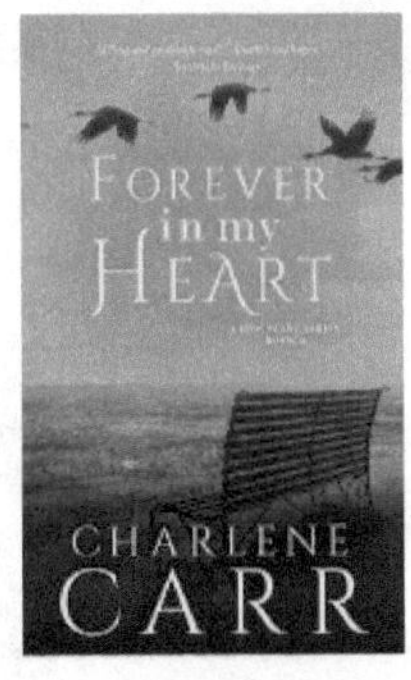

**Tracey Sampson has finally met the man she's ready to start her life with. He's perfect.
But is she?**

Struggling with the unknown and desperate for answers, Tracey embarks on a journey to reveal the secrets of a past she vowed she'd never explore.
Heartfelt and honest.
Courageous and compelling.
Forever In My Heart, book 4 in the *A New Start* stand-alone series, is a deep and passionate read about coming to terms with your imperfections and insecurities in order to let love in.

The act every woman is supposed to be capable of, she's failing at, over and over again.

A year ago, Tracey Sampson met and married the man who helped her finally believe she is worthy of love, just as she is.

But she's yet to fulfill her greatest dream—to hold her own child in her arms.

As month by month that dream drifts further and further away, Tracey is forced to acknowledge that not everyone gets their happily every after.

Engrossing and inspiring.

Heart-wrenching and passionate.

As real as it gets.

Whisper of Hope, book 5 in the *A New Start* stand-alone series bares the heart and soul of a woman heartfelt and emotional story of a woman pursuing her life's dream despite heartache and disappointment. Witness the power of hope to transform a life.

ACKNOWLEDGMENTS

I would like to thank my wonderful beta readers who gave generously of their time and provided invaluable feedback. It amazes me, the little nuances you are able to see that help me make these stories so much more than what they were. I would also like to thank my editor and her keen eye.

BOOK CLUB DISCUSSION QUESTIONS

1. Do you think Eloise is a workaholic? Or do you think she's just viewed that way because she's a woman? Does her attitude towards work, promotion, advancement and her family and future seem different than most men in high pressure jobs?

2. Do you think there would be a major problem if Moses and Eloise's positions were reversed with Moses needing to move for a promotion and expecting Eloise to give up her job which she loved? Why or why not?

3. In Chapter 20, Moses demanded that Eloise make a decision on whether she wanted children or not, stating twice 'You need to figure that out'. Was this fair?

4. What are your thoughts regarding Eloise's relationship and feelings toward her family? Were they understandable, or do you feel she was misguided?

5. A lot of Eloise's emotional issues and her drive to succeed came from feeling abandoned and rejected by her mother and ashamed of her father. Do you think that Eloise needed to go through intensive therapy to help her handle the traumatic death of her mother? What type of therapy? She did have meetings with a psychologist as a child, but did it seem enough?

6. Was Tracey being a true friend by consoling Moses and not telling Eloise about the situation? Or do you think she should have been more upfront about how close they were much sooner?

7. Do you think there was more Eloise could have done or should have done to protect and guide her sister so Lori could have avoided teen pregnancy?

8. What do you think of the way the grown children of Pop and Evelyn responded to their parents' upcoming marriage?

9. What do you think of the quote Eloise reads on the locket in the final chapter: "*We are shaped and fashioned by what we love*"? Do you agree with it? Obviously that's where the book gets its title, what relevance do you feel it holds for the story as a whole and for Eloise's realizations at the end of the novel?

If you have any questions about the discussion guide or would like a chance at having Charlene visit your bookclub through a webcall, email contact@charlenecarr.com

ABOUT THE AUTHOR

I'm a lover of words. Pursuing this life-long obsession, I studied literature in university, attaining both a BA and MA in English. Still craving more, I attained a degree in Journalism. After travelling the globe for several years and working as a freelance writer, editor, facilitator, and starting my own Communications business, I decided the time had come to focus exclusively on my true love - novel writing.

My goal is to write books that are almost impossible to put down, not because of some great mystery, or high-speed chase, or sexy scene, but because they're full of characters who enrage and delight you; Imperfect people in circumstances that could hit any one of us.

Characters full of human frailties who make awful, sometimes stupid choices …

But who don't give up when they're knocked down. Who struggle and fight and come out on the other side stronger, braver, ready to live a life of their own making.

Read more at www.charlenecarr.com/books

www.ingramcontent.com/pod-product-compliance
Lightning Source LLC
Chambersburg PA
CBHW061618190726
48288CB00007B/2380